A WOMAN'S NEEDS

"And what about you? Do you want to marry me?"

"I—yes, I do," she whispered as she remembered the promise she had just given her father. She would not waste one second. Her gaze rose up until it was locked with his. She tossed her head back and sighed deeply before she gave into the urge that she could not deny any longer. She leaned closer to him and Black Horse's hand immediately slid around her waist as he pulled her the short distance to him. Then, his lips descended on hers with abandon.

Although she hadn't been able to comprehend that their second kiss could even begin to compare with their first one, Meadow was certain Black Horse was trying to outdo himself. They were standing in the middle of the village where everyone could see them, yet she gave no thought to modesty. His strong arms were surrounding her again, and his mouth was doing the most amazing things. Meadow let her own lips imitate his and returned his kiss without reservation. She had her own hunger to satisfy, and it was obviously equal to his appetite.

VERONICA BLAKE

BLACK HORSE

LEISURE BOOKS NEW YORK CITY

For Albert . . . my hero

And for my amazing grandsons . . .
Derek, Devin & Kaden Blake

A LEISURE BOOK®

January 2008

Published by

Dorchester Publishing Co., Inc.
200 Madison Avenue
New York, NY 10016

ISBN 10: 0-8439-6167-8
ISBN 13: 978-0-8439-6167-6
E-ISBN: 978-1-4285-0749-4

The name "Leisure Books" and the stylized "L" with design are trademarks of Dorchester Publishing Co., Inc.

Printed in the United States of America.

10 9 8 7 6 5 4 3 2 1

Visit us online at www.dorchesterpub.com.

ACKNOWLEDGMENTS

I would like to thank my parents, Ortencia and Cecil Bettger; my children, Brian, Tiffany and Jason Blake; my daughters-in-law Heather Blake and Charlotte Thomas for their love and support and for always believing in me. Thanks to my dear friend, Helena Silva Bond for being my biggest fan and giving me the extra push that I needed to finish this book. And, a special thanks to my editor, Alicia Condon, for giving me a chance to pursue my dreams.

BLACK
HORSE

Chapter One

"See? That's him, that's Black Horse," Gentle Water whispered. She put her hand over her mouth and stifled a giggle.

"Quiet! He might hear us," Meadow warned with a stern glance. She tried to look serious, but the sight of the young war chief on the other side of the thick brush sent her heartbeat racing and caused a strange fluttering sensation in the pit of her stomach. She turned away from Gentle Water and focused on the man down by the riverbank.

Even from this distance he appeared to be slightly taller than most of the Sioux men in their village. Two thin braids wound with brass wires framed his handsome face and dangled over his bare chest. The rest of his dark hair hung to his waist. A large necklace of grizzly-bear claws encircled his neck—potent medicine for a warrior to posses. Black Horse was a chief warrior, which at his young age meant that he held a powerful position in the tribe.

Everything about him was impressive, Meadow noticed. His shoulders were outlined with bulging, sinewy muscles, his belly lean and defined. A white breechcloth encircled his hips, and tan leather leggings hugged his muscular thighs.

"Do you want to meet him now?" Gentle Water

asked. Her voice rose slightly above a whisper. She muffled another giggle when her friend shook her fist at her. Gentle Water leaned close to the other girl. "Your face is red, Meadow. I think you want to do more than just meet him."

"I'm leaving," Meadow whispered through gritted teeth. Before she could turn around to crawl back through the thick brush, a deep voice bellowed from the riverbank below.

"Who's there?"

Meadow instinctively fell down flat on her stomach and held her breath. Pressed against the hard ground, she could feel her heartbeat thudding uncontrollably. Beside her, Gentle Water was also lying facedown in the underbrush. But now she was also being quiet as death. Meadow silently cursed herself for letting Gentle Water talk her into coming down to the river today. Nothing could be more humiliating than getting caught in this compromising position.

When his cry was met with silence, Black Horse grew wary. He pulled his antler-handled knife from the sheath at his hip, bent his knees and began to inch up the sloping riverbank. His dark eyes darted back and forth. The dense brush of alders and willows made it difficult for him to see. Black Horse knew how easy it was to hide in heavy brush such as this. He had done so on many occasions when he had been hunting game, or waiting in ambush for an enemy.

Sensing there was someone—or something—hiding in the bushes, Black Horse didn't call out again. He continued to take cautious steps toward the bushes. He had moved only a few feet, though, when his keen ears picked up the slight sound of rustling brush. His footsteps halted. Every muscle in his body tensed. A light sheen of perspiration broke out on his chest and face as he prepared to go to battle again.

For several moments Black Horse did not move. When another faint sound came from the bushes, he pinpointed his prey's location. He moved like a crouched mountain lion toward the bushes to his left and then peered into the heavy underbrush. He smiled.

Through the low-hanging branches of the willows he could see the distinct forms of two females lying face-down on the ground. He studied them for a moment. Black Horse was certain they were just a couple of curious young girls. His smile widened.

"I must have been imagining things," he said out loud. The girls did not move a muscle. The urge to chuckle tickled the back of his throat, but he resisted.

As he sheathed his knife, he turned and walked back to the river with a nonchalant stride. Humming to himself, Black Horse untied the belt that held his elaborately decorated knife sheath. He placed the weapon down on the ground, then presented his observers with a full view of his hind side as he bent over to pull off his tall, beaded moccasins. He kept his movements slow and provocative. *I'll give them something to see*, he thought.

Unable to keep the smirk from his lips, Black Horse kept his back to the bushes until he could control his expression. He wanted to make sure that the girls were still watching. He didn't want to waste all this effort if he no longer had an audience. With a feigned look of indifference, he turned around. There were still no signs of movement on the hillside.

Black Horse untied the belt that held up his leggings. He rolled the fringed leg coverings down past his knees, lifted one foot up, then the other, until he was free of the leggings. Clothed only in his breechcloth, he turned toward the river again. He remained in this position for a moment to give the two visitors a chance to leave before they saw more than they were expecting. Or maybe that's what they want, he told himself. Why else would they be hiding in the bushes while he was preparing to take a bath? He turned sideways to the bushes where his audience hid, and slowly untied the strings at his hip.

In the scanty cover of the bushes, Meadow watched every one of Black Horse's movements in breathless awe. He was the most magnificent man she had ever seen, and the way he was undressing was like nothing she had ever witnessed. In the pit of her stomach, and even lower, she felt an unfamiliar ache. Her insides were on fire, and every time Black Horse discarded another article of clothing, the heat within her grew more consuming.

He was facing the bushes now, and Meadow knew there was no way they could leave without being seen. They would have to wait until he was in the water. Then, they could flee. Once they were away from the river, she planned to tell Gentle Water what a troublemaker she was to have suggested this scheme. But now that they were here she could not tear her gaze from the warrior's seductive movements.

His stark white breechcloth made the young chief's smooth skin shine like glistening copper. His legs were long, with well-defined muscles along his thighs and on the backs of his calves. As he moved, every muscle of his body strained and contracted with exact precision. At that moment, Meadow could not have taken her eyes off him even if the bushes around her had caught on fire and burned to the ground.

When the ties that held his breechcloth together were dangling long and loose in his hands, Black Horse was still facing the bushes. He parted his powerful thighs as he slowly pulled the breechcloth out from between his legs and then casually let it drop on the ground at his feet.

Meadow felt perspiration running down her body as she continued to stare. She had seen very young boys running around naked in the village, and she'd helped her adoptive mother prepare dead men for burial. She knew what a male looked like without his breechcloth. But little boys and dead men did not even begin to compare to the virile male who stood at the river's edge now.

Yearnings that Meadow had never experienced before ballooned inside her until she thought she would burst apart. It seemed as if Black Horse knew he had an audience. But that was ridiculous; he had no idea they were hiding here in the bushes. As soon as he dove into the water, they would get away from here, and this embarrassing situation could be forgotten. Even as that thought passed through her mind, Meadow knew there was no way that she would ever be able to forget the sight of this handsome man, who now stood before her naked as a newborn babe.

The gasps coming from the thick brush almost made Black Horse laugh out loud. More than anything, he wished he could see the faces of his inquisitive observers. He knew, however, it would not be long before he would encounter at least one of them again. When he saw them hiding in the underbrush, he had noticed one of them had hair that was the shade of the prairie sun—a half-breed, most likely. She would be easy to find in the Sioux village, where most of the women had hair as black as midnight.

Smug and filled with satisfaction that he'd given the curious virgins an eyeful, Black Horse lingered for a second longer. As though he had grown bored with the charade, he turned and sauntered to the river's edge. Without pausing, he walked into the cool water until it was up to his hips and then dove under the surface. Staying completely submerged, he swam out to the middle before coming up for air. He turned back toward the bushes.

A deep laughter escaped Black Horse when he glimpsed the two spies hurrying up the hillside on the other side of the thick clump of bushes. They were both dressed in the long fringed dresses and knee-high moccasins worn by all the females of the tribe, but the thing that caught his attention the most was the alluring way the buckskin dress caressed the curvy hips of the taller one—the one with the long yellow hair.

Black Horse began to splash around in the deep water of the river. He let the cool water wash away the dirt from the last of the long, hard trails he had ridden for the past few months. For a while, he let his mind clear. At dawn this morning he had crossed the Canadian border. He hoped Canada would offer a peaceful haven where he could rest.

Barely more than three months ago he had ridden

with his comrades in the battle at Greasy Grass River—the battleground the white men called Little Bighorn. But victory over the long-haired General Custer and his men had been short-lived. Within weeks of that successful attack, Black Horse's people had been defeated again and again.

But for the first time in a long time he had something besides fighting and killing on his mind. He was thinking of the two girls in the bushes, and of the fun he would have when he had a chance to meet the light haired one face-to-face. His mind recalled the way the wavy locks of her flaxen hair had swung back and forth above her shapely hips as she scurried up the hillside. He hoped she looked as enticing from the front as she did from behind. Another carefree laugh escaped from his mouth. He was looking forward to his stay here in Canada.

Chapter Two

"I will never forgive you!" Meadow yelled as she stomped back toward the camp. "If he had found us hiding in the bushes—oh!—I can't even imagine what would have happened."

Gentle Water giggled. "You are so funny, Meadow. I saw how you were looking at his—"

"I don't want to talk about it," Meadow interrupted. She covered her ears with her hands. Her mind, however, could not help but recall Black Horse's well-endowed physique. Just the thought of him caused the strange ache to inch through her body once more. She was drenched in sweat again. Her steps faltered, and her legs started to feel shaky. She hoped she would never see him again, because she knew there would be no way she could look at him without remembering every single detail of his muscular body.

"He'll be the guest of honor at the ceremony tonight," Gentle Water said. "Would you like me to braid your hair with leather and feathers?"

"I don't need my hair braided, because I won't be there."

Gentle Water gave her friend a smug glance. There was no chance her friend would intentionally miss the festivities tonight. Their band of Hunkpapa Sioux—led by the fierce war chief, Sitting Bull—had been camped here in the North-West Territories since early summer. Now, it was the beginning of the fall season, and this was the first celebration since they had fled across the Canadian border from their homelands in the Dakota Territory.

When Black Horse and his small band of Oglala warriors had arrived earlier that day, they had brought with them an abundance of freshly killed buffalo. Meat of any kind was becoming more and more scarce. The buffalo meat, along with the flasks of whiskey the warriors had also brought to the camp, was more than enough reason for a celebration. Since the battle a few months ago at the Greasy Grass River, it seemed the reasons for celebration among the Sioux were growing fewer and fewer.

"Your hair is prettier when you wear it loose, anyway," Gentle Water said, even though Meadow did not seem interested in pursuing this conversation. "I will brush it with a dry-grass brush until it shines like dancing moonbeams," she added as she found herself wishing that her dear friend had beautiful straight black hair like the rest of the Sioux women.

It was rare that Gentle Water thought of Meadow's white heritage, but there were times when she was reminded of how different they really were in appearance. Gentle Water knew that walking side by side, as they were now, only their clothes were similar. The summer sun had lightened Meadow's hair to a pale golden hue, and the thick tresses fell down her back in heavy waves that were impossible to brush smooth. Her complexion, even suntanned, was also several shades lighter than the skin of anyone else in the tribe.

Meadow's jade-colored eyes made her even more distinct within the Sioux tribe that she had lived with for the past fifteen years. The vibrant color of her eyes had been the inspiration for her name. Her adoptive *ate ate*, or father, White Buffalo, had thought that looking into her eyes was like looking at the beautiful blades of tall grass in a summer meadow.

"I will come for you when I've finished helping my grandmother with preparations for tonight," Gentle Water said as they walked cautiously through the tall pine trees. She noticed that Meadow kept looking back over her shoulder, even as they reached the edge of the encampment. Gentle Water had already pushed their spying escapade to the back of her mind and assumed Meadow's nervous behavior was due to the unusual location of their new campsite.

The large gathering of Sioux that had recently settled here had created a vast sea of tepees. There were seven tribes that made up the Great Sioux Nation: the Oglala, Brulé, Hunkpapa, Miniconjou, Oohenonpa, Itazipco and Sihasapa. Members of nearly every one of those tribes were camped in this vicinity. It was the usual custom of the Sioux people to camp out on the open plains, where there was less chance of ambush, and this camp in the dense forests of Canada made them wary.

By the time they had arrived back at the village, Meadow was more determined than ever to stay away from tonight's festivities. Just the thought of seeing Black Horse again made her insides quiver. Surely these abnormal feelings were the beginnings of an illness that she could use as her excuse to avoid the celebration tonight.

Without looking at Gentle Water, Meadow waved good-bye and hurried toward her own tepee. The hide-covered lodge Gentle Water shared with her *kunci unci*—grandmother—was on the opposite side of the encampment. Because they had no husbands to care for them, the husbands of other women looked after Gentle Water and her elderly grandmother, Sings Like Sparrow.

Meadow's adoptive father was an honored Hunkpapa Sioux medicine man. Their tepee was close to the main circle of lodges. Sitting Bull, the most powerful of all medicine men and the great war chief of the Hunkpapa tribe, was their closest neighbor.

But even the presence of so many Sioux did not make Meadow's uneasiness fade. She prayed constantly that here in Canada the fighting would cease. They were all so tired of living like hunted animals. Even after their victory over the yellow-haired Custer, they were still constantly on the run from the angry white soldiers. It was rumored that now the Canadians were desperately trying to convince the American government to negotiate with the Sioux to get them to return to the other side of the border, because they did not want them to remain here in Canada.

"Is that you, *mi-cun-ksi*?"

Meadow smiled when she heard her adopted father calling her daughter. Since soldiers had killed his wife, her adoptive mother, Little Squirrel, a little over two years ago, he had become even more devoted to Meadow. The Indian attack that had killed her real family when she was barely two years old was not even a hazy memory. "I have been with Gentle Water," she said as she entered through the hide flap in the doorway of their tepee. The cozy interior of the lodge welcomed her, and White Buffalo's smiling face filled her with a sense of comfort.

"Have you and Gentle Water been off teasing the young men?" White Buffalo asked without looking up from the bowl where he was mixing up some medicinal concoction. "The village is full of them since all the tribes have been gathering here."

Meadow stifled a gasp as she felt a rush of heat flood her cheeks. Drawing in a deep breath, she looked down at White Buffalo. He concentrated on the mixture of herbs in his bowl. Meadow chuckled nervously when she realized he was only joking. If he really knew what she'd been doing, he probably would be too ashamed to speak to her.

"We've been—uh—we went down to the river," she answered. She had never lied to White Buffalo, and she hoped she would not have to start now.

"It is dangerous, even here in Canada, to go out of the camp alone," White Buffalo said sternly. "Don't forget those evil Blackfoot people have followed us up here and are probably lurking about in the forest." He glanced up and added, "Be careful."

His tender gaze did not match his gruff voice as he looked up at her. Meadow nodded her head and then turned away quickly. She did not want him to see her embarrassment. It had been stupid for her and Gentle Water to be wandering around in the forest, especially since the Sioux' most hated enemies, the Blackfoot, had also taken up residence in this part of Canada. Even worse was that they had taken such a terrible risk just so that they could spy on that man—that beautiful vision of a perfect man. Stop thinking about it, Meadow told herself. She swallowed hard and wiped away the sweat on her upper lip.

"I will help you," she said when she felt she was regaining a bit of her composure once again. As she knelt down beside White Buffalo on the soft elk furs that blanketed the floor of the tepee, she noticed he was mixing a simple recipe consisting mostly of crushed yarrow plant. White Buffalo kept his medicinal supplies well stocked, and one corner of their tepee was stacked with pouches containing medicines to treat everything from broken bones to ailing horses.

"I don't need help," White Buffalo said. An amused smile curved his mouth.

"I'll go help Gentle Water and Sings Like Sparrow, then," Meadow said as she shrugged her shoulders and rose up to her feet. She moved toward the doorway.

"*Mi-cun-ksi*," he called out. "Are you bothered by something?"

Meadow paused. It always astounded her that he seemed to know her better than she knew herself. She wanted to talk to him about the feelings that had been rushing through her ever since she had been to the river, and she wished she could ask him why the sight of Black Horse's naked body affected her in such a dramatic way. Even now, her mind continued to cling to the sensuous image of him stripping his clothes from his muscled frame.

"No," she lied without turning around to face him. A deep sense of shame filled her. "I'll be back soon," she said as she shoved aside the hide flap and hurried outside again.

* * *

White Buffalo stared after her as Meadow exited the tepee. He had noticed the troubled expression on her face, but he assumed it was just because he had once again refused to let her help him. Ever since she had been a small child, she had always offered to help him mix his medicines or to assist him in collecting the herbs and roots he used in his recipes, and he always declined. If he had a son—or even a nephew—White Buffalo would be eager to pass on his vast medical knowledge. But a daughter was different. Soon, she would find a young man who would teach her all that she would ever need to know about life.

White Buffalo knew he was lucky to have had her all to himself for this long. She was seventeen—already several years past the normal age of marrying. Lately, however, the young warriors had been too preoccupied with fighting the whites to take notice of the blossoming females who were overly ripe for marriage. But soon there would be a young brave who would realize that there were more important things in this world than war. When that day arrived, he hoped he would not lose a daughter, but gain a son.

The thought filled White Buffalo with joy, yet at the same time gave him much sorrow. Meadow was all he had left, now that Little Squirrel and their own children were gone, and his greatest worry was that she would decide to leave the tribe entirely. She did have a choice, White Buffalo reminded himself, and someday she might choose to go back to her own people. He hoped that he would not be alive if that day ever came. But, he reminded himself, his beloved Meadow could not be more devoted to the Sioux if she had been born from his own seed. There was only one thing missing from her life, and if White Buffalo had anything to do with it, she would not be deprived of this necessity much longer. For the first time since she had become a woman, there was a village full of eligible young men. He had a feeling that Meadow would soon meet the man she would spend her life with. White Buffalo smiled. He had a way of knowing these things.

Meadow took a deep breath of fresh air once she was out of the tepee, but it didn't help. She still felt as if she was going to suffocate. If White Buffalo didn't need her, perhaps Gentle Water and her grandmother would have a job for her to do. There had to be something that would help to keep her mind off of Black Horse. Tonight—and forever—she'd have to make sure she stayed far away from him, because she was certain she could never look at the man again without wanting to die of humiliation. She scowled down at the dirt as she stomped away from her tepee.

A low chuckle reached her ears, and her heart skipped a beat. Black Horse stood directly in front of her, no more than a foot or two away. He wore only his claw necklace, white breechcloth and tall moccasins. A beaded knife sheath hung at a careless angle from his hip, and his fringed leggings dangled over one of his arms. Little droplets of water dripped from the ebony tips of his braids, forming wet trails down his bare stomach.

Black Horse leveled his gaze at the woman's face. She was not a half-breed as he had first suspected. She was *wasichu*—white—but obviously not a captive who was kept here against her will. Her pale complexion was streaked with red. He watched as her pink lips parted with a startled gasp and her green eyes grew wide with horror. He had to remind himself of the reasons he had come to Canada. He was here to rest his tired body and renew his spiritual devotion to *Wakan Tanka*, the Sioux god, not to find a woman—especially one with eyes as green as a moss-covered lake that could drown a man in their depths.

Black Horse stared at her for a moment longer as he tried to remember his plan. He let his gaze travel lower, until he had skimmed every inch, every curve, of her firm young body. The effect she was having on him was not going to be easy to hide when he was wearing nothing more than a breechcloth. He had to force himself to assume a nonchalant attitude as he looked into her unusual eyes. It was obvious to him that she was afraid and humiliated, but from the way her gaze kept flitting from his face down to his body, he also guessed that she had been enthralled by the suggestive show he had given her and her companion.

A taunting grin curved his lips. He could just tell her that he had seen her at the river today, but it was much more fun to wait and see how long it would take her to admit to it. He could be patient—sometimes. His eyes raked up and down her body one last time, and then he stalked past her without a single word.

Meadow could not move. In the time Black Horse had looked brazenly into her eyes and scrutinized her entire body, she had experienced a multitude of new emotions; fear had lasted only a second, embarrassment just a moment longer. But the desire his presence summoned forth was not so easy to escape. She wanted to flee, but her legs were too weak and shaky.

She turned to watch as he walked casually past the nearby tepees. His bronzed body still glistened with droplets of river water. Her fingertips tingled with a yearning to rub those tiny bits of moisture into his smooth skin and to feel the taut muscles that rippled underneath. But all she could do was stare at him until he disappeared through the narrow doorway of his tepee. Symbols of fierce animals and images of warriors engaged in battles were painted on the sides and were signs that an important man lived in this dwelling.

The fear that Black Horse might be watching her from inside his tepee was strong enough to snap her out of her trance. As a sense of panic gripped her, Meadow twirled on her heels and ran as fast as her feet would carry her away from him.

The emotions she felt were too powerful to control, and they were still too new for her to understand. But as she raced past the tepees, she was sure of one thing, one devastating thing: somehow, Black Horse knew she had been watching him when he was down at the river today.

Chapter Three

When she reached the far side of the village, Meadow saw Gentle Water and Sings Like Sparrow working over a simmering pot at the fire pit in front of their tepee. She could not go charging up to them in this frantic state. Sings Like Sparrow was a wise old woman, and she would immediately sense that there was something wrong. The last thing Meadow wanted was to get Gentle Water in trouble. If they told the old woman what they had done today, Meadow knew that both she and Gentle Water would feel Sings Like Sparrow's whipping stick.

Moving quickly behind the nearest lodge, Meadow wondered how she would be able to act normal, now that she knew Black Horse was staying in a tepee only a short distance from her own lodge. She had to find a place where she could be alone while she attempted to free herself of Black Horse's memory—and cure herself of these strange new longings.

Meadow knew that most of the men would drink themselves into a stupor at the celebration tonight. Even White Buffalo, who was normally a levelheaded man, would eagerly succumb to the temptation of the whiskey. If she could just stay out of sight until the men were too drunk to notice anything or anyone around them, then maybe she wouldn't be missed.

With any luck, Black Horse would leave the village soon, and she could work on forgetting the way he had looked when he pulled his breechcloth from between his muscled legs. Meadow drew in a deep, shaky breath and glanced back toward Gentle Water and Sings Like Sparrow. They were still oblivious to her. Taking several cautious steps backward, she ducked behind the nearest tepee. How long would she have to hide and how far would she have to run to escape from the feelings Black Horse had roused in her?

If she were a man, Meadow thought with an aggravated huff, she could say she was going on a vision quest, and then she could just disappear into the forest or the mountains for as long as she wanted. When she returned, the rest of the tribe would anxiously crowd around her, wanting to hear about the mystical visions she had seen while on her spiritual journey.

She sighed in defeat. The men had it much better than the women. Many times she had dreamed of being able to jump onto the back of a horse and ride as fast as the wind across the open prairie. As a woman, however, she had little opportunity for this sort of adventure. Cooking, tanning hides, hauling water and firewood, tending children and doing all the other chores that needed to be done in the camp—this was the life of a Sioux woman.

Knowing there was no escape, Meadow decided to give up her crazy scheme to run away. She had no alternative but to go back to her own tepee and try to conceal her turmoil from White Buffalo. Sneaking toward her lodge, Meadow felt like a naughty child. She could see that nearly everyone was already gathered in the center of the village. A large fire had been lit; several long spits held buffalo quarters that were roasting to crisp perfection. The enticing aroma filled the air and made Meadow's mouth water. Rows of drums were lined up on one side of the fire. They would accompany the flutes and provide music for the dancers this evening. A pang of disappointment shot through Meadow's breast. She hated the thought of missing the celebration tonight. But, because of that awful Black Horse, she had no other choice!

Her chest tightened as she held her breath and hurried past his lodge. She exhaled heavily when she noticed he was nowhere in sight, then she quickly ducked through the doorway of her own tepee. Her relief grew when she saw that White Buffalo was no longer there. As she plopped down on the soft furs that made up her bed, a sense of peace settled around her. She had always felt safe in her tepee, even when there had been battles raging outside.

Fleetingly, she recalled a time when a soldier's sword had sliced open a large hole in the side of this very same tepee. White Buffalo, younger and quicker then, had pulled the soldier away from it before he had a chance to enter. Little Squirrel had huddled with Meadow in the furs while White Buffalo had defended his home and family. Meadow glanced at the far wall where the hole, now stitched up tightly, was a grim reminder of that close brush with death.

A noise outside the tepee door drew Meadow's attention back to the present. A familiar voice called out.

"Meadow? Are you ready to go to the celebration?" Gentle Water leaned down and entered without waiting for an invitation.

"I'm not going," Meadow announced. She returned

Gentle Water's look of annoyance with her own defiant one. To reinforce her position, she grabbed a colorful woven blanket and pulled it up under her chin.

Undaunted by Meadow's display, Gentle Water chuckled. "No one will ever know what we did this afternoon."

"He knows," Meadow retorted. She clutched the material of the blanket tighter in her fists.

"White Buffalo knows?" Gentle Water gasped. She dropped down on her knees in front of Meadow. She was wearing her best dress, a light, fringed buckskin gown with an elaborately beaded yoke. Her leggings and moccasins were also covered with intricate beading.

"*He* knows! Black Horse knows!"

Gentle Water clasped her hand over her mouth to stifle her shocked cry. When she lowered her hand again, she whispered, "He can't know. How is it possible?"

"He stopped me, and—and . . ." She shivered under the blanket when she thought of him again.

Scooting closer, Gentle Water whispered again. "Did he say if he was going to tell on us?"

"He didn't say anything at all. He just laughed and looked at me like he wanted t-to—" Her voice grew too hoarse to speak, and she swallowed, hard.

"If he didn't say anything to you, then how do you know that he—?"

"He knows!" Meadow interrupted. "He's going to make us pay for spying on him. You didn't see the way he looked at me. It was almost as if he knows everything about me."

Meadow could tell that the tone of her voice and the

expression of fear she undoubtedly wore on her face was enough to convince Gentle Water that they had been caught. Gentle Water glanced frantically around the darkening tepee as if she hoped to find a way to escape, but Meadow sensed they were not going to get away this time.

"What are we going to do? If my grandmother hears about what we did today, she'll have my nose cut off."

Before Meadow had a chance to reply, the flap of the tepee swung open. White Buffalo's grinning countenance appeared in the opening. He nodded toward Gentle Water with a friendly acknowledgment, then focused all his attention on Meadow. "*Mi-cun-ksi*! Come, I have someone important for you to meet."

The lump that formed in Meadow's throat prevented her from answering for several seconds. "Wh-who?" she finally asked in a raspy voice, as her stomach twisted with a sense of impending doom.

"Hurry, my daughter," White Buffalo said as he pulled the flap wider. "Black Horse is an impatient young man." The excitement he clearly felt over this introduction, along with the alcohol he had already consumed, made him oblivious to the tense atmosphere inside the tepee.

The blanket slipped from Meadow's limp hands. Her terror-filled gaze settled on Gentle Water. The other girl's look of senseless panic did nothing to reassure Meadow. She looked toward the front of the tepee and fearfully glanced through the doorway.

Black Horse stood in full view. He was dressed in a magnificent suit of clothing, including a red and yellow painted society shirt. Long locks of ebony horsehair formed the fringe on the shirtsleeves. His leggings were beaded in shades of white and black, and a porcupine-quilled bag was tied around his waist.

Meadow's gaze moved up to his bonnet of eagle feathers. The crown of the headdress was made from the skull of a horned buffalo. Only the strongest warriors were permitted to wear a horned bonnet, and those who did were believed to have the strength, the dignity and the stamina of a bull buffalo. Flaring out from the back of the headdress was a brilliant display of gray, white and black eagle feathers that extended down Black Horse's back and stopped only a couple of inches above the ground. Meadow began to tremble.

"I apologize for my daughter," White Buffalo said to Black Horse. "She is very shy and modest," he added.

Black Horse cast the elderly medicine man a forced smile. The faded light in the tepee did not permit him to see inside, but he was anxious to finish there so that he could continue his search for the green-eyed woman. The whiskey he had already consumed warmed his amorous nature, and the thought of the curious young white woman caused his blood to boil. His night would not be complete until he saw her again.

Feeling as though she were caught in a bear trap, Meadow reached over and grabbed Gentle Water's arm and pulled her along as she rose up to a standing position. "You're coming out there with me," she said between clenched teeth. With a forceful shove she pushed the other girl out through the doorway. In her shocked state, Gentle Water stumbled out of the tepee without resistance.

Black Horse stared at the young woman as she straightened up to face him. He nodded his head curtly. His gaze quickly scanned her face and body. She was, he noticed, a pretty girl, and not fat like many of the Sioux women. But when he looked into her dark eyes, the memory of the woman with catlike eyes claimed his thoughts once again. His brows drew together with impatience.

"This is Gentle Water—a dear friend," White Buffalo said in an anxious tone of voice. Then, in a proud announcement, he added, "And this is my beloved *mi-cun-ksi*, Meadow." He grabbed Meadow's arm as she stumbled from the tepee and pulled her up beside him.

A deafening silence followed as Meadow's gaze ascended and settled on the face of the tall chief once again. In the brief interim of quiet, Meadow was sure her heart had stopped beating and every drop of blood in her body had just rushed into her face. She detected a slight narrowing of Black Horse's dark eyes and a barely noticeable smirk curling one corner of his full lips. She could only imagine the thoughts that were going through his mind at this moment.

Black Horse crossed his arms over his chest and leaned back on his heels. His casual stance did not even begin to match the turmoil he was feeling inside. He felt his breath lodged tightly in his dry throat, and there was something fluttering wildly in his stomach like the wings of a bird. He had always prided himself on his common sense, but now his mind was spinning with the seductive things he had been thinking about ever since he had first glimpsed this woman in the bushes. But that was before he had known that she was White Buffalo's daughter. Shy and modest . . . ha!

Instinctively, Black Horse glanced at White Buffalo. He hoped the wise old medicine man was not able to guess the immodest thoughts that were filling his head at this moment. When he noticed that White Buffalo was looking at him with a look of expectation, Black Horse was overcome with embarrassment. He glanced away quickly.

The strange exchange between Black Horse and Meadow did not go unnoticed. White Buffalo assumed Black Horse's behavior was due to surprise over seeing that his daughter was not Sioux. He had grown accustomed to this reaction throughout the years and was not hesitant to declare that Meadow was his daughter in every way, regardless of her true bloodline or the color of her skin. But he had other things on his mind right now.

"Black Horse is to be thanked," White Buffalo said, intruding into the strained silence. "He has provided us with enough meat to fill our bellies for many sunrises. With the white man's whiskey we will be able to forget for a time about the pain and hunger of the past few moons. He has truly given us a reason to celebrate," White Buffalo said in an excited tone as he looked at his daughter and Gentle Water.

"My grandmother and I thank you," Gentle Water said in a raspy tone of voice. She stepped back from the others as she bowed her head meekly and mumbled that she had to go help her grandmother, then twirled around and made a hasty retreat before anyone had a chance to stop her.

Meadow tore her attention away from the chief and stared at her father. He was still unaware of her panic, and she knew that she must also acknowledge Black Horse's generosity before her father became suspicious. She turned to Black Horse. His dark penetrating stare was focused directly on her again, and his mouth still wore a crooked smile. His eyes twinkled—probably in anticipation of the payback he was planning. She took a trembling breath and swallowed hard.

"Th-thank you for—for your kindness and generosity," she murmured. His expression did not change, nor did her feeling of helplessness. Without blinking, she continued to stare up into his dark, twinkling eyes.

His patronizing attitude cut Meadow's pride, but the humiliation she felt quickly turned to anger. They had just thanked him for the gifts he brought to the village. Yet, instead of accepting their gratitude graciously, he acted as if he wanted them to fall down to the ground and kiss his feet. She clenched her hands into tight fists at her sides. It had been wrong to spy on him today at the river, and she would readily admit this to him. But she refused to be intimidated by him now. Most of all, she would not allow him to be rude when they were in the presence of White Buffalo. She glanced back and forth between the two men. Compared to the wisdom and greatness of her father, Black Horse was nothing more than a strutting rooster.

Black Horse's taunting grin grew even wider. The fire in this woman's bright eyes and the scarlet blush in her pale cheeks excited him in a way he had never known. She had spirit, and he liked a feisty woman. Now, more than ever, he wanted to see how the flames of passion would also light up her face. He glanced nervously at White Buffalo. He had to break free of the spell this woman was casting on him before he made a complete fool of himself. He was a fearless warrior, the youngest war chief in the entire Sioux Nation! Nothing could distract him when he was in battle against his enemies. Why was he letting this green-eyed woman affect him so profoundly now? Drawing on the last of his waning control, he pulled himself up to his full height and raised his chin up to a proud tilt.

Turning toward White Buffalo, Black Horse wiped the crude smile from his face. He bowed his head humbly toward the older man, carefully choosing each of his words before he spoke. White Buffalo was a man to reckon with, especially since Black Horse hoped to make him a strong ally—in more ways than one.

"You and your daughter are very kind to thank me, but I gladly bring food to my people." Black Horse's expression grew serious. Then, hitting a closed fist against his chest, he added in an emotional tone, "I will do anything for my people. I will die for my people." Though his words were not spoken to impress, Black Horse could not miss the look of admiration on the older man's face.

Briefly, Black Horse let his gaze settle back on Meadow. She did not seem to impress as easily as her father. A growing sense of determination flooded through him. He had never been injured seriously in battle, and he would not allow this woman to wound his pride now. Proving to her that he was a good man was a challenge he was looking forward to.

White Buffalo turned toward his daughter, and words began to tumble rapidly from his mouth. "Black Horse is very brave, and his medicine is very strong." The old man smiled widely, and little lines crinkled around his dark eyes. "I would be proud to call him my son . . . and my daughter's husband." White Buffalo's announcement seemed to surprise the medicine man as much as it did everyone else. He understood now why earlier today he had had such a strong sense that Meadow was about to meet the man she would marry.

Meadow was speechless as she turned to stare at her father. She dared not look in Black Horse's direction, because she did not want to see his reaction to her father's ridiculous proposal. He couldn't be serious—could he? An uncomfortable silence followed.

"I—I would also be proud to be related to s-such a great medicine man," she heard Black Horse stammer. Meadow remained rooted to the spot. This could not be happening. She was even more shocked when Black Horse leaned toward her and almost touched his face against hers as he added, "And I would consider myself the luckiest man in the Sioux Nation to have such a beautiful, shy and modest wife."

The shame his words induced made Meadow's anger return. She tried to think of a way to get out of this terrible predicament. Then, she thought of her aging father. To disagree or refuse this proposal would be to go against his wishes. She would also be disobeying the customs of the tribe, as it was not uncommon for parents to arrange marriages for their children. She drew in a trembling breath. There was only one thing she could do now.

She focused on the depths of Black Horse's intense gaze. His expression was set in a determined mask that told her he would not be swayed from this course.

She forced a weak smile and nodded her head as she stared at the ground in resignation.

White Buffalo chuckled with satisfaction and caught his daughter in a loving embrace. Meadow glanced up at her father but could not even begin to fake a tiny bit of the happiness that he was obviously feeling at this moment.

The old medicine man released his hold on Meadow and reached out to slap Black Horse playfully on the forearm. "We will have a smoke to celebrate this forthcoming marriage."

"And another drink," Black Horse added. Had he imagined the high-pitched tone in his voice? He glanced at Meadow. Her face was drained of all color. She looked as dazed as he felt.

When she glanced his way, the sparks of anger that flashed in her eyes excited him. Her hostile feelings were quite obvious, and Black Horse was sure she would rather be eaten by a grizzly bear than marry him.

The last thing he had planned to do was to take a wife, but White Buffalo was an honored man among the Sioux, and Black Horse would never disrespect the elder man. Nor could he dishonor his daughter. Maybe it was time for him to think about something other than fighting his enemies. He glanced at Meadow again. She looked at him as if she considered him her enemy. To his surprise, Black Horse realized that if this marriage was really going to take place, it was important to him that she wanted him as badly as he wanted her. He sensed he had his work cut out for him.

He would be responsible for this woman in all ways, and for her family, too. He glanced back at White

Buffalo. In spite of his advanced age, it did not appear that the powerful and capable medicine man would require too much of his attention. His gaze moved to Meadow again. He would like to be responsible for teaching her the ways of lovemaking between a man and a woman. She had already taught him something. Until a few short minutes ago, he never would have believed that there was a woman alive that he would actually think about marrying. His heart began to beat faster. Well, if he was going to take a wife, she might as well be one that made hot lava rush through his veins.

White Buffalo pulled a catlinite pipe from the sash that was tied around his waist. The long pipe was adorned with a carved eagle's head. Porcupine quills and feathers dangled from leather ties at one end. He grabbed the beaded pouch that was also hanging from his belt, which contained the potent tobacco they would pack in the pipe. "Come then, *mi-cin-ksi*, we have more to celebrate now."

Black Horse nodded obediently. White Buffalo had just called him *mi-cin-ksi*—son. Without looking at Meadow again, he began to walk away with long strides. He felt a desperate need to sit by the fire with the other warriors, to drink and smoke and let his pounding heart become calm. Then, maybe, he could escape from the emotions that were raging through him now . . . the ones he once thought he would never allow himself to feel. He had already lost too many people that he cared about in his lifetime. The thought of marrying and starting a family only increased his fear that he would lose more people that he loved. Un-invited, thoughts of living a peaceful life with the green-eyed woman here in the lush forests of Canada filled his mind. Was that possible?

Then, reality intruded. He remembered what the white men had done to his people, and why he could never find peace again.

How could he even think of taking a white woman to be his wife? Underneath the Indian dress, Meadow was still a white woman—and so his greatest enemy. But the thought of what was underneath her doeskin dress redirected his attention. He felt the swell of his manhood tighten against his breechcloth. The color of her skin would not matter once he had her firm young body pinned beneath him on the soft fur robes in his tepee.

He glanced at White Buffalo once more and was reminded of how different his people were from the white men. The Sioux judged one another by what was in a person's heart. Meadow must have a heart like a Sioux, or else White Buffalo would not have accepted her as his own daughter so easily.

Yes, Black Horse told himself, he could claim *this* white woman for his wife.

White Buffalo handed the younger man the long pipe. Smoke trailed up from the narrow end and the strong odor of tobacco filled Black Horse's nostrils. He took the pipe and was reminded of how it was customary for a Sioux man to court a woman by playing love songs on a flute, bringing gifts to her father and engaging in silly courtship games. An impatient grunt escaped from Black Horse at the thought of partaking in these useless rituals. Meadow probably wouldn't appreciate the lengths to which he was willing to go for her, but his intuition told him that she was worth it.

Chapter Four

"I cannot marry him!"

"But you must not disobey your father," Gentle Water replied. She pulled the woven blanket from Meadow's head. She had been hiding under it for most of the evening. "White Buffalo sent me to get you now. Get up before you get us both in trouble."

Meadow shook her head defiantly. "No, I will not go. It's too humiliating to be around that man after we watched him—you know?"

A giggle escaped Gentle Water as she attempted to pull Meadow to her feet. "Do you really think a man like Black Horse would marry you just to pay you back for watching him take a bath?"

"Maybe," Meadow retorted. Her logic sounded ridiculous even to her own ears. She satisfied her friend by allowing her to pull her up to a standing position. With her hands on her hips, Meadow faced the other girl. She had not lit a fire, so only a faint sliver of moonlight shone through the smoke outlet in the top of the tepee, and she could not see Gentle Water's face clearly.

"Why would a man like Black Horse want to marry me?" Meadow asked. Because she still had no intention of going, she had not changed into her ceremonial gown or fixed her hair for the evening's festivities.

"Maybe he likes you," Gentle Water said with an accompanying shrug. She did not tell her dear friend that many members of the tribe were also baffled as to why the chief would want to take a woman who was not a Sioux as his wife. She had heard whispered comments at the celebration tonight, but no one wanted to anger Black Horse or insult White Buffalo, so they were careful not to voice their opinions too loudly.

Meadow wished now that she had lit a fire so that she could look into her friend's eyes as they talked. Something else was bothering Gentle Water, and she could usually read hidden thoughts in her friend's expression.

"Have you heard Black Horse talking about me tonight?" She drew in a worried breath. What did he really think of her?

Since they were still holding hands, she pulled Gentle Water to the tepee entrance and yanked back the flap to allow the pale moonlight to enter. "You must tell me if you know something!"

Gentle Water shrugged and glanced down at the ground. Meadow had been here almost all of her life, and because of White Buffalo's complete devotion to her, no one had ever dared suggest that she didn't belong here. Until tonight, Gentle Water had never heard a word said against Meadow, but regardless of how much they all loved and accepted her, it did not change the fact that she was not a Sioux.

"I know of nothing that he has said," Gentle Water said. It was true. Black Horse had not said anything about the impending marriage at all. Only White Buffalo had been raving all evening about the upcoming union. The young chief sat at his side, merely smiling and nodding and looking as if he was in some sort of a trance.

Meadow drew in a deep breath. She was certain Gentle Water was keeping something from her. "What has been said about the marriage?

"Your father is very, very proud that his future son-in-law is such an admired man in the tribes. He has told everyone!" Gentle Water followed her out into the open as Meadow exited the tepee. "Let's go before he comes to see why I have not yet returned with you."

Meadow turned toward the other girl. Now, with the full force of the pale moonlight shining down upon them, she could study her face more closely as she asked, "Black Horse has said nothing—nothing at all about the marriage or about me?"

Gentle Water shook her head and repeated, "No, Black Horse has not said a word about you or the marriage. Why do you care so much? I thought you didn't like him."

"I never said that I didn't like him." Meadow threw her hands up in the air in an exasperated gesture. This was all too confusing. At her age, she should be thrilled that she was getting married, and especially to a powerful, virile war chief.

Meadow's stomach started to ache. Maybe his reluctance to speak about the proposal meant that he had no intention to follow through with her father's plan.

Gentle Water eased her arm around her friend's shoulder and gave her an affectionate hug. "I think you like Black Horse more than you care to admit."

"I don't even know him," Meadow returned. "The only thing I know about him is that he is—" Her words faltered as she began to recall the sight of his muscled, naked body.

"He's the most handsome of all the warriors and chiefs, and he looks wonderful without his breech-cloth, and—" She giggled when she heard Meadow's gasp. "Oh, you didn't notice that, did you?"

"I don't ever want to think or talk about it again," Meadow retorted as she started back into the tepee. She did not want Gentle Water to know just how affected she was by the dangerously handsome chief.

Laughing, Gentle Water grabbed her arm as she tried to escape. "Oh, no you don't. Your father said to bring you back with me, and I'm not leaving here without you."

Meadow pulled Gentle Water along with her as she ducked back through the tepee door. "No, I will not go, so you might as well go back and tell my father that I am not coming!"

Gentle Water dropped her arms down at her sides in exasperation. "Some are saying that you should be grateful that such a great man even wants to marry a white wo—" She cut her words off and threw her hand over her mouth.

Meadow's footsteps faltered as the other girl's words took meaning. Gentle Water had never spoken to her about the differences in their nationalities in all the years they had known each other. "Gentle Water, does it matter to you that I'm not Sioux, that I . . . am white?" she asked in a low voice.

Gentle Water reached out in the darkness and put her arm around Meadow's shoulders. "I'm so sorry, my dear friend. I do not judge you by the color of your skin, you have to know that."

"But . . ." Meadow turned to face Gentle Water, once again wishing that she could clearly see the other girl's expression as they spoke. "Obviously there are others in the village who do judge me because of this, and Black Horse is probably one of them." Gentle Water's silence was not the answer she had hoped for.

Meadow drew in a trembling breath and moved away from her friend. She made her way to the mound of fur robes at the far corner of the lodge that served as her bed. She knew the location of every item in this tepee and did not need light to see where she was going. As she slumped down on the furs, she tried to force back the tears that were threatening to fall. "Please let me be alone now, Gentle Water."

"I can't leave you like this," Gentle Water said as she cautiously made her way across the darkened lodge. "It was not my intent to say something that would hurt you. It's just that I overheard a few comments tonight about Black Horse not marrying one of his own. They did not mean anything bad by their words." Her foot touched the pile of robes, and she sank down and reached out until she had located Meadow's hand. As she clasped it, she added, "Even though you look different, you are still one of us. Please believe me."

Meadow wanted to believe her friend, but there were so many mixed emotions clouding her thoughts. Since she knew nothing other than the desperate plight of the Indians she had lived among for almost her entire life, and because of the horrors she had witnessed due to the white man's hatred for the Indian race, she had been able to rationalize the tragic events that had brought her to the Sioux village all those years ago.

White Buffalo had told her that her real family had

been traveling with a wagon train that was headed west. Just days before the attack on the wagons, white soldiers had massacred an entire Sioux village less than thirty miles away. Most of the Sioux who had been killed were women, children and elderly men. The Sioux retaliation against the wagon train was as senseless as the soldiers' actions against the defenseless Sioux village.

Several years ago, Meadow had asked her adoptive mother if there had been other captives taken from the wagon train. Little Squirrel had told her that there had been several other children, along with a couple of young women. When she'd asked Little Squirrel what had happened to them, the older woman had replied, "Sometimes, the things we do not know are best kept that way."

She often wondered if White Buffalo and Little Squirrel would have felt the same toward her if their own children had lived. Sadly, both of their offspring— a three-year-old son and an infant girl—had died of smallpox many years before Meadow's capture. They had not been blessed with any other children. When she had been brought to their village, White Buffalo and Little Squirrel had made her a member of their family in the Making Relatives Ceremony. After smoking from a sacred pipe, sharing food and praying to *Wakan Tanka*, the adoption had been complete. Meadow had no doubt that her life would have been drastically different if it had not been for White Buffalo and his dear wife, Little Squirrel.

As Meadow had grown up in her adopted Indian world, she was constantly made aware of why the Indians were forced to react so violently: they were losing their homelands, their families and even their heritage. The only thing the whites had not yet stolen away from them was their dignity.

Now, for the first time, Meadow wondered why she had not been killed with the rest of her family. "Gentle Water," she said in a low tone, "I'm just realizing that I don't know who—or what—I am. I'm not Sioux, but yet I don't feel anything like a white woman, either. I suddenly feel like an outcast with all people."

Gentle Water tightened her hold on Meadow's hand. "I feel terrible that my careless words have caused you so much pain. Next to my grandmother, you are the person I love the most. You have more than proven your loyalty to our people, so I do not understand why some members of the tribe would care if Black Horse takes you as his wife. I think they are just jealous."

Meadow clutched her friend's hand in the dark tepee. She did not doubt White Buffalo's love, or Gentle Water's either, but she wasn't sure how she would ever feel at ease with the rest of the tribe, now that she knew that they did not accept her completely.

"It does not matter anyway," Meadow said. "I will never be Black Horse's wife, so there is no need for anyone to worry. He is still free to marry one of his own kind. When my father suggested this, and when Black Horse accepted, they had probably drunk far too much whiskey. I'm sure that once they are both thinking clearly again, they will realize that White Buffalo's suggestion is not possible, and then this whole crazy thing will be forgotten."

Gentle Water sighed heavily before answering. "Perhaps you are right about your father, but I don't think

Black Horse is that drunk. Anyway, for now, you must obey your father and come to the celebration."

"Yes," Meadow agreed. "You go on ahead, and I'll come as soon as I change into my ceremonial gown." She squeezed Gentle Water's hand reassuringly. "I will come, I promise."

Gentle Water hesitated for a moment. "I can help you get ready."

"If you don't trust me, I guess—" Meadow began in a hurt tone.

Gentle Water released her hold on Meadow's hand. "I trust you, and I will go back and tell your father that you will be there soon." The two girls stood up together and hugged affectionately.

"Thank you," Meadow said as she pushed Gentle Water toward the opening in the tepee. She watched as the girl ducked through the doorway, then followed her out into the open. Wrapping her arms around herself, Meadow watched until Gentle Water disappeared from her sight. A heavy feeling settled in her chest— she hated lying to her best friend. But she could not go to the celebration tonight.

Off in the distance, where the celebration was taking place, she could see the spiral of smoke rising up above the tops of the tepees. The delicious aroma of the roasted buffalo still filled the entire area, and she could hear the pulsating beat of the drums. She could envision the members of the tribe dancing with abandon around the fire pit. A part of her longed so much to join them, to laugh and dance and gorge herself on the delicious meat. She wanted to forget about Black Horse, and most of all she wanted to forget about the things that Gentle Water had told her. How would she be able to go on living contentedly among these people, knowing that they judged her by the color of her skin?

A deeper ache lodged itself in Meadow's breast. Of all the things she had worried about throughout the years—ambush, starvation, disease and death—she had never once thought that she would have to worry about where she belonged.

Chapter Five

Black Horse had consumed enough of the white man's whiskey throughout the course of the evening to make him even more daring than usual. But he always tried to stop drinking before he got too drunk to be aware of what was going on around him. If there was an attack from an enemy, he had to be capable of fighting. However, the only war he fought tonight was the one within himself. He had sat quietly beside White Buffalo all evening and listened to the older man brag about his daughter's beauty and kindness, and about what a good wife she would make him. Black Horse did not doubt that she would be a good wife in every way. But now the moon was high in the night sky, and Black Horse wanted nothing more than to see this green-eyed beauty that he had agreed to take as his wife.

All evening he had been watching for her, but he was growing tired of waiting for Meadow to appear. When he attempted to push himself up from the ground, his arms felt like weak twigs. He plopped back down and squeezed his eyes shut in an attempt to stop the world from spinning around him. Maybe he had drunk more whiskey than he thought he had. When he slowly reopened them, he found that his vision still had not cleared. The dancers around the fire pit were one constant whirl of color, and the flames in the center of the circle looked as though they were intertwining with the dancers. *Sha*—yes—he had definitely had too much to drink.

An aggravated huff escaped from Black Horse. He rubbed his eyes with clenched fists, which only seemed to make the pounding in his head grow more intense. Although he had planned to drink, eat and dance until the morning hours, right now he only wanted to lie down on the soft fur bed in his lodge. He imagined a lovely young green-eyed woman stretched out beside him like a lazy cat. Her pale skin would shimmer in the darkness, and it was not difficult to imagine how silky and smooth she would feel to his touch. He moaned out loud.

With more determination, Black Horse pushed himself up to a standing position. His lopsided headdress tumbled to the ground unnoticed. When he glanced down at White Buffalo, he saw that the medicine man was lying flat on his back with his mouth wide open, and snoring loudly. Black Horse had the urge to do the same thing, but he had important business to tend to first.

He stepped over the older man and concentrated on watching where he put his feet down until he had managed to avoid stepping on the other inebriated men who were passed out from too much celebrating. Finally, he was away from the center of the village and the hub of the activity. Some of the men had already found their way home and were slumped on the ground in front of their tepees. Their wives and children had probably retired long ago and were sleeping peacefully in their fur-covered beds. Black Horse smiled as he wandered through the maze of tepees. It felt good to be here among his people. His band of warriors spent most of their time in secluded hideouts between battles and raids. He was enjoying meeting members of the different Sioux tribes—especially one lovely young maiden. He might end up liking Canada much more than he had thought he would.

When Black Horse reached his own lodge, he did not stop—he had other things to do before he retired tonight. White Buffalo's lodge stood quiet and dark, as if no one was there. He drew in a deep breath and glanced around. The area was quiet and dark. His steps were slow as he made his way to the medicine man's tepee, but his heart pounded rapidly in his chest. The image of the beautiful young white woman dominated his thoughts.

"Meadow, are you in there?" he called out when he reached the other tepee. "Why are you hiding from me?" he asked as he pushed open the door flap and stepped inside. He was not expecting the stillness and the complete darkness, and he stumbled forward until his foot caught under the edge of a stack of logs. He did not realize his predicament until he crashed hard against the ground.

The impact made it impossible for him to catch his breath for a moment, and as he struggled to regain the ability to breathe again, he slowly became aware of a dull throbbing in his temple. A moan escaped from him when he attempted to move. The fall, combined with the liquor he had consumed, made getting up more trouble than it was worth. Within minutes, he was sound asleep.

* * *

Since she had not wanted to be at the tepee if Gentle Water came back to insist that she go to the celebration, Meadow had escaped to the edge of the forest, where the horses were kept in a roughly built corral. Although she longed to jump on the back of one of the animals and gallop far away, the fear of what might be lurking in the darkened forest kept her from wandering from the village. She had spent the evening in the company of the Sioux ponies.

When the sounds were beginning to die down from the night's festivities, she figured it was safe to sneak back to her tepee. Black Horse was probably so drunk that he had forgotten all about her by now.

Gentle Water was probably mad at her for lying, so no one would bother her for the rest of the night. As Meadow made her way back to the tepee, she noticed that the drums were finally silent and most of the lodges were dark and quiet. She sighed with relief that she had not encountered Black Horse again. The only thing she wanted was the comfort of her soft bed. Tomorrow she would worry about the things that Gentle Water had told her regarding her white blood, and with any luck, this ridiculous situation with Black Horse would be forgotten.

Entering the dark tepee, Meadow could hear breathing coming from the vicinity of where her father's bed was located. At least he had made it back to his own tepee for the night, unlike some of the men that she had seen passed out on the hard ground around the encampment. As quietly as possible, Meadow made her way to her own bed and slipped under the covers. Since she had not made a fire all evening, the inside of the tepee was freezing. She decided to sleep in all of her clothes and removed only her tall moccasins. As she burrowed farther down under the thick covers, she wondered how they would ever survive the winter in this part of the country. It was only early fall, and already the temperature was dipping down to almost freezing at night.

Once her bed began to warm up slightly from the heat of her own body, Meadow fell into a deep but troubled sleep. Her dreams were tormented with images of wandering aimlessly between the white man's world and the village of the Sioux people. In each location, she would be chased away like a rabid dog, until she had nowhere to go and found herself all alone, huddled under an ominous-looking tree in a darkening forest. Then, as though some invisible force had surrounded her, she felt someone's strong arms wrap around her. She felt so safe—safer than she had ever felt before. Meadow snuggled deeper into the strong arms that held her and slipped into a peaceful slumber.

Black Horse's nose felt like a chunk of ice, and his hands were even colder, when he awoke sometime during the night. He was surrounded by darkness, and he couldn't force his eyes to stay open. His head hurt, and he didn't feel like moving. But the freezing temperature prompted him to make the effort to find some source of heat. He felt around with his hands and located the rocks surrounding the fire pit in the center of the lodge. He could see the soft glow of moonlight where the flap in the doorway was located at the front of the tepee and through the smoke hole at the top.

Assuming that he was in his own lodge, Black Horse

began to crawl toward the back of the tepee, where he knew his soft bed was waiting. The comfort of his bed was much more desirable than the cold, rock-hard ground he was lying on now.

When his searching hand felt the edge of the thick furs, he exhaled a deep sigh. This bed was going to feel so good, he thought as he discarded his shirt, breechcloth and leggings before he crawled under the warm covers. He rolled over on his side and realized that a soft feminine body was curled up under the furs with him. This was a nice dream. Without a second thought, he wrapped his arms around her in a comforting embrace. The last thing he vaguely remembered before he dropped off into a deep slumber was the way the woman's body molded up against his as if they were meant to be this way forever.

Before she even opened her eyes, Meadow felt a strange presence in her bed. A large arm was slung across her breast, and a muscled leg was pinning her to the ground. Her eyes flew wide open. A dim glow from the early-morning sun outside the doorway and through the smoke hole overhead barely lit the interior of the tepee, but it was still not enough light for Meadow to see who was sprawled all over her. Her mouth instinctively opened with the intent to scream for help, but then the man moved slightly and spoke softly.

"Green-eyed woman," Black Horse whispered without opening his eyes. His breathing grew even and quiet again.

The scream that had been in Meadow's throat a moment ago was now a huge, choking lump. Her arms and legs felt frozen in place, and she could not make a sound because her breath was caught somewhere in the back of her throat. Black Horse was in her bed . . . with her?

This was not possible! Was she still sleeping and having a nightmare?

She became aware of every tiny inch where their bodies were touching: his face was pressing into her neck, and she could feel his soft breath brushing against her skin; his arm was resting intimately across her breasts; and worst of all, she could feel the outline of his manhood pressing against her thigh. The memory of his naked body down by the river yesterday came rushing back to her in vivid color.

In spite of her attempt to keep silent, a choked gasp escaped. She clamped her eyes shut tightly, but she could not erase the realization that those very same parts were now so close to her own most private area that they were almost touching. Nothing—absolutely nothing—was separating the lower portion of their bodies. Meadow's dress was hiked up around her waist, and Black Horse was completely naked!

Mindless panic engulfed any coherent thoughts she had left. The dream that she had enjoyed so much during the night—the strong arms, the sense of security—had *not* been a dream. It had been real, and she had managed to sleep through it all!

Meadow brought her free hand up to her mouth to stifle any sound she might make. The Sioux people did not look kindly on promiscuous behavior among the women of the tribe. After learning about her precarious position with some of the tribal members from Gentle Water last night, Meadow knew that being in the situation she was in at this moment could very well mean her exile from this village forever. Then where would she go?

Black Horse mumbled something inaudible, then pressed even closer against her than Meadow thought was humanly possible. His manhood felt enormous against her leg, and the strange ache between her legs returned. Meadow had never felt so helpless in her entire life. She had to get away from him before the entire population of the village was up and moving about, but she could not even breathe, let alone move.

From the faint light breaking through the doorway and the smoke hole in the ceiling, she assumed the first rays of the morning sun were already here. Normally, most of the village's population would be up by now, but because of the late celebration last night, almost everyone except the old women and mothers with little ones were probably sleeping off the effects of too much celebrating.

Black Horse smelled faintly of whiskey, which was probably why he had stumbled into the wrong tepee. Would she be able to convince anyone else of that?

Meadow tried to calm herself. There was really only one thing that she could do: get out of Black Horse's tight hold and then get as far away from him as possible. She used her free hand to push against Black Horse's shoulder. He was a deadweight, and she was hardly able to raise him up more than an inch or two. He plopped back down against her the instant she released him. Meadow coughed when all her air was knocked out of her body. She drew in a deep breath and refocused all her energy on the man who was sprawled on top of her. With every ounce of her strength, she shoved against his chest and kicked her legs until she felt his limp body begin to roll off of her.

She shoved him the rest of the way and panted as he thudded against the hard ground beside her thick mattress of furs. A loud groan was his first response. Then, to Meadow's horror, he began to make noises as if he was waking up.

"Wh-what happened?" he mumbled. He tried to force his eyes open, but even the limited light in the tepee was too much for his blurry eyes. As the cold from the ground underneath him began to seep into his bones, he shivered visibly. His hand reached out and touched on the edge of the soft fur blankets beside him. He started to push himself up to a crawling position.

"Stop right there," Meadow ordered through clenched teeth. She scooted to the far side of her bed in an effort to keep as much distance between them as she could.

The sound of her voice stopped Black Horse's sluggish movements. "Who's here in my tepee?" he demanded as he struggled to sit up.

"Your tepee? You are crazier than I thought," Meadow retorted with more bravery than she actually felt. Her whole body was shaking uncontrollably. She crawled to the bottom of her bed, which was closer to the exit if she needed to make a quick escape.

Black Horse managed to sit up. "Green-eyed woman?" he muttered. He rubbed at his eyes and stared at her again. "It is you. I had a dream about you. But why are you here now?"

"Because this is my father's lodge, and you will be a dead man if he finds you here." Meadow scooted a few inches closer to the doorway.

She could tell that Black Horse was confused. He glanced around at the strange surroundings and began to rub nervously at his forehead. Meadow took this opportunity to inch closer to the doorway.

"Wait," he said, then grabbed his head again at the sound of his own voice. "Don't go," he said in a quieter tone.

"My father—"

"I will make him understand . . . that is, once I am able to understand why I am here."

"Could you at least, you know—" Meadow motioned toward his exposed manhood as she made a useless attempt to look the other way.

Black Horse's gaze followed hers. He did not bother to respond with words as he reached over and grabbed the fur blanket to cover himself.

"Thank you for that, at least!" she huffed.

Black Horse ignored her indignation as he shut his eyes and tried in vain to recall the details of the previous night. He remembered coming to look for Meadow, and then he had tripped and fallen down . . . but that was all he remembered. He didn't think he had drunk that much.

"I must have gotten lost when I was going to my own lodge last night," he said with a shrug of his bare shoulders. "White Buffalo probably saw me wandering around and took pity on me, so he let me—"

"My father would not leave you alone in here with me, so I don't think that's what happened." Meadow crossed her arms over her breast and drew in a nervous breath, adding, "And, he certainly would not have let you sleep in here like that." She motioned with a quick wave of her hand toward his naked body, which was partially covered by the blanket.

"Maybe I—" Black Horse dropped his hands down on his thighs. He had no explanation for this. "I am sorry if I have put you in a bad way with your father. White Buffalo is a respected man in the tribe."

"I'm sure he does not know you're here. I think he must have slept in the center of the village with the other drunks."

"I should go, then," Black Horse said in hardly more than a whisper. He scooted closer to where Meadow was sitting. She was so close now that he could reach out and touch her again, and this was a temptation he could not resist. His hand shook as it rose up in the air and reached out for her hand. To his amazement, she did not try to stop him as he picked it up and clasped his fingers around hers. An odd sensation passed through him as he gently held her hand, and it had nothing to do with the obvious way she affected him physically. He just wanted to hold her hand—to hold onto her— forever.

As the sun from the smoke hole brightened the interior of the lodge, Meadow could plainly see the tenderness in his handsome face. He was staring at her so intently, and he seemed so confused. She wondered if it was possible he really didn't know what tepee he had bedded down in last night. He looked so different from yesterday, when he had stood proudly outside the tepee in his finest garments and enormous headdress.

Now, sitting here on the hard ground, a bewildered expression on his face and his long ebony hair tousled around it, he reminded Meadow of a lost little boy.

She had the urge to put her arms around him and tell him that everything would be well. Instead, she began to focus on the way he held her hand so gently in his own—and of the way this simple gesture set all of her insides ablaze with that odd feeling of pain and pleasure.

Meadow ran her tongue across her parched lips and held her breath for a moment. She knew he had to leave before someone caught them like this, but she could not force herself to pull her hand away. Her gaze met his, and it was as if the rest of the world did not exist. She leaned forward, instinctively drawn to him.

His lips touched hers lightly at first, as if he ached to be near her but was slightly unsure of her reaction. He reached up and placed his hand around her head. She could feel the strands of her long hair entwined in his fingers. His lips pressed harder against her soft mouth, and she leaned in even closer to him.

Never had Meadow imagined that she would experience such an overpowering feeling of bliss from her first kiss. All of her fears dissolved, and every inch of her body felt like a million hot coals had just invaded her. The feel of his lips against hers was like a magical journey that she wished would never have to end.

When they were forced to part for air, Meadow thought she could live forever without taking another breath if it meant she could feel his lips against hers for the rest of her life. She felt his hand slide under her chin, raising her face up so that they were staring into one another's eyes again. His dark gaze caressed her, and everything outside of this moment was mute.

"Oh, green-eyed woman, what strong magic you

must possess. You have put me under a spell," Black Horse said softly.

The sound of someone from a nearby tepee coughing brought Meadow back to reality. "Maybe you should go now," she said in a hoarse tone. She cleared her throat, but not the sensuous feelings that were still surging through her body.

Black Horse nodded his head and cleared his throat gruffly, too. "*Sha*, I should go." A faint smile touched his lips as he added, "But this is only the beginning for us." He reached out and tenderly caressed her cheek with the back of his fingers.

Meadow remained unmoving on the ground as Black Horse slowly rose to his feet. She did not even have to avert her eyes while he dropped the fur, quickly donned his breechcloth and scooped up the remainder of his clothes. Her attention was held captive by his tender gaze. All the doubts she had first had about him seemed to disappear and were replaced with the realization that she never wanted to hide from him again. When he backed toward the doorway to leave, there were no words that needed to be spoken; his kiss had just sealed her fate.

Chapter Six

Today had to be the most glorious day ever, Meadow decided as she stirred a pot of stew with large, succulent chunks of leftover buffalo meat. She had made corn cakes earlier while the stew was simmering, and now she was ready to prepare herself for the evening ahead.

As she braided her hair into one thick braid that hung down her back, Meadow relived every second of her last encounter with Black Horse. She could still feel the way his hand had caressed her face and see his loving expression as he told her that this was only the beginning for them. A wide smile settled on her lips every time she thought about seeing him again. What a difference a day could make. The way she had acted yesterday seemed so silly now, and she was grateful that she would have another chance to show him what a good wife she would be. She would prove to the entire tribe that she was the right woman for him, regardless of their prejudice against her white blood.

Although most of the men had spent the day trying to recuperate from massive hangovers, White Buffalo had found his way home shortly before the midday meal, taken a short nap and awakened after a couple of hours feeling good as new. He had then gone to Black Horse's tepee to invite him to dinner tonight, and his invitation had been accepted.

Meadow could tell that he had no idea Black Horse had spent the night with her in their tepee, and she was determined to keep this latest episode with Black Horse a secret from her father. Was it only yesterday morning that she could not have imagined keeping anything from him?

While she was sitting in the tepee braiding her hair, Meadow saw Black Horse coming out of his own lodge. She had purposely tied the door flap open so that she could watch for him. He was wearing only a breechcloth and carried a small blanket that was draped over one arm. Meadow knew he was headed down to the river to bathe again. She drew in a deep breath as she watched him approach. The attraction she felt toward the chief was something she could not deny, but it went far beyond the way he looked—with or without his clothes on. She already knew what a beautiful man he was on the outside, and she was looking forward to finding out if he was as appealing on the inside, where it really mattered.

When he walked past her tepee, Meadow noticed that he took a peek in the huge pot that was simmering over the fire pit outside. He smiled as though the contents pleased him greatly. Then, he looked toward the tepee. His smile widened when he caught sight of her through the open doorway.

"Would you care to join me at the river again today?" he asked with a sly smile and then a wink of one eye.

A gasp was Meadow's only verbal reply as she shook her head rigorously from side to side. She hoped White Buffalo was not close by. Black Horse's laughter reached her ears as he walked away. She was just grateful that she was sitting in the tepee, so that he wouldn't have to see the immense shame that had undoubtedly lit up her face again. Would he never allow her to forget that stupid episode?

Probably not! But once they were married she would relish the idea of bathing with him.

By the time Meadow saw Black Horse returning from his bath, she had managed to calm her racing heart. But she still did not trust herself enough to leave her tepee to stir the stew again until she was sure he was back in his own lodge. She told herself that she would have to learn to accept the fact that he would always have that little incident at the river to hold over her head. Of course, if they did get married, the sight of his naked body would be a daily occurrence. She grabbed a rag and wiped away the sweat from her entire face and neck. At this rate, she was going to melt away before she even had a chance to become Black Horse's bride.

"Are you ill, *mi-cun-ksi*?" White Buffalo asked worriedly as he walked up to their tepee.

Meadow threw the rag down on the rocks surrounding the fire pit and attempted to answer him in a coherent manner. "*Sha*. Well, maybe . . . I don't think so," she finally admitted. There was no use trying to hide everything from her father any longer—he was far too wise and intuitive.

"Then come, sit with me and tell me what is bothering you." White Buffalo motioned for her to join him on the ground in front of their tepee. He sat down in a cross-legged position and patted the spot next to him.

Meadow hesitated before sitting down beside her father. How would she explain these strange feelings without dying of embarrassment? Finally, she sat down and plucked at a weed that protruded from the ground, as she mulled over what she would say. But White Buffalo did not give her any more time.

"So tell me, *mi-cun-ksi*, about these feelings that you get every time you think about Black Horse, or when you see him."

Meadow drew in a sharp breath. "How did you know?"

His ability to sense what was going on in her head was unnerving.

White Buffalo chuckled. "You might find this hard to believe, but I was young once. And Little Squirrel's ripe young body made my blood boil faster than that stew bubbling over there in the pot."

His words made Meadow giggle nervously. Thinking of her father and mother experiencing these same fanatical emotions seemed very odd to her. "But that was different."

"How so?" White Buffalo asked in a surprised but amused tone of voice.

"Well . . . because you met each other and fell in love," Meadow began. She had to be careful not to say anything that would make him suspicious about her adventure at the river yesterday or her encounter with Black Horse in their tepee. "And then you courted Mother and married her in the normal way."

A hearty laugh emitted from White Buffalo. "The normal way?" He reached out and grabbed his daughter around the shoulders to pull her close to him in a tight hug. "And you think these things that you are feeling for Black Horse are not normal?"

Meadow allowed herself to snuggle into her father's embrace just as she had when she was a little girl.

"Well, I just saw him—I mean, met him yesterday," she answered. "Shouldn't these feelings develop slowly over time?"

A sigh escaped from White Buffalo before he spoke. "Not always, and in these crazy days, our people do not have the luxury of time." He rubbed her back affectionately. "Time is so precious that we should not waste one minute of it. Love all you can today, *mi-cun-ksi*, because we never know if there will be a tomorrow. That is why I knew I had to take matters into my own hands and propose marriage for you and Black Horse."

The full meaning of his words struck Meadow like a bolt of lightning. She was reminded once again of how wise this wonderful man was, and of how lucky she was to have been adopted by him. "Thank you, Father," she said. "I will not waste even one second, and I will not deny my feelings, even if they did arrive without warning."

"I think that is called love at first sight. I sensed it from the first moment I saw the two of you together yesterday. I believe Black Horse is just as taken with you. I saw him walking toward the river earlier with a huge smile on his face, and then he began to sing an old Sioux song about his heart being stolen by the *Wakan Tanka* of love."

Goose bumps broke out all over Meadow's body. She felt so happy at this moment that she wanted to jump up and burst into song, too. "So, you believe that he really does want to marry me?"

"I do not do anything that I do not want to do."

At the sound of Black Horse's voice behind them, Meadow let out a cry and jumped to her feet. "W-we didn't see you there," she gasped.

"Well, I think I'll let the two of you be alone for a bit," White Buffalo said as he pushed himself up from the ground. He smiled at the couple as he walked past them. "I'll be back for dinner, though, so don't start eating without me."

Meadow stared at her father in disbelief. How could he leave her here alone with Black Horse when he knew how this man made her feel? She suddenly became aware that Black Horse had come up close behind her. Her heart stopped beating for an instant when she heard his deep voice directly behind her.

"As I said before, I never do anything that I don't want to do."

Meadow turned around to face him. He stood barely more than a few inches away from her, and her first thought was that they were almost close enough to kiss again. His next words snapped her out of this sweet reverie, however.

"And what about you? Do you want to marry me?"

"I—I— Yes, I do," she whispered as she remembered the promise she had just given her father. She would not waste one second. Her gaze rose up until it was locked with his. She tossed her head back and sighed deeply before she gave in to the urge that she could not deny any longer. She leaned closer to him, and Black Horse's hand immediately slid around her waist as he pulled her the short distance to him. Then, his lips descended on hers with abandon.

Although she hadn't been able to imagine that their second kiss could even begin to compare with their first one, Meadow was certain Black Horse was trying to outdo himself. They were standing in the middle of the village where everyone could see them, yet she gave no thought to modesty. His strong arms were surrounding her again, and his mouth was doing the most amazing things. Meadow let her own lips imitate his and returned his kiss without reservation. She had her own hunger to satisfy, and it was obviously equal to his appetite.

The sound of a man's laughter interrupted their passionate interlude. Meadow felt Black Horse's lips pulling away far too soon, and to her dismay, his tight hold on her grew slack. She turned to face the man who had caused the interruption.

"*Hunda wanzin ya!*" Black Horse exclaimed as he pulled Meadow up to the other man. A broad smile claimed his mouth as he glanced back and forth between the man and Meadow. "This is Walks Tall," Black Horse stated.

"Y-your brother?" Meadow stammered. "I did not realize you had a brother," she added as she politely bowed her head toward the man. She realized that she knew nothing about her husband-to-be, except the rumors she had heard about his brave and dangerous exploits.

"And you are Meadow," the man said in a soft tone. He also bowed his head in a courteous manner. When he looked up again, his gaze drifted to Black Horse and he nodded and winked. "You did not exaggerate her beauty."

A smile came easily to Meadow's kiss-swollen lips as she looked up at Walks Tall's friendly countenance. She guessed his name was due to his towering stature; he stood even taller than Black Horse. He did not, however, have the well-muscled body of the war chief, and although he was a good-looking man Meadow did not think him nearly as handsome.

"It is truly an honor to meet the brother of Black Horse," Meadow said. She noticed the possessive way that Black Horse held onto her; he did not allow her to leave his side for one instant.

Walks Tall leaned toward Meadow and chuckled as he said, "We're not related, but we do consider ourselves as close as brothers."

"We have been blood brothers since we were small boys and cut our fingers to join our blood," Black Horse added. "And Walks Tall is also my head warrior. He is at my side in all battles."

Walks Tall nodded his head and straightened his stance in a proud manner. As head warrior, he had ridden with Black Horse on every raid and battle they had fought since they had been inducted into manhood together during the Sun Dance Ceremony, in which boys became men in an ancient ritual that involved having hooks stuck in their chests, then being hung from a pole by the hooks. The boy would dance around the pole until the skin was ripped from the hooks. All Sioux men carried the scars from this sacred rite.

"Will you eat with us tonight?" Meadow asked, knowing that her father would not mind another guest for the evening meal. She glanced up at Black Horse and was relieved to see that he did not seem to mind her extending the spontaneous invitation to his close friend. He smiled down at her when their eyes met, and nodded slightly.

"You are kind, but my sister—my real sister—has insisted that I come to eat with her family tonight.

I have not seen her for many moons, and I have a young nephew that I did not even know had been born."

"There will be time," Black Horse said. He hugged Meadow tighter and smiled down at her.

"I will look forward to it," Walks Tall answered.

As he turned to leave, Walks Tall glanced back at his friend in wonderment. It seemed almost impossible that Black Horse had gone through such a complete transformation in the last two days. The man he had known his entire life had said on many occasions that he did not have time for a wife and family because he considered the fight for his people his only quest. Now, in just the short time since they had arrived in Canada and he had met this woman, the chief was like a different man. Walks Tall had never known a woman to affect Black Horse in such a manner, although there had once been a young Blackfoot girl who had held his interest for a while. Even though she was supposed to be Black Horse's captive, they had enjoyed a very passionate time together. Black Horse had kept the girl, Shy Deer, for several moons, and even missed her when her own people had finally recaptured her.

Last night, Walks Tall had heard the comments about this woman's white heritage, and he hoped this would not present any problems. But, as Walks Tall looked at the beautiful woman at his friend's side and the way they were looking at one another now, his heart filled with happiness. This marriage was a good thing. It was time for Black Horse to have some peace and contentment in his life—even if it was for only a little while.

Chapter Seven

Brandon Cornett wished he could shed every stitch of his clothing. The heat of the midday sun felt almost unbearable, and the heavy woolen coat he was wearing made him feel like a million miniature irons were pressing into his skin. He sighed, deep and hard. What he would give to take off his coat. But then, he reminded himself, he would be out of uniform. With a sense of aggravation, he glanced at his superior officer, Superintendent Walsh. Instead of the formal uniform worn by the other North-West Mounted Police, the flamboyant leader of the troop at Fort Walsh preferred to wear a fringed buckskin outfit.

A frown tugged at Brandon's mouth as he continued to study the man who led the troop. Even now, on this solemn mission, the commander wore his unorthodox suit as he rode at the head of the small brigade. Brandon thought his attire was in gross defiance of the rules.

"What'd ya think that savage will be like?"

Brandon glanced absently at the man who had just ridden up beside him, interrupting a daydream about his future as the superintendent of his own fort. "Who?"

"Old Sitting Bull," the sergeant replied. "I heard he looks meaner than a rattler and is twice as deadly."

Brandon shrugged. "Seems like he's been a might docile since he's been up here in Canada." His voice, deep, and heavy with a French-Canadian accent, contained an obvious note of annoyance.

"He's just waitin' to strike," Sergeant Rattan said. He gave his head a firm shake. "You mark my words, Lieutenant, Sittin' Bull's calm now. But he's still lickin' his wounds from the Little Bighorn. Once he's had time to regroup, he'll grow strong again. Then, he'll wipe out everything—and everybody—who gets in his way."

Brandon kept his eyes focused on the road ahead. "I hope you're wrong," he answered. An icy shiver raced down his spine. He kept recalling the rumors, or truths, that had been circulating around the fort. Over five thousand Indians, mostly Sioux, had crossed over the Canadian border in the past few months. Their enormous number meant that before long, sickness and disease would likely erupt; starvation was inevitable, too.

To make matters worse, they had also heard that the Sioux' worst enemies, the Blackfoot, had also taken up residency in the area. The two warring tribes would undoubtedly continue with their murderous raids on one another's villages, especially since all the Indians were restless, angry and tired of running away from the relentless American soldiers on the other side of the border.

A sense of doom caused a heavy knot to settle in the pit of Brandon's stomach. How could the measly hundred and two Mounties who were stationed at Fort Walsh ever hope to control an invasion of thousands of vengeful Indians? Newly built here in the Cypress Hills, the stockade that housed Fort Walsh represented the only form of law and order in the North-West Territories.

Sergeant Rattan rode beside Brandon without making any further comments about the Indians. Brandon sighed with relief. He did not want to dwell on what might happen when they reached the Indian encampment. They had sent a scout to the village to warn the Indians that they were coming, and he had returned unharmed, so Brandon hoped there was nothing to worry about. If the sergeant was right about Sitting Bull, this entire mission was foolish and suicidal.

Once again Brandon noticed how intolerable the heat was today—or was it just his nervousness? He squirmed uneasily in his saddle and then tugged hard on the high collar of his coat. It seemed abnormally warm for Canada at this time of year; during the day it felt more like July than September. But at night the temperature dipped significantly, and the chill in the air was already hinting at the approaching winter.

The announcement that the Sioux village was near snapped Brandon's thoughts back to the business at hand. A nervous twitch in his stomach made him feel queasy. Since becoming a Mountie, this was by far the most dangerous mission in which he had ever been involved. His fear continued to grow as he listened to Superintendent Walsh's instructions.

"We are here on a peaceful mission," Walsh called out to his troops. "Under no circumstances are we to initiate any trouble."

"What if they start it?" Rattan asked, then added in a slightly belligerent tone, "Sir?"

Walsh cast the sergeant a narrowed-eyed glare. "There are thousands of them, and a dozen of us. If they want to fight, I guess this will be the day we all meet our Maker."

Walsh's blunt retort left the troop silent and looking as if they all wanted to turn tail and run. The superintendent didn't give them the chance. He raised his arm up into the air. The long suede fringe that decorated his shirt waved like a flag from his sleeve as he signaled for his men to follow him into the Indian encampment.

Brandon's horse fell in line as they began their march into the village to meet with Sitting Bull and other important leaders of the Sioux tribes. The nausea in his stomach expanded. Now he felt a hard knot forming in his chest, too. What was it he had heard that the Indians always said before going into a battle? "It's a good day to die," he whispered as a cold sweat broke out on his forehead. The sun continued to beat down on his fevered face, yet he shivered. It did not seem like such a good day to die, Brandon thought as he clenched his horse's reins tighter in his sweaty hands.

As the troop neared the village, the sound of drums could be heard echoing through the dense forest. Expecting to be surrounded by warriors who had murder ruling their thoughts, Brandon was surprised when they continued to approach the village without being stopped or killed. The pounding of the drums seemed to rival the pounding of his heartbeat, but Brandon wasn't sure which one was louder. The horrid stories of the recent battle at the Little Bighorn on the American side of the border kept flashing through his mind. General Custer and his troops had not fared well against Sitting Bull and his warriors. What made this little troop of Mounties think they would do any better?

The thick, towering pines began to grow sparse, and the noises coming from the village grew closer. Columns of smoke could be seen rising up through the treetops. Brandon was beginning to think they were going to be able to ride right into the center of the camp, when a loud shout halted their progress. Within seconds, Indians surrounded the Mounties. The sea of dark faces blurred before Brandon's eyes. He blinked nervously and tried to focus on the Indian standing nearest to him. Blinding panic gripped Brandon when his gaze met with the piercing dark eyes of the Indian who had suddenly appeared at his horse's side.

As his vision cleared, Brandon realized he was now staring down the barrel of a .44 Winchester. He had never seen an Indian carrying a gun until now, and the sight of the Sioux warrior holding one was unnerving. He remembered hearing that most American Indians were usually well armed with guns they had either stolen from soldiers or obtained from unscrupulous traders.

From the corner of his eye Brandon noticed his comrades were all being ordered to dismount. Using the gun he held, the Indian beside Brandon motioned for him to do the same. With slow, cautious movements, he dropped to the ground. His gaze remained on the gun, but his thoughts were going in a dozen directions at once. Mostly, he was thinking about how the Indians tortured their captives. When the Indian shoved his gun in his side, Brandon prayed he would just shoot him now.

All activity ceased when the Mounties were led into the center of the camp. Superintendent Walsh made several attempts to speak to the Indians but was ignored. Now, they were surrounded by a large group of women, children and barking dogs. Walsh fell silent as he watched the crowd grow in number, although the Indians made no attempt to harass the soldiers. The Sioux spoke to one another in whispers that were not audible to the soldiers. Shortly, the group of Indians began to part, making a path for several others.

Brandon watched the men approach in fascination and fear. It was obvious by their elaborate costumes and headdresses they were important men in this tribe, but it was their dignified manner that impressed him the most. There was no doubt the man who walked in front was Sitting Bull. Brandon had heard that the powerful medicine man and chief walked with a limp as a result of a bullet wound from a Crow's gun during a horse raid when Sitting Bull was just a young man. When the feared leader stopped before the Mounties, Walsh stepped forward.

Sitting Bull nodded a curt greeting to Walsh, which the superintendent imitated. An exchange of Sioux words followed, with Walsh speaking first, then Sitting Bull. There appeared to be no harsh words spoken, and since the superintendent spoke to the Sioux leaders in their own language, Brandon had no knowledge of what was being said until Walsh turned around and repeated the brief conversation in English.

"Sitting Bull has assured me that his people have abandoned their fight on the other side of the border."

In spite of his calm manner, Brandon noticed a heavy mask of sweat coated the superintendent's face as he spoke.

"Are we free to leave, then?" one nervous-looking Mountie asked.

"Sitting Bull has asked us to stay for a wedding that is about to take place. I've accepted his invitation," Walsh announced. The obvious tension that was apparent in his expression and tone of voice began to fade as he added, "He said his people are too tired to fight anymore—and I honestly believe him."

After Brandon watched Walsh turn around and follow Sitting Bull toward the center of the village, he glanced at the crowd of Indians who had slowly backed away to make passage for the soldiers. An overpowering sense of sorrow washed through him. He had been prepared to hate these savages, but there was nothing savage about these pitiful-looking people. The sea of dark faces around him were not hostile and murderous. Many of the women—especially the older ones—looked as if they had borne the weight of a thousand pounds throughout their lifetimes. There was emptiness in their eyes and a look of hopelessness on their haggard faces. Most of the men looked old and walked with hunched shoulders and slow steps. But it was the children Brandon found the most pathetic. In spite of their tiny bodies, the haunted expressions they wore on their faces made them seem as though they weren't really children at all. It was as if their youth had been stripped away and they had forgotten what it meant to play.

Walking through the village, Brandon was amazed

to see how many tepees were crowded into this wooded area. He guessed there had to be several hundred lodges scattered among the trees. His nervousness returned as he settled down on the ground beside the rest of his comrades. The Indians joined them, all sitting down in a huge circle around a large fire pot. Several large buffalo hindquarters roasted over the hot coals, giving off a scrumptious aroma. Brandon had heard the Sioux were at the point of starvation, but it did not appear that they were doing without food now. Buffalo were rare in this part of Canada, so Brandon was even more surprised to see that there seemed to be such an abundance of this type of game in the village.

When a long pipe was handed to him, Brandon obediently took a puff. The tobacco was potent and it felt as if it had lighted his throat and nose on fire. Trying to keep from choking, he handed the pipe to the next man. A gruff cough escaped from him in spite of his attempt to hold it back. He kept his attention focused on Superintendent Walsh and Sitting Bull.

He was not able to hear their voices because of the drums that had resumed beating. The Mountie sitting closest to Walsh, however, began to pass bits and pieces of the conversation down the line as the superintendent relayed information to him. When the tidbits reached Brandon's waiting ears, he learned that the wedding they were about to witness was that of a war chief and the daughter of an elderly medicine man. He was one of the men who had accompanied Sitting Bull out to meet them when they had first arrived in the village. That same medicine man was sitting next to Sitting Bull now. Brandon eyed him thoughtfully.

He looked slightly older than Sitting Bull, and not nearly as fierce. Sitting Bull, with his hawk-like nose and perpetual frown, seemed almost ominous.

The pounding of the drums grew more intense, drawing Brandon's attention to the opposite side of the fire pit. Through the rising smoke he could see a man walking toward the head of the circle where the chiefs and Superintendent Walsh sat. The man walked tall and straight. Brandon guessed he was young because he still moved with a sense of pride—unlike many of the men he had noticed in the village. When the man stepped out from the veil of smoke, Brandon finally got a clear view. A cold chill whipped through his body as he stared at the young chief. He wore the most magnificent costume Brandon had ever seen. As his gaze traveled down from the huge feathered headdress to the beaded and fringed moccasins the chief wore, his sense of foreboding increased. When Brandon looked back up, he caught a glimpse of the man's face. Another icy shiver shook through Brandon. This man was the epitome of the dangerous savage he had always feared.

"Who is that Indian?" one of the Mounties closest to Brandon asked in a low voice.

With a shrug, Brandon leaned toward the man on his other side and asked the same question. The inquiry was repeated until it reached the man closest to Walsh. When the name Black Horse was echoed back through the circle, Brandon felt another deep sense of foreboding settle in his chest. He had never heard the name before, but he had the distinct feeling that this man was not just another Indian. There was a dangerous aura about the young chief, a sense of something reckless, powerful . . . and memorable. "He's the one who brought the buffalo," whispered Sergeant Rattan. "There was whiskey, too, but they already gulped all that down."

"Thank goodness," Brandon replied. He knew the Indians' reputation for drinking. If they had arrived while the Indians were still drunk, the Mounties might have received a far less cordial greeting.

The beating of the drums intensified as all eyes turned toward the opposite side of the fire again. Brandon was eager to get a clear view of the bride, whom he could see moving through the smoky haze. When she stepped up to the chief, Brandon felt his breath catch in his throat. She wore a light-colored buckskin dress that looked as if it had been tanned until it was as soft as melted butter. Beads and long fringe hung from the neckline, and also from the sleeves and the uneven hemline that hung down to the top of her high moccasins. Her hair was braided on both sides of her head with leather thongs that matched her dress, and long white feathers hung from the sides of the beaded headband that encircled her head. She was, Brandon decided in that instant, the most beautiful sight he had ever seen . . . and she was a white woman!

For the past couple of weeks Black Horse had allowed himself to engage in the silly courtship games that his people's tradition insisted he play. He had played love songs on a cedar flute outside Meadow's tepee and had given White Buffalo some of his best horses as a wedding gift. To Black Horse's surprise, he had not minded doing any of these things, in spite of Walks

Tall's constant teasing. As final preparation for the wedding, Black Horse had undergone the Rite of Purification to cleanse him of all his wrongdoings. When he left the sweat lodge after the rite, he had felt as if he was reborn, and he had been eager to assume his role as Meadow's husband.

He watched her walk toward the sacred fire circle where he waited for her with growing anticipation. Although her beauty made his knees weak, and the honor of being the man to take her maidenhood caused his loins to throb with impatience, Black Horse was amazed at how much he was growing to love all the other things about her. Her laughter, even just her smile, made his heart sing, and it was contagious. He had laughed and smiled more in the last couple of weeks than he had for years, and he hoped he could provide his new wife with a life that would make her smile often. Her gentleness and kind nature touched his heart, but Black Horse admired her strength most of all. He had no doubt that she had suffered many hardships in her young lifetime, but she was still full of optimism that the future was somehow going to be better. He wished he could tell her she was right.

Black Horse continued to stare at his beautiful bride-to-be as she stopped beside him. He could see a glimmer in her pale gaze that he was sure was admiration and, most definitely, the excitement of their blossoming love. A shy smile curved her lips, and a guilty pang shot through his chest. What if he could not give her the life she deserved? He knew that he would not be content to live here in Canada—in hiding—for the rest of his life. He took a deep, heavy breath. If she expected these things of him after they were man and wife, she would be gravely disappointed. He would not hide in a foreign country like a scared dog, nor would he stand idle while his people died of starvation and sickness. Black Horse intended to fight back against the white men until his dying day. After this ceremony, his life would become hers, too. He only hoped she understood the commitment she was making this day.

Meadow's gaze lowered when she saw the odd way Black Horse was staring at her. She still found it hard to believe she was actually going to be the wife of this brave and powerful chief. Other than the few kisses they had shared, and a few stolen moments alone now and then, they had spent the majority of the past couple of weeks in the company of others or engaged in preparations for the wedding. But she had been with him enough to know that she was already in love with him. Her father had been right when he had told her that she had fallen in love with Black Horse the moment she had first set eyes on him, but that had only been the beginning of the feelings she was developing for this man. He was a proud man, with a good heart, and she had no doubts that he would be a good husband. He made her feel safe, and she knew as long as he was at her side, there would never be any doubts about where she belonged. She already knew how much she enjoyed his naked body, and the thought of being truly intimate with him tonight filled her with excitement.

Meadow tried to push the thoughts of her wedding night from her mind as she tore her attention away from Black Horse briefly and glanced around. Her gaze swept over the red-coated soldiers who sat beside the fire. Gentle Water had told her about their arrival and the purpose of their visit. Even though they had heard the soldiers in this country were not hostile, their presence made Meadow uneasy. Just knowing they were here conjured up terrifying memories of the soldiers in the American army, and of all the tragedy and heartbreak they had caused for her adoptive people.

When Sitting Bull walked up to them and began the simple ceremony that would unite her with Black Horse for all eternity, Meadow happily pushed the soldiers' presence to the back of her mind. Having such a great man conduct the ceremony was considered a special honor. The simple ceremony began with Sitting Bull wrapping each of them in a blue blanket. The blankets were symbols of the lives they had lived before they met. White Buffalo stood behind Meadow holding a single white blanket.

Sitting Bull raised his arms up to the sky and asked *Wakan Tanka* to bless the couple. Then he motioned for them to remove the blue blankets and shed themselves of any sorrow and shame from their pasts.

White Buffalo stepped forward and started to wrap the white blanket around the couple. This blanket would symbolize the beginning of their new life together. They would pull the blanket over their heads and engage in the kiss that would unite them in marriage. After the ceremony there would be a huge feast, and the newlyweds would sneak away into the forest to begin their new life together.

Meadow felt a joyful tear roll down her cheek as her father began to drape the white blanket over her head.

She saw the proud expression on his aged face and knew that he was as happy as she was at this moment. This truly was a new beginning for all of them.

"Wait—this marriage must be stopped!"

The pulsating drum beat ceased, and a strange quiet settled over the village as the interruption turned everybody's attention toward the Mountie who had called out. Yet, even as he stumbled to his feet, Brandon Cornett was not sure of his own actions or what he would do, now that he had allowed his impulsive statement to escape from his mouth. He was only sure of three things: this young girl was white, she did not belong here, and there was no way he could allow her to marry this savage!

Chapter Eight

The unnerving silence following Brandon's outburst lasted only a few seconds before the angry shouts of the Indians began to fill the air. Panic engulfed Brandon as he realized the danger he had just created for himself and his comrades. In barely more than a heartbeat Brandon knew that these Indians could slit their throats, toss them all in the fire pit and get on with the wedding ceremony as if nothing had happened. The possibility of being slaughtered within the next few seconds eclipsed his gallant motive for interrupting the wedding.

"What do you think you are doing?" Walsh demanded as he stopped in front of Brandon. His face was flushed a deep shade of scarlet, and the raspy tone of his voice made his panic and anger evident.

Brandon could not speak for a second because of the lump of fear that had formed in his throat. He met the other officer's gaze as he stuttered, "I—I—well— Sh-she is a white woman, sir."

"I know," Walsh said in a hoarse voice.

"What if she is being held here against her will?" Brandon asked in a panicked tone of voice. He could tell by the conflicting expressions flashing through his commander's face that he, too, was wondering the same things.

Turning slowly around, Walsh looked toward the woman. "Are you being forced to marry this man?" he called out to her. A look of confusion and her silence was the only reply the Mountie received from her.

The rage Black Horse felt at having a stranger, especially a white man, interfere with his wedding flashed across his face like a death mask as he stalked to where the soldiers stood. As he approached the Mounties, Black Horse grabbed a long, feathered lance from one of the other warriors. He stopped before the man who had jumped up and shouted for them to stop the ceremony, and leveled his dark gaze so that he was staring directly into the other man's eyes.

All movements and noise ceased while the two men stared at one another. The obvious hatred toward the soldier radiating from the chief made the tension around the fire pit seem as thick and suffocating as the smoke spiraling up from the flames. Black Horse clutched the lance tightly in his right hand as he faced the soldier, and as he began to raise the lance up into the air, the look of sheer terror on the Mountie's face filled him with a deep sense of satisfaction. The man's terrified gaze followed the blade at the end the lance as it raised up into the air above his head. His face seemed to drain of all color, and his mouth opened in what appeared to be a silent scream.

For an instant Black Horse considered fulfilling the man's expectations. He envisioned himself plunging the lance into the man's chest. Many times he had killed an enemy in this manner.

But common sense overruled his anger. He remembered what he had been told shortly before the wedding about Sitting Bull's promise to the Mounties that they would not cause any trouble while they were here in Canada. Although he felt he had a justifiable cause to kill this man, Black Horse also knew that he could not ignore the promise that Sitting Bull had given to the soldiers. Right now Canada was a temporary haven that his people desperately needed.

Black Horse's gaze studied the face that he would not allow himself to forget. When the Mountie's face was imprinted deeply in his mind, Black Horse brought his arm down sharply and drove the lance into the ground only inches away from the toes of the soldier's black boots. He heard a frightened gasp escape from the other man as he turned and walked away from the group.

Low murmuring from his tribesmen reached Black Horse's ears as the men reacted in surprise to the way he had managed to control his rage. He, too, was shocked by his own actions. Though he prided himself in using good judgment in battles, he was rarely so tolerant when he was personally assaulted. The blond-haired Mountie better hope that they never crossed paths in the future. Next time their encounter would not end on such friendly terms.

Taking his first full breath since this near tragedy had started, Superintendent Walsh turned around to face Sitting Bull. "I sincerely apologize for the disturbance and"—he glanced briefly at the lieutenant before facing the older chief again—"you have my word that nothing like this will ever happen again."

The expression on Sitting Bull's face gave no clue to the way he felt about this turn of events. For a few seconds he made no comment or movements. When he did acknowledge the superintendent's apology, it was with a quick nod of his head, before he turned around and walked away without speaking another word.

Brandon watched the departure of the fierce chief with a feeling of despair. He knew his impulsive actions might be the end of his career—if not his life. Superintendent Walsh was a compassionate man, but he did not tolerate insubordination. Brandon was sure the superintendent would consider his outburst a direct defiance of the peace agreement he had just worked out with Sitting Bull. His feelings were confirmed when he glanced in Walsh's direction. The superintendent was looking directly at him, and the hostile expression on his face made his position clear.

"I suggest we move out of here immediately," Walsh said. With a narrow-eyed glance at Brandon, he added, "And without making any further trouble."

Brandon avoided looking at his superintendent as he gave his head a sharp nod. Before he followed the rest of the Mounties, however, he looked back to where the girl had been standing. She was being led away by several of the Sioux women. As if she sensed that he was staring at her, Brandon noticed that she glanced back over her shoulder. He could not tell if she was looking at him in that brief instant before she turned away and disappeared into one of the tepees.

Brandon remained rooted to the spot. His head spun with indecision, and his heart pounded against his chest. What was the look he had seen in her gaze? Could it be that she had been praying she would be saved from this marriage before it was too late? Her expression did not look like appreciation. Maybe it had only been sympathy he had seen in her glance, because she knew he had just sealed his own fate.

With the thought of his own death planted firmly in his mind again, Brandon glanced down at the feathered lance at his feet. It protruded at an awkward angle from the ground, with the end feathers hanging directly in front of his face. Thinking of how easy it would have been for the chief to stick the weapon into him instead of the ground, Brandon sidestepped the lance and stumbled blindly behind the rest of his troop.

He was fearfully aware of the Indians who escorted them from the center of the village, but he was oblivious to any other activities around them. To his amazement, he found himself standing beside his horse. When he realized the other men were mounting up, he wasted no time pulling himself up into his own saddle. He glanced around again, still expecting to be murdered at any second. The Sioux men who had escorted them to their horses did not look sociable, but they did not appear to be in a killing mood either. As Walsh motioned for his men to follow him back through the dense forest, Brandon felt a sense of relief begin to inch into his trembling body. When the Indians were out of sight, and the threat of his own death started to fade, he began to think about other possible repercussions of his foolish actions. He expected to be putting in a lot of extra guard duty, as well as enduring a host of other undesirable jobs.

He glanced around at his comrades, but none of them looked back at him. On their faces were solemn expressions, and their goal was obvious: to put as much distance between themselves and the Indian village as possible.

Brandon tried to focus his attention on the trail ahead of him. He attempted to clear away the memory of the white girl, but her image had fixed itself in his mind. Even now that they were a safe distance away from the village, he still had the feeling that he needed to do something—anything—to bring her back to her own people.

Chapter Nine

The reason the Mountie had felt compelled to stop the wedding did not matter to Meadow. She only cared about being with Black Horse, and he was nowhere to be found. After he had confronted the Mountie and driven the lance into the ground, he had disappeared into the forest, and Meadow had been led back to Sings Like Sparrow and Gentle Water's tepee to wait for his return. It seemed as if she had been alone in the tepee forever. She still clutched the white blanket against her breast and planned to hold it until she was with Black Horse again and their wedding ceremony was completed. But did Black Horse still intend to go through with the wedding, or was he so angry that he had changed his mind about marrying her?

She kept recalling how handsome he had looked as he waited for her to walk up to him during their wedding. When she had taken her place at his side, she had felt such an overwhelming sense of pride and hope for their future together that it had been difficult to contain her joy at the thought of becoming his wife. A fluttering sensation erupted in her stomach even now as she thought about him, and it was followed immediately by a crushing sense of sadness. If not for the Mountie's interference, she would be Black Horse's wife, and they would be spending their first night as husband and wife.

In Sings Like Sparrow and Gentle Water's tepee, Meadow listened to the pounding of a lone drum. Even though there had not been a wedding today, the tribe had carried on with the celebration that had been planned for tonight. Meadow wrapped her arms around herself in a tight hug and fought back another round of weeping. Her eyes burned from the sad tears she had already cried today. She should be dancing with her handsome new husband right now, and they should be planning to sneak away together to spend their first night as man and wife in one another's arms. Instead, she was making plans to sneak away from the village alone so that she could look for Black Horse.

Meadow pulled back the flap at the tepee door and stuck her head outside to glance around. The daylight had long ago faded into night, and not even Sings Like Sparrow or Gentle Water were close by the tepee. Everyone, it seemed, was partaking in the festivities that were meant to be in celebration of her marriage. She felt the sting of more tears forming in the corners of her eyes, but she blinked them back and forced herself to concentrate on the one thing that would take away this emptiness and pain.

Turning away from the sounds of the celebration, Meadow took a deep breath and stepped out of the tepee. She took the white blanket and wrapped it around her shoulders as she headed toward the river. Though she didn't know why the feeling was so strong, Meadow was almost sure that she would find him in the same place he had been when she had seen him for the first time.

Unlike that first day, when his boldness had shocked her, Meadow had every intention of being the bold one tonight. Although their wedding had not taken place as planned, Meadow knew that she would become Black Horse's woman tonight. She had a nagging feeling that if they waited . . . it might be too late.

The forest at night seemed eerie and unfriendly to Meadow. Even though she thought Canada was beautiful and she was growing used to the dense forests, she missed the wide-open plains of Montana and the Dakota Territory where she had grown up. There, she could look out across the prairie and see so far off in the distance that it looked as though the sky and the land had merged into one. Not being able to see what lurked behind each tree in the forest filled Meadow with anxiety. The gibbous moon, however, was nearly full on this autumn eve, and it cast pale patches of light through the treetops, so the dense woods were not as ominous as they would have been in complete darkness.

With each step Meadow took toward the river, the thumping of her heart grew more intense. She was not sure what to expect when she did find Black Horse. Clutching the long fringe on the hem of her wedding dress tightly in her hands so that the delicate strands would not hook up on the tall dry grass, Meadow stepped cautiously over twigs and protruding rocks.

A couple of times she had to pause to get her bearings to make sure she was still going in the right direction. With every step, though, her uncertainty increased. What would she do if she got lost in the forest at night—or worse, what if she encountered a group of the hated Blackfoot warriors when she was out here alone? White Buffalo's dire warnings echoed through her mind. She clutched at her throat and took a trembling breath in an effort to calm the panic she could feel building inside of her like a cannon that was about to explode. Then, as if to answer her prayers and calm her fears, she heard the calming sounds of running water. The bushes where she and Gentle Water had first watched Black Horse bathing loomed ahead of her, and everything looked familiar again.

She sighed with relief, but the lump that remained in her chest reminded her of the dangers she could still encounter. Pushing aside the leafy branches, Meadow bent down and eased through the brush as quietly as she could. The fringe on her dress kept catching on the branches, and several times she had to stop to untangle the leather strips from the long, skinny twigs of the willows. The upper branches kept tugging on her hair and had pulled most of it out of the thick braids that had held it neatly against her head earlier. Now, the long strands were tangled in disarray around her face and most of the pretty leather strips that had adorned her braids were lost among the trees.

Whenever she paused, she noticed how the rapid thudding of her heartbeat sounded deafening to her ears in the quiet of the night. At times, it even seemed to drown out the lulling sound of the nearby river. Feeling certain that her building sense of excitement was because she would find Black Horse on the other side of the bushes, Meadow shoved the last of the branches out of her way. Nothing but the dark rolling waters of the river greeted her anxious eyes.

Meadow's footsteps halted as her disappointment settled heavy in her heart. She scanned the area in breathless anticipation of seeing Black Horse sitting on one of the rocks scattered among the willows and alders that created a craggy ebony barrier along the riverbank. Moonbeams shimmered on the river like silvery spiderwebs. The soothing sound of the water, combined with the moonlight and the isolation of this secluded spot, seemed almost magical to Meadow. She pulled the white blanket tighter around her body and glanced around again.

Her feeling that Black Horse was close by continued to grow even though she could not see any sign of him. "Black Horse," she called out softly. "Are you here?" The absence of his reply was her only answer. A chill rapidly spread through her body, and the sinking feeling that she was alone filled her with emptiness. She had been so sure she would find him here.

Turning around slowly, Meadow hung her head down and drew in a defeated sigh. She did not notice the man who had just emerged from the bushes.

"I'm here," Black Horse said quietly as he approached her from behind.

A startled gasp escaped from Meadow as she twirled around to face him. He had removed his feathered headdress and ceremonial shirt. His bare chest was a shimmering shade of dark bronze in the moonlight, and his leggings and breechcloth hung low on his narrow hips. He had released his long hair from the tight braids, and now the thick raven tresses framed his handsome face and tumbled down over his shoulders. A wide tribal armband of black and gold encircled one of his upper arms.

"I—I was looking for you." Meadow met his unwavering gaze and felt the breath catch for a moment in her throat as she waited for him to speak again. From the strange expression on his face, she wondered if he somehow blamed her for the trouble with the Mounties. Before he finally spoke again, Meadow felt as if she had died a thousand deaths.

"It is not safe for you to be in the forest alone, especially at night," Black Horse said in a formal tone. His gazed traveled up and down her entire body.

"I don't care," she retorted, not caring that he was looking at her as if he could see right through her clothes. "Tonight is supposed to be my wedding night—remember?" She paused and waited for him to respond. His only reaction was to continue to stare at her in a way that left her feeling completely naked.

"Why did you run away today?" she asked in a tone edged with the hurt and disappointment she could no longer hide.

"I have never run away from anything or anyone in my life!"

He stepped closer, and although Meadow was tempted, she did not back away from him.

"You ran away today," she repeated. She forced herself to remain unmoving, even though his obvious rage made her tremble inwardly like a frightened rabbit. Even in the dim moonlight, she could see the way her words affected him. She raised her head up in a defiant manner that belied the nervousness she felt inside and clutched the blanket even tighter, as if it would somehow protect her from his wrath.

Black Horse had never known a woman who would confront him in this manner, and even in his fury, he was impressed that she would not back down. He would not, however, allow her to accuse him of running away. He had merely sought refuge down here by the river while he tried to sort through his troubled thoughts. In spite of his growing love for her, the Mountie's outburst had made Black Horse's doubts about their wedding resurface.

Although he had heard many stories in the past few days about how Meadow had come to live with the Sioux, and he could see for himself that she was more than content to be living with his people, Black Horse still could not ignore the fact that the Mountie had blatantly pointed out: she was white. Even Walks Tall had hinted to him in the beginning that his marriage to a woman who was not Sioux could be a mistake. What worried Black Horse even more was knowing that, once he claimed her as his woman, his love and devotion to her would never allow him to give her up again, especially if she bore him any children. He drew in a ragged sigh. What if they did have children and she someday decided to return to her own people? Would she try to take his children with her?

An odd sense of fear filled Black Horse, a feeling he did not know how to acknowledge. He had trained himself to feel hatred toward the *wasichu*—whites—but he had never feared them. This woman made him fear that he would let himself love her even more than he already did, and then he would lose her.

Black Horse stared down at her. Words eluded him, and emotions he had never known left him feeling vulnerable and defenseless. He had sensed a joining of his soul with this woman's from the first moment he had looked into her unforgettable green eyes, and the feeling was growing stronger with each passing second.

A defeated sigh escaped from his parted lips. He shook with the realization that he was falling so completely in love with her that nothing else mattered. He cleared his throat loudly, but could not clear his confused thoughts.

"Why were you looking for me tonight?" Black Horse asked. His voice had dropped to barely more than a whisper now, and he trembled as he waited for her reply.

Meadow drew in a quivering breath as she stared up at his face. "I—I came because . . ." Her mind groped for the right words to express the way she felt at this moment. "Because I cannot imagine waking up to another sunrise if I am not in your arms. I want nothing more than to be your wife and spend the rest of my life with you," she said in a shaky voice.

Black Horse remained silent and unmoving as though he was contemplating her words. His eyes never left her face as he said, "You must know that to be my woman—my wife—in every way means that you will have to deny your true heritage for as long as we are together, for as long as we live."

"I have proven my loyalty to the Sioux," Meadow retorted. "White Buffalo has never kept me here against my will."

"When the last of the Sioux are dying of starvation and there is nowhere else to hide, will you still be so loyal?"

The meaning of his question cut deep into Meadow's pride. It pained her to think that he doubted her devotion to the Sioux in any way. She had never once considered returning to the whites if life here became too difficult. Somehow, she had to make Black Horse realize her true feelings if they were going to have a future together.

"I have not forgotten that the Sioux killed my white family," Meadow said with a slight quiver in her voice. "But I have also seen what the *wasichu* have done to the Indians. And like you," she continued with a forceful tone as she brought her fist to her chest, "I will die for my people." Her stance straightened in a proud manner as she added, "And the Sioux are my people now and forever!"

He stared at her in silence for a moment. "As my woman," he said in a hoarse voice, "you will have to understand that there are things that I must do."

"As your woman, I would make it my duty to understand and support whatever it is that you must do." She imagined that he was referring to the raids that he had been conducting down in Montana on the ranchers' and the American soldiers' livestock and supplies. The thought of him leaving her for these dangerous escapades was not something she looked forward to, but she knew he would expect her to accept that this was his way of helping his people.

"It's more than killing the white man's cattle or stealing his whiskey," he said, as if he could read her thoughts. He added more forcefully, "I am not ready to admit defeat against the *wasichu*."

As his meaning became evident, a worried gasp escaped from Meadow. "But Sitting Bull has said that there is to be no more fighting with the whites."

Black Horse dropped his head down and stared at the ground. "I understand why Sitting Bull and the other chiefs have brought our people here to Canada.

The old ones and the women and children are weak, and too tired to fight anymore." His head rose up as he looked at her again. "But I will never understand their decision to give up completely." Black Horse shook his head slowly. His voice was low and determined when he added, "I will never stop fighting for my people and the land that is rightfully ours. Never!"

An icy chill whipped through Meadow. She knew Black Horse meant every word he said, and she had no doubts that he was prepared to face the consequences. If he went against Sitting Bull's orders, he could be cast out of the tribe, and she along with him, if they were married.

Letting his words settle in her mind, Meadow turned away from him and stared out at the calm waters of the river. Life here could be so peaceful and easy if the Canadians would allow them to stay. But she knew that would not happen. When they were forced to return to the other side of the border, they would undoubtedly encounter the same hatred they had run away from in the first place. Meadow exhaled a burdened sigh as she tried to imagine what the future might hold for the Sioux, or even if they would have a future at all.

"Do you think you are strong enough—brave enough—to be the woman of a war chief?" he asked as he moved up behind her.

She was much smaller than he was, and he could almost rest his chin on the top of her head. Meadow could feel his breath touch lightly against her hair. She yearned for his arms to encircle her, to turn her around, and for him to kiss her until her lips begged for mercy. But he was waiting to hear her say the words that would tell him that she truly understood what he must do, and that nothing—or no one—could stop him.

Her buttocks were brushing against his thigh, and her knees felt almost too wobbly to hold her weight. Still, the thought of him leaving her to go into another battle with the whites dominated her thoughts. She heard him draw in a heavy breath. When he exhaled, the warmth of his breath engulfed her. She could feel the heat radiating from his body and infusing every inch of her own body with a raging wildfire. But there was so much more involved here than the immense physical attraction they felt for each other.

She recalled a discussion she'd had with White Buffalo earlier that day, when he had paid her a visit shortly before the wedding ceremony. He had told her how proud he was to have her as his daughter. As he often did, he spoke of the hardships and pain their people had suffered, of how uncertain every day of their lives was, and of how important it was for them to live each day as if there might never be another tomorrow.

White Buffalo also explained why he wanted her to marry Black Horse, and he had asked her to forgive him for his selfishness for wanting her to stay with the Sioux forever. As she thought about the conversation she had had with White Buffalo, her thoughts kept wandering to the handsome man who stood so close, and to the question he had just asked her: are you strong enough and brave enough to be the wife of a war chief? She wondered why she hesitated so long in answering. There was only one choice she could make. "*Sha*," she answered as she turned to face her warrior.

"You give me the courage and the strength to face anything, as long as I know that you are at my side. I love you, Black Horse, and nothing else matters."

For a few seconds he seemed too surprised by her admission to make another move. When his instincts took over, though, he clasped her by the shoulders and pulled her toward him. Her head tilted back and her gaze met his for just an instant before his mouth descended on her waiting mouth. Meadow's response to his kiss was immediate. Letting him pull her tighter into his embrace, Meadow allowed her passion for this man rule all of her actions. The strict customs of their people did not enter her mind, nor would she permit them to interfere with the plans for tonight. In her mind, and in her heart, she would become his woman with or without the completion of a wedding ceremony. The white blanket fell into a crumpled heap at their feet.

Instinctively, Meadow's arms slid up to encircle his neck. She did not resist when he crushed her body against his. The way he kissed her now was completely different from the tender kisses they had shared before, and as his mouth seemed to devour hers, she mimicked his actions with exuberance. When his tongue slipped into her mouth, she was unsure how to react, but after it began to tease and entwine with hers, she discovered she was enjoying this strange new game. She was not hesitant to let Black Horse teach her the ways of love, and she eagerly let her own tongue begin to taunt his as they continued the wet, heated kiss.

Though his kisses caused the most wondrous sensations to erupt throughout her body, they were almost forgotten when Meadow felt his hands moving down to her waist and then along the curve of her hips. She gasped inwardly when she realized he had grabbed onto the fringe on the bottom of her dress, and was now raising the garment past her thighs. She wore nothing under her wedding dress, and his large hands eagerly clutched at her bare buttocks. He pulled her even closer as his fingers kneaded her soft skin. A moment of panic and fear gripped Meadow when she felt the rock-hard core of his manhood pressing against her stomach.

Fleetingly, she remembered all the strict rules that governed the women of her tribe. She made a feeble attempt to pull away, but he ignored her efforts, and she quickly gave up the weak fight.

Black Horse seemed vaguely aware of her mild protests. Tearing his lips away, then drawing in a ragged breath, he leaned back slightly. "Did you change your mind—?"

"Never," she interrupted without hesitation. She was vitally aware of the way his hands still clasped her buttocks, and even more aware of the way his manhood was no longer throbbing against her stomach. "But I can't help being a little frightened," she said in a raspy voice. Her mind whirled with indecision while her body sang with new and wanton yearnings.

A tired sigh escaped from Black Horse. He did not release his tight hold on her. "I know, and I understand your feelings," he admitted. "But if not for the Mountie, we would be married right now. And we should be living in our own homelands and carrying on the customs that have ruled our people since the beginning of time." Black Horse's voice was just a whisper as he added, "Nothing will ever be the same again for the Sioux. All that matters now is survival and this. . . ." His head tilted down as his lips claimed hers in another demanding kiss.

Black Horse's words had almost the same meaning as the things White Buffalo had said to her before the wedding, and at this moment their reasoning had never made more sense. There might not be a future for the Sioux, and tomorrow might never come . . . and tonight was all that mattered.

Without further delay, Meadow raised her arms up as Black Horse lifted her dress up over her head. A shiver claimed her as the chill of the autumn night brushed against her skin. Her breath caught in her throat as anticipation and nervousness made her entire body quiver. She crossed her arms over her breasts when she no longer had her dress to cover her. Black Horse reached out and pushed her arms back down to her sides. An intense anxiety bolted through Meadow as she stood completely exposed before him. Even in the near darkness, she could see the twinkle in his dark eyes as he closely surveyed her trembling body. The smile on his face suggested that he definitely liked what he saw.

When he reached out to her again, she eagerly sought his arms. She felt her bare breasts flatten against his hard body, felt his swollen, hard manhood straining against his breechcloth again. There was no turning back.

Black Horse let his hands roam freely over her soft skin. He could feel her tremble, and he could sense her complete surrender. An anxious quiver shot through him as he thought about the beautiful sight of her firm young body. The silken paleness of Meadow's skin excited him more than he'd ever thought possible. He wanted to make her his woman now in every way, without another moment's hesitation.

In a single movement, Black Horse pulled his breechcloth away from his hips. He tossed it into the darkness of the night.

The warmth of his bare manhood touched Meadow, and jumbled thoughts of the whisperings she had heard from the women of the tribe regarding the intimacy they shared with their husbands, combined with the realization of what he would soon be doing to her, made her knees grow weak. Not one coherent thought entered her head as she felt Black Horse begin to lower her down to the ground. She glimpsed the moon in the starlit sky overhead for just an instant before his kisses stole away the sight. She clung to him, unsure and frightened, yet too overwhelmed with desire to stop him.

This magical night, the moon overhead and this man were her entire world at this moment.

When his hips settled between her thighs, Meadow was vitally aware of the tip of his manhood pressing into her most private parts. She knew there would be pain; she had heard new wives talk about their first night with their husbands. With this thought, she tried to brace herself as he pressed farther inside her. His mouth covered hers again in a kiss that demanded her complete attention. Within the next instant his hips plunged down, and a searing pain ripped through her body. Her shocked cry was stolen away by his kiss, but the pain was worse than she had imagined.

Black Horse remained inside her for a time, unmoving, as he let her adjust to the invasion. But just as quickly as it had exploded inside her, the searing pain began to subside. Then, slowly, he began to rock his hips up and down until her stiff body began to relax.

Even though he was still kissing her, Meadow was only aware of the awakening sensations in her body. Now that the pain had faded away, she was experiencing an ache of a different nature. With each of his deep plunges she felt as if something uncontrollable was building up inside of her. She let her hips arch up to meet his. They began to move in unison, melding tightly together as if they were one.

Black Horse's kisses had ceased, and it felt to Meadow that his total concentration now was on driving himself down into her. Clinging to him as they moved together, Meadow lost touch with anything other than the overpowering passion she would never again be able to deny. She felt his movements grow more intense and held on tighter, clenching her teeth together to keep from crying out as ecstasy swept through her.

Black Horse could not hold back any longer. Giving into the raging need that had climaxed to the highest summit, he released himself with abandonment. With a shudder, he began to relax against Meadow. He felt her grow limp in his embrace and sigh with contentment. For a moment, he was content, too.

Tonight, as he had planned, he had made Meadow

his woman. But now, as he had not planned, she had also awakened something in him. He knew for certain now that he would not be able to leave her behind when he left here—not even for a little while. But he would not give up on his war against the *wasichu* either. From this day forth, he decided, this woman would ride at his side. Then, he would know the true extent of her devotion to his people . . . and to him.

Chapter Ten

With the first hazy gray streaks of dawn came another awakening of their passion as Black Horse made love to her for the third time since they had met at the riverbank the night before. Each time they indulged in this sensual ritual, Meadow noticed that his actions became more loving and more attuned to her pleasure. He explored every inch of her body, and then taught her how to touch him and please him in the same manner. By morning, she had no doubts about the night they had just spent together or about her love for this man.

Meadow found it incredible that such a fierce warrior could also be such a considerate and gentle lover. The things he taught her and the feelings he aroused went far beyond the physical contact they shared. She knew she had found her life's mate . . . her reason for living. And she knew Black Horse was also growing to love her as much as she loved him. His actions were proof. Knowing this man loved her would be the strength she could draw upon, no matter what the uncertain future held.

"You are so beautiful, my green-eyed woman, inside and out," Black Horse whispered as he held her close.

Meadow snuggled up against him. They had used a patch of soft grass for a flimsy mattress, and the white blanket to cover themselves. The blanket did not provide them with much protection from the chilly early-morning air, and the ground beneath them was cold from the nighttime temperature.

"So are you," Meadow replied.

"Men are not beautiful," he retorted indignantly.

"In my eyes you are beautiful," she answered. A smile curved her lips when she heard Black Horse huff at her comment. She knew he would never agree with her, but everything about this man—his dangerously handsome appearance, of course, but also his strong beliefs and his exuberant passion—all made him beautiful in her mind.

"We need to find White Buffalo," Black Horse said, his voice growing serious. "I will ask him to marry us quickly so that you will not be considered a loose woman." He pinched her nose teasingly, adding, "I would hate to see that pretty nose cut off."

A fiery blush rushed through Meadow's face, and her nose twitched at his implication. Women who did not behave according to Sioux etiquette were sometimes disfigured so that everyone would know they had been disobedient, adulterous or loose with their feminine wiles. Sioux men, however, could have as many wives as pleased them, and it was not considered immoral. Meadow planned to be the only woman Black Horse would ever need.

Now, however, she knew the time had come to be accountable for the previous night. She just hoped White Buffalo would understand and forgive them, because Meadow knew that she would not do one thing differently, if she had a choice.

"He will be at the rock bluff overlooking the river at this time of the morning," she said reluctantly. White

Buffalo went to the bluff most mornings at the crack of dawn to contemplate the plight of their people and to seek inspiration. Some days he would have a vision, which he would anxiously repeat as soon as he returned to the village. In the past, Little Squirrel and Meadow would eagerly await his return so that they could listen to his amazing stories.

"Would this be a good time to approach him?"

Meadow shivered. "No time will be good to tell him that I have disgraced him."

"Do you regret—?"

"No," Meadow cut him off before he could finish. Black Horse's hold on her tightened as she added, "Not one single minute of last night."

"If not for that Mountie . . ." Black Horse said between clenched teeth.

Meadow felt the way his body stiffened. She understood his anger, because she felt the same way toward the man who had interrupted their wedding. Her feelings, however, were not so intense and deadly. Right now, she just wanted the episode with the Mountie to be forgotten, and with any luck, they would never have to see that man again. But most of all she wanted to be Black Horse's wife as soon as possible.

"I would prefer to talk to my father when he is alone, rather than once he is back at the village."

Black Horse mumbled his agreement, but Meadow sensed that his thoughts were still focused on the Mountie.

"We should go now," she added.

A sharp pang had shot through Black Horse's chest when Meadow said that she had disgraced her father.

He wanted her to feel pride and joy on this first day as his woman, not disgrace. Her torment filled him with a feeling of guilt, leaving him more determined than ever to make her happy and proud to belong to him. It was hard for him to not blame the Mountie for all their problems, but now was not the time to dwell on the revenge he would seek if he ever encountered the man again.

Forcing his thoughts back to the present situation, Black Horse eased his tense hold on Meadow. He turned away when his gaze met her worried one. A heavy frown settled on his face as he thought about White Buffalo's probable reaction to their passionate night together. Telling the old medicine man about their impulsive behavior was not a task he was looking forward to. Still, he wanted to do it soon, so that the matter would be behind them and they could live their lives together without scandal.

"Do you wish to bathe in the river first?" he asked, reluctant to leave this special spot. "But maybe we shouldn't take the time," he decided. There would be more than bathing going on if he was in the water with this beauty, and they had more important business to attend to now. He sighed heavily and released his hold on her.

Meadow nodded in agreement and clutched her dress against her breast as she sat up. His smoldering look told her that he was thinking along the same lines as she was about the two of them taking a bath together.

As the morning sun peeked over the horizon and began to brighten the countryside with its golden rays, Meadow's natural modesty claimed her.

Black Horse, however, did not grant her one moment of privacy as she dressed. His raven gaze glistened like black diamonds while he watched her every move, and he chuckled boldly when he caught her sneaking a peak at him when he stood up to put on his breechcloth. Since Meadow had already determined that bashfulness was not a trait he possessed, she was not surprised when Black Horse made sure he presented her with a full frontal view once again, just as he had on the first day they had been in almost this exact same spot. She could feel her face grow red with embarrassment. The instant he looked at her, his yearning to make love to her again became evident; his swollen manhood protruded shamelessly against the white material of his loose-hanging breechcloth.

Meadow tried to avert her eyes from him, but that did not erase the virile image of him from her mind. If only one night with this man filled her with such great passion and longing, she wondered how she would ever function as a normal person again, once she was allowed to spend the rest of her life in his arms. Maybe, once they were properly married, they could just spend every night—and every day—among the soft furs in their tepee. The wanton thought made the glorious ache in her loins throb unmercifully.

With a loud cough, Black Horse made an attempt to bring his racing emotions under control. What this woman did to him was causing him more than a little concern. How could he continue to be a ruthless war chief and a leader of his people, if the only thing he could concentrate on from this day forth was corralling this green-eyed woman in his arms?

Black Horse reached down and picked up the white blanket and threw it over his shoulder. "It's time to go see White Buffalo now, or else we might never leave." He let his gaze meet with Meadow's for an instant before they began to walk hand in hand away from the spot where they had spent their first night of lovemaking. As their eyes met now he felt an engulfing sense of oneness. He trembled at the realization that he would never feel whole again unless he was with this woman.

They walked in silence through the forest, enjoying every sight and sound around them on this glorious day. The Canadian forest was in full bloom with autumn growth. The last of this season's wild flowers in hues of yellow, blue and white opened their petals toward the sun, and the tall blades of grass shimmered in shades of bright green as the last dewdrops evaporated with the warming of the air. The day was flawless—at least where the weather was concerned.

"We were so close to finishing our wedding vows that I really do believe my father will understand why we had to be together last night," Meadow said as they neared their destination. Her trembling voice did not sound as convincing as she had hoped.

White Buffalo sat atop a large boulder. If not for his graying hair, he could almost have been mistaken for a much younger man. His back was completely straight, his legs crossed with his arms resting upon his thighs, and his head was tilted upward toward the sky. He did not seem aware of anything around him.

"I had hoped you would come here to see me this morning," the old medicine man said without opening his eyes or moving.

His unexpected words caused Black Horse and Meadow to halt abruptly. They remained rooted to the spot until the older man finally lowered his head and opened his eyes to look down at them. Only the loud chattering of an angry squirrel in a nearby pine tree broke the silence of the morning.

In an attempt to break the awkwardness, Meadow stepped forward. "Father, I—I— We—" She motioned toward Black Horse while her words faltered in her dry mouth.

"I know," White Buffalo said with a slow nod of his head. He stared at his daughter for a second, and then glanced at Black Horse. "And I do understand." He saw the tense look fade from the young chief's face as their eyes met. "As I've told Meadow before, I was young once, too." He smiled. "And Little Squirrel and I looked at one another the same way I see the two of you look at one another." He looked back at Meadow in time to see the glowing blush color her pale cheeks. Another smile curved his lips. He uncurled his legs and slid down the front of the boulder.

Standing in front of the young couple, White Buffalo focused his attention on Meadow. He noticed she stared down at the ground as if she was ashamed to look at him. With a gentle touch he lifted her chin up. Her troubled expression, along with the wide array of emotions he could glimpse in the depths of her jeweled gaze, told him the extent of her shame—and also how much she cared for the powerful man who stood at her side.

The knowledge that she was falling so deeply in love with Black Horse was proof that intuition had not failed him. A wide smile claimed his mouth as relief flooded through him. He had gotten this one right.

"Do not regret anything, *mi-cun-ksi*," White Buffalo said as he tenderly cupped Meadow's small chin in his rough hand. He shook his head. "As I have told you in the past, our people do not have time for regrets. We must seize every opportunity for happiness." He grinned again, then glanced up at Black Horse. The younger man nodded his head in agreement. White Buffalo's attention returned to Meadow. Her worried frown had not disappeared.

"Do you want to finish getting married today, then?" White Buffalo asked.

Meadow nodded her head, because she did not trust herself to speak. A large lump had formed in her throat, and she could feel the stinging sensation of tears welling up in her eyes. White Buffalo's kindness and understanding never ceased to amaze her. She stood on her toes and kissed him softly on the cheek. When she glanced up at him again, she noticed his eyes were also shiny with moisture. How lucky she had been to be raised as his daughter.

"I have the authority to perform the marriage ceremony, if you want me to do it," White Buffalo suggested.

"Can you conduct the ceremony right now?" Black Horse asked.

White Buffalo nodded his head. "Yes, we need to finish what was started yesterday—to right the wrong that was done to both of you by the soldier." He glanced at Meadow again, then looked back to Black

Horse. "But I would like to talk to my daughter first. Will you give us a few moments of privacy? We'll meet you at our tepee soon, and then we'll get on with the important business of getting you two properly married." He motioned toward the white blanket that still hung over Black Horse's shoulder. "That will finally serve the purpose it was meant for," he added with a chuckle.

Black Horse did not acknowledge the medicine man's attempt at humor, but he did feel his face grow hot. He didn't even glance in Meadow's direction, because he could only imagine how embarrassed she was at this moment. He did not want to go back to the village alone. To delay this wedding any longer seemed like a bad idea to him, and as he observed the loving exchange between the medicine man and his daughter, a strange sense of urgency began to overcome him. The feeling of foreboding continued to grow inside him and made his uneasiness expand until he felt as if he couldn't breathe.

He glanced around at the forest, then down toward the river. Everything was as calm, quiet and natural as it had been earlier. But the tightness in his chest and the fluttering in his stomach told Black Horse that something was not right. Many times his instinct had kept him from riding into an enemy ambush, or kept him safe from some other type of harm. He stared at White Buffalo for a moment longer, wondering if the medicine man sensed danger. But from White Buffalo's expression, it was plain the old man was not experiencing the same type of anxiety that he was feeling at this time. Black Horse told himself that if a wise, insightful man like White Buffalo did not feel uneasy, it must be only in his imagination.

"I will be waiting for you back at the camp," Black Horse said, silently reprimanding himself for feeling so negative and afraid. As he started to walk away, he gazed once more at Meadow. Their eyes met and seemed to hold one another prisoner for several seconds. The strangling sensation passed through Black Horse again. He shivered visibly. Standing there in the glow of the early morning sun she looked so beautiful . . . and so vulnerable.

The vigorous night of lovemaking had left her long hair tangled around her shoulders, and she had faint purple smudges beneath her lower lashes from lack of sleep. Even now, standing here in the presence of her father, Black Horse yearned to carry her back into the forest and make love to her again. An odd sense of sadness inched through him, mingling with his feelings of desire.

When Meadow met Black Horse's piercing stare, a radiant smile lit up her face. He forced himself to smile back, but he was finding it increasingly difficult to conceal his growing panic.

Though he hated to leave, Black Horse tore his gaze away from her face and reluctantly walked toward the camp. Several times he stopped and thought about going back, but he did not want White Buffalo and Meadow to think he was acting like a fool, and so he forced himself to continue on to the village.

As Meadow watched Black Horse's departure, she wondered why he wore such an odd expression. For one instant, she had a wild urge to run after him, throw her arms around him and never let him go again. But then the pounding sensation in her breast calmed, and her frantic thoughts ceased. She told herself she was becoming fearful because of what had happened with the soldiers yesterday. There was nothing that could interfere with their wedding today, especially now that she knew White Buffalo was not angry with her.

"Black Horse is coming to love you very much," White Buffalo said. "I think he worries about losing you."

Meadow sighed and turned away from the direction where Black Horse had just disappeared into the dense forest. Was that what she had glimpsed on his face—love entwined with fear? "I love him very much, too. I will never leave him," she said quietly. "Or you and my adoptive people."

White Buffalo did not reply to her comment. He motioned toward the river. "Come, let's walk down by the water and talk." He took her arm as they began to walk.

A worried frown settled on Meadow's face. She could only think of one reason why her father would want to postpone the wedding any longer, or why he would need to talk to her in private. "I'm sorry if I have brought you shame," she said in a trembling tone of voice.

"You have not shamed me. I meant it when I said that I understood what was happening between you and Black Horse," he insisted. "And I cannot tell you how happy it makes me. As for last night . . . Well, I do not think that anyone else even suspects that you were with Black Horse. Sings Like Sparrow and Gentle Water think that you came back to our tepee last night, and I did not tell them any differently."

In spite of White Buffalo's generous attitude, Meadow could not help but feel as if she had dishonored him by spending the night with Black Horse. She knew it must have been hard for him to hide the truth from Sings Like Sparrow and Gentle Water. It was not in his nature to lie to anyone.

"I had a vision this morning," White Buffalo said.

Meadow paused beside her father at the river's edge. The morning sun reflected across the smooth surface of the deep water with such brilliance, it was impossible to stare at the shimmering water without blinking. "What did you see in this vision?" she asked with enthusiasm. She would never grow tired of hearing her father's insightful revelations of past or future events.

White Buffalo hesitated for a few seconds before he answered. He was still trying to sort through the jumbled thoughts and images that had passed through his mind earlier this morning while he had been in a deep trance. When he had first closed his eyes and cleared his head of all thoughts, his mind had wandered as it usually did to the bleak future of his people. But then his thoughts had become focused solely on his daughter. He envisioned her disrupted wedding and the Mountie who had caused the disturbance. He tried to push away the image of the blond soldier, but for reasons he could not comprehend, he sensed that somehow the Mountie would play a future role in Meadow's life.

As his vision progressed, White Buffalo saw a large triangle in the middle of a vast field. At the tip of the triangle he could see Meadow. Her hair was braided

Indian-style with feathers and leather strips adorning her pale tresses; she wore beaded, fringed moccasins on her feet. But she was wearing a white woman's flowered gown instead of her usual deerskin dress. Her odd mixture of white and Indian garments concerned White Buffalo. He had seen his daughter many times in his visions, but she had always been wearing the customary Sioux garments. Even more confusing was that Black Horse stood at one point of the triangle and the fair-haired Mountie stood opposite him on the other point.

The persistent presence of the soldier in White Buffalo's vision caused him much distress. He hoped the vision was only influenced by yesterday's events and not by something that was yet to happen.

"My vision could have many meanings," he said with a slow nod of his head. He turned toward Meadow so that he could watch her as they spoke. "You were in my vision, and Black Horse, too."

She chuckled nervously. "Wh-what did you see us doing?" she asked.

"You were standing in a field, and you were wearing a white-woman's dress. Black Horse stood across from you, and the Mountie who ended the wedding yesterday was standing at the other end of the field."

Meadow stared at him and shrugged. This vision could not have any importance.

"I do not understand it, either," he replied. "At first it made me wonder again if you might be having doubts about marrying Black Horse and staying here with the Sioux. But when I saw the way you and Black Horse looked at one another a few minutes ago—" He paused when he heard her muffled cry of despair, and he gazed into her eyes. "I will never bring up this subject again—your answer is clearly written on your face. Forgive me for ever doubting you, *mi-cun-ksi*." He glanced down at the ground in shame, inwardly cursing himself for bringing up this painful issue again.

"I forgive you always," she answered softly. "Your vision obviously means something entirely different."

"Maybe it means nothing at all." White Buffalo knew this was not true. His visions always had a meaning, even if they did only in a very trivial sense, but this one was too complex for him to understand right now. He tried to push the disturbing vision to the back of his mind for the time being. After he married Meadow and Black Horse, he could take the time to ponder the troublesome revelations he had envisioned this morning.

"Your man is waiting for you, and we have a wedding to attend," White Buffalo said. He reached out to take Meadow's hand, but he suddenly grew nauseated and weak-kneed. He knew this dreaded feeling well: each time their village had been attacked by enemies, this same feeling had passed through him in the preceding moments. Sometimes, he had time to warn his people, but now the feeling was far too strong, and he knew the danger was imminent.

Why hadn't he sensed it sooner? Had he been too consumed with his needless worries about losing Meadow to be aware of an impending attack on their village? Panic raced through him, but there wasn't even time to call out a warning to his daughter.

The Blackfoot war party emerged from the cover of the dense forest without warning. There were at least a dozen braves in the group, and White Buffalo knew their brazen appearance this close to the Sioux camp could only mean serious trouble. With a cloud of dust rising up around them, the warriors stopped their horses several hundred feet away from White Buffalo and Meadow. For a moment there was no movement or conversation from the intruders as they focused their cold, raven eyes on the medicine man and the girl. Then, the two men who rode at the head of the group began to whisper back and forth. Lecherous grins curved their thick lips as they pointed at Meadow.

White Buffalo did not need to hear their conversation to know what was in their evil minds. He knew precisely what they planned for his daughter, and his only thought was to defend her. Without a thought to his own safety, he pulled his knife from its sheath at his waist. He lunged forward, but was stopped in his tracks when an arrow sliced through the air. Darkness engulfed the great medicine man as he tumbled face-first toward the ground.

When she saw the Blackfoot warrior grab for his bow, Meadow screamed a warning to her father, but it was too late. The warrior pulled an arrow from his quiver, aimed and sent the arrow flying through the air. She would never forget the swooshing sound as it headed for White Buffalo, and the unnatural thud when it hit its target. A burning pain ripped through her own breast when her father fell forward. She screamed again, this time in torment, as she fell on her knees at her father's side and gently rolled him over. The arrow had broken off when he fell, so only a short, jagged stick protruded from the torn material of his beaded shirt. Her eyes blurred with the sight of the dark red blood that was spreading out across the front of his shirt.

Before she could do anything, she was grabbed roughly around the waist and yanked up to her feet. She began to kick and swing her closed fists at the warrior who held her prisoner, but it was useless. The man easily overpowered her and then tossed her on the back of his big Appaloosa as if she were no more than a rag doll. She attempted to push herself back down from the horse, but the warrior was too quick. He swung up behind her, crushing her back against him until she was sure her ribs were breaking with the pressure of his brutal embrace.

As the Appaloosa twirled around and began a rapid retreat, Meadow got one last glimpse of her father's crumpled body lying on the ground. In her shocked state she saw only the growing circle of red on the front of his shirt. She began to claw and punch at the arms that imprisoned her, but the Blackfoot warrior merely tightened his strong arms around her until she heard a cracking sound and then felt excruciating pain in her ribs.

She ceased fighting, knowing that she was wasting her energy. But unlike all the times in the past when her village had been attacked, or even the time when her family's wagon train had been ambushed, this time Meadow knew that she would have to fight alone.

Chapter Eleven

From experience and training, Meadow knew that being passive might be the only way her life would be spared, at least for a while longer. The Blackfoot warrior kept her restrained in a relentless grip that made her broken ribs throb unmercifully with each racing step of the horse's hooves.

Her mind was clouded with pain, and her clearest memory was still that of White Buffalo lying on the ground, and of the growing puddle of blood on the front of his shirt.

The war party rode at breakneck speed for what seemed to Meadow to be an eternity. As her physical pain grew, she tried to focus on her injured father.

Please, please, she prayed to *Wakan Tanka*, don't let him be dead. Meadow could not imagine life without White Buffalo. She tried to focus on only positive thoughts. He was going to recover, and she would escape and be reunited with him—and with Black Horse. How long would it be before Black Horse would come to look for them when they didn't return to camp? And how long before he came after her and saved her from what she knew would be a fate worse than death?

Why had the small band of Blackfoot warriors been so close to the Sioux campsite? If they had been planning to ambush the village, they would have needed to bring ten times more warriors. But it seemed as if this group had come there just to take her captive.

The war had raged between the Sioux and the Blackfoot throughout history, and she knew her fate if she failed to escape. A Sioux woman taken captive by a Blackfoot warrior was usually treated no better than a dog. And she was also a white woman, which made her their enemy two times over.

The sun was high in the sky before the Blackfoot stopped to water their horses. Meadow was dropped to the ground with a rough shove. She tried to brace herself in an attempt to protect her broken ribs, but her legs were weak and unable to support her weight, and she crashed down on the hard riverbank. The new injuries to her knees, however, did not even begin to compare with the agony the fall had caused her crushed ribs. She bit the inside of her lower lip and forced herself not to cry out, though it took every ounce of her will not to show her captors how much she was suffering.

Drawing in a deep breath, gritting her teeth against the pains shooting through her body, Meadow pushed herself up from the ground. Standing, she could feel the throbbing and burning in her cut knees, but that was minor compared to the rest of her injuries. Still, she refused to show any weakness in front of these animals.

For the first time since this nightmare had started, she turned to face her captor and met his dark, penetrating gaze. His face was decorated with streaks of red and black paint in jagged lines shaped like lightning bolts. He wore his hair in two braids that hung over his bare shoulders. Framed by the thick braids was a broad face, with sharp, high cheekbones and very small close-set eyes. Even with the paint on his face, it was apparent that he was not a handsome man. He wore only a tanned-hide breechcloth, leggings and moccasins; his bare chest was painted in warlike symbols of red, black and yellow. His shoulders and upper torso were taut and ridged with bulging muscles, and although he was not a tall man, his arrogant stance made him appear much bigger. As he stared back at Meadow, a smirk curled his thick lips, almost as if he enjoyed watching her suffer.

In spite of her misery, Meadow narrowed her eyes and held her head up high. She returned the warrior's brazen stare until he mumbled under his breath and motioned for her to get a drink from the river. Grateful for his small show of kindness, Meadow exhaled the breath she had been holding, but the gesture made the pain in her ribs flare like wildfire. It took all her strength to keep from doubling over and falling back on the ground. Instead, she took several short breaths, and then made her shaky legs move toward the water. Her progress was slow, and she wrapped her arms around herself to keep the movement of her broken ribs to a minimum. When she reached the river, she found it nearly impossible to bend down so that she could take a drink of the cool water. Even the slightest movement made sharp spears of pain rip through her upper body.

Someone walked up beside her, and Meadow stiffened. She remained unmoving as the man stopped next to her. Glancing out of the side of her eye, she noticed it was the same man who had caused all of her agony. To her surprise, he bent down, scooped up a handful of water and then pressed it to her lips. Her parched lips welcomed the cool drink, and in spite of her reluctance to accept his unexpected gesture of kindness, Meadow gulped down the few drops of moisture his cupped hands contained. She looked up at him again, but his expression was emotionless. She quickly looked away.

The woman's bravery impressed Strong Tree. He knew she was in terrible pain; her actions were proof, and he could see the pain in her green eyes. Still, she did not give into her misery, nor did she beg for mercy. It was no wonder Black Horse had chosen to make her his woman in spite of the fact that she was white. Not only was she beautiful to look at, but she was also strong and brave, unlike any other white woman Strong Tree had ever encountered.

Black Horse would want her back, and when he came for her, Strong Tree would be waiting for him. Then, Strong Tree told himself, he would finally have his revenge for the things Black Horse had done to his woman, Shy Deer.

His captive's ribs were broken, but he hesitated over whether or not he should help her. He recalled how Shy Deer had told him that Black Horse had not mistreated her, but had only used her for his pleasure. Strong Tree's hand drew into two tight fists at his sides.

He called out a gruff command and motioned for the woman to go back to his horse. Without looking at her again, he stomped back to the Appaloosa and waited for her to make her way slowly back to where the horse stood. Her brow was coated in sweat and her face was unnaturally pale. Briefly, he regretted his decision to let her suffer. But if he showed her too much compassion, his comrades might think him weak.

Strong Tree was as gentle as possible when he lifted her onto the back of his horse. He heard her moan softly, but she sat up straight in the saddle and made no further sounds as she waited for him to mount. He swung up and scooted close behind her. Using his bare legs to hold her securely against him, he was able to avoid squeezing her too tightly around her injured midriff again.

When they started riding once more, Strong Tree noticed that she seemed to relax slightly and did not seem to be getting any worse. This was good, he told himself, because if she died all of this would have been for nothing, and his revenge would never be complete. He let his horse fall behind the others with the hope that the slower pace would make her ride a bit easier. He had many plans for her when they reached the Blackfoot village, and he wanted to be sure she was completely aware of everything he did to her.

As they continued to ride, however, Strong Tree noticed that his captive's body had grown limp, and she seemed to be completely unconscious when he shook her arm to rouse her. He yanked on the reins, halting his mount's steps. She fell forward against the long blond mane. Strong Tree pulled her back up and slapped her face lightly with his hand. A soft moan escaped from her. He exhaled the breath he had been holding, once he realized that she had only fainted. His sense of relief increased when he glanced up and noticed that none of the other men had stopped to see what was going on.

She was unconscious, and so Strong Tree did not see any reason to go so slow. He kicked the Appaloosa in the sides and attempted to catch up with the other riders. Riding was still difficult, though, because now his passenger was unable to hold herself up in the saddle. Strong Tree did not want to alert his companions to her deteriorating condition, especially since they had all tried in vain to discourage him from carrying out this raid and had been reluctant to take part in his scheme.

It was common knowledge that Black Horse was a fierce enemy, and the Blackfoot warriors had no doubt that he would retaliate. But they had finally agreed to come along because Strong Tree was their comrade, and he had been greatly shamed by Black Horse.

Two days ago, Strong Tree had learned from a Canadian trapper that Black Horse was in Sitting Bull's village on the banks of the river. The trapper had also relayed news about Black Horse's impending marriage to a white woman who was also the adopted daughter of the medicine man White Buffalo. This was the day he had been waiting for, and Strong Tree wasted no time in planning his trip to the Sioux encampment to seek revenge.

Now, the deed was done, and Strong Tree had no doubts that he must prepare for the inevitable battle with Black Horse. Although he had wanted this for a long time, Strong Tree still could not push away the feeling of fear that gripped him when he realized that there was no turning back now and he would finally confront the man that had ruined his life.

The Blackfoot war party planned to ride all the way back to their own village before daybreak, but with the unconscious woman it was almost impossible for them to travel at night. Strong Tree decided that if he was going to keep Black Horse's woman alive long enough to fulfill his plan, they would have to let her rest for the night.

"What is wrong with this woman?" Long Feather asked as he took her limp form down from Strong Tree's horse. He held her in his arms as he studied her face in the disappearing daylight. Even for a white woman, her skin was ghostly pale.

Strong Tree slid down to the ground and shrugged his broad shoulders. "I think she broke her ribs when she was trying to get away from me."

Long Feather's disapproving expression told Strong Tree what his friend thought of his rough actions. Like the other warriors, Long Feather had not kept his feelings about this revenge raid a secret, but because he was Strong Tree's closest friend, he had helped to convince the others to come along. If the woman died before they even got back to their own village, though, Long Feather would not be proud of his part in this scheme.

"Broken ribs will be the least of her complaints by the time I finish with her," Strong Tree said in a harsh tone. He grabbed the woman's limp body away from his friend and dropped her on the ground. A barely audible whimper was her only reaction.

Ignoring Long Feather's disgusted grumble, Strong Tree grabbed his horse's reins and led the animal to the nearby narrow stream. He studied the area as his horse drank. At daybreak they would continue to travel upstream, and by midmorning they would be back in the Blackfoot village.

When his brown-and-cream-colored Appaloosa was through drinking from the stream, Strong Tree joined the rest of his comrades as they cared for their own mounts. The horses' needs almost always came first, for in this harsh country a man's survival sometimes depended on a strong and capable horse.

Once he finished tending to his horse, Strong Tree had no choice but to make another important decision regarding his captive. He could let her suffer, and as a result she could get worse. He could, however, bind her ribs so that they could begin to heal. He hadn't meant to hurt her so badly, and the condition she was in now made her useless for the type of vengeance he wanted.

Standing beside the small, clear stream, Strong Tree tried to sort through his tormented memories. He had loved only one woman in his twenty-seven summers. When he had taken Shy Deer as his wife several years earlier, their lives had seen many happy days.

Black Horse had changed everything. Strong Tree drew in a deep breath and tried to quell his rage as he recalled the day Black Horse's band of renegades had swooped down on a group of Blackfoot women while they were washing clothes in the Missouri River, down in northeastern Montana. Being the youngest—and the prettiest—Shy Deer had been claimed by the chief who was leading the warriors. When Strong Tree learned of Shy Deer's capture, he had been filled with heart-wrenching pain, and even more with rage. He just hoped that Black Horse was suffering the same type of tormented feelings at this very moment over the loss of his woman.

For over four months Strong Tree had searched

throughout northern Montana and into the Dakota Territory for some sign of Shy Deer. Black Horse kept outsmarting him. For Strong Tree, the chase became more than just a quest to reclaim his woman; he was obsessed with the idea of winning an even-greater victory over the feared Sioux war chief. Strong Tree wanted the fame that would be bestowed on the Blackfoot warrior who killed Black Horse.

Much to Strong Tree's disappointment, Black Horse was on a hunting expedition the night that he had finally located the renegade band's campsite. Shy Deer, along with two other Blackfoot women, had been reclaimed that night. But Strong Tree's thirst for a settling of scores was not quenched.

After they returned to their own village, Strong Tree realized he had lost more than just his chance to be the one who killed the dreaded war chief of their enemy tribe. He had also lost Shy Deer's devotion and love. Her time with the handsome Sioux chief had changed her drastically, and although she told Strong Tree that she hated Black Horse, her actions had proved this was not the case. She lay beneath her husband like a wooden doll in their tepee at night. On more than one occasion, Strong Tree had caught her staring dreamily off in the distance as if she was waiting—or hoping—to see someone riding in her direction. It enraged him to think that she was probably wishing that Black Horse would be the one to ride over the distant horizon.

The feeling that someone was staring at him drew Strong Tree's attention away from the past. He turned around slowly. Even the fading light of day did not hide Long Feather's unwavering and accusing stare.

"Do you have something to say to me?" Strong Tree demanded.

"If she dies, Black Horse will wage another war between our tribes that will affect many innocent lives."

"Since the beginning of Mother Earth there has been a war going on between our tribes." Strong Tree's mouth drew into a fierce frown as he turned away from his longtime friend. The disapproving tone in Long Feather's voice, combined with his accusing stare, did not ease Strong Tree's torment.

In the uncomfortable silence that followed, Strong Tree once again mulled over his true reasons for seeking retaliation against Black Horse. He glanced toward Long Feather. This had become a private war that involved only Black Horse and himself. He did not want this private feud to create more problems for his people.

"I won't let her die," Strong Tree said in a gruff voice. He turned toward the still form of the girl. She had not moved since he had dropped her on the ground. A cold chill swept through him, and a sense of urgency made him rush to her side. He rolled her over and studied her ashen face in the nearly obscure light. Her delicate beauty touched his heart. For a moment he truly felt sorry for what he had done to her. But then Shy Deer's emotionless face intruded into his thoughts.

He clenched his teeth tightly together and fought back the anger that rose up in him. Shy Deer had not deserved what Black Horse had done to her, either. Strong Tree doubted that the Sioux chief had ever once regretted anything he did to Shy Deer, so why should he care about Black Horse's woman now?

"Does she have a fever?"

Strong Tree jumped at the sound of Long Feather's voice. He had not heard him approaching. Touching the girl's forehead, Strong Tree shrugged. "She feels warm." He rose to his feet and avoided looking at Long Feather. "I will make her comfortable for the night. By morning she will be ready to travel the rest of the way to the village." He grabbed the fringed pouch that hung around his waist. From the bag he took out a strip of tightly wound leather. The leather strip served many purposes. It could be used for a tourniquet to help stop bleeding, or it could be wound around his head like a headband. He had once used it for a lead rope for his horse. Now, it would bind the girl's broken ribs.

Although he was aware of Long Feather's presence, Strong Tree did not speak to the other man as he un-rolled the long leather strip. When he lifted the girl up to a sitting position, Long Feather knelt down beside him and held the girl up while Strong Tree slipped her beaded gown down from her shoulders. The sight of the young white girl's firm, rounded breasts drew both men's attention, but neither of them made a comment.

As Strong Tree began to wind the leather around her ribs, the girl moaned. Her head rolled to the side, and for a moment it seemed as if she was going to re-gain consciousness. Hope flooded Strong Tree, but it fled almost instantly when she fell limp again. He swallowed the lump that had formed in his throat.

"Bear Woman will make her strong again," Long Feather said, as if he sensed his friend's worry.

Strong Tree nodded, but inwardly he was not so sure. Bear Woman was the wisest woman in their tribe, and she possessed strong medicine, even stronger than most of the Blackfoot medicine men. However, Strong Tree knew that if even one of her broken ribs had punctured something inside of the girl, she might not survive, in spite of Bear Woman's great healing powers.

He carefully pulled her beaded gown back up over her shoulders. He had not realized until now that she was wearing a ceremonial gown. For a moment he was not sure what this could mean. Then, like a gust of wind, it hit him: she must have been dressed for her wedding to Black Horse. Did this mean that she was already married to the war chief, or was today to have been her wedding day? Another shiver raced through Strong Tree. He glanced up and noticed that the men who rode with him were standing in a tight group around them. Their obvious expressions of lust told Strong Tree that they had enjoyed the brief exposure of the girl's body. He glared at them until the warriors backed away, playfully hitting each other and mumbling rude comments about the tempting young captive they had taken today.

As the night wore on, Strong Tree grew more concerned about the girl. He had tried to force water down her, but he had not been very successful. Most of the water had merely rolled down the sides of her face, and she had nearly choked on the few drops that he had managed to pour down her throat. Occasionally she groaned, but when morning came, she did not even make this small effort. When Strong Tree placed her on the back of his horse for the remainder of the journey to the Blackfoot village, he was not sure if she would survive. The entire group of warriors rode in solemn silence, each seemingly occupied with his own thoughts.

With the girl cradled in his arms, Strong Tree rode directly to Bear Woman's tepee. He ignored all the questions called out as he made his way through the maze of tepees. The other warriors who rode with him could tell them the details. The purpose of this raid had been to kidnap Black Horse's woman, and they had succeeded, which meant there would be a celebration tonight. Strong Tree, however, would not be celebrating in the manner that he had originally planned.

He pulled on the reins and halted his Appaloosa in front of Bear Woman's tepee. Before he swung down to the ground, his attention was drawn to the woman who had just walked up to his horse. Shy Deer's brooding face tilted up toward him. Her dark gaze moved to the girl in his arms. Shy Deer made no effort to hide the contempt and jealousy she held for this captive. Her thick lashes narrowed over her flashing black eyes. Strong Tree was once again reminded of the obsession Shy Deer must still harbor for Black Horse.

"Bear Woman?" Strong Tree called out in a loud voice. He tore his gaze away from Shy Deer's flushed and angry face. Holding his captive's limp form, he carefully slid down to the ground. He shifted her weight as he tried to balance himself with the extra burden. He wondered why he had thought this act of revenge would win back Shy Deer's love and respect. More than likely, having Black Horse's woman here would only prove once and for all how much Shy Deer still wanted to be with the Sioux chief.

"Is she sick?" Bear Woman's deep, gruff voice broke into his tormented thoughts.

He turned away from Shy Deer's piercing stare. "She is hurt, Bear Woman, hurt bad."

The old woman leaned forward as she looked closer at the girl. Her dry, cracked lips pursed into a heavy frown as she shook her head in a disapproving gesture. Sighing heavily, she turned around and motioned for Strong Tree to follow her into the tepee. The inside of the tepee was hot, and the smell of herbs hung heavy in the air.

Strong Tree laid the girl down on a bed of elk hides, and then quickly got out of Bear Woman's way as she knelt down to examine the girl. "Her ribs are broken," he said.

"You did this to her?" Bear Woman did not look up at Strong Tree, but surely she could hear the shame in his voice when he answered.

"I did not realize how hard I grabbed her."

"She's nothing more than a Blackfoot slave now, so why should you care?" The old woman glanced up and her knowing gaze focused on the warrior's face.

"True, she is just my slave. But I want her to be strong so that she can serve me in every way."

A disgusted huff emitted from Bear Woman. She turned back toward the girl as her gnarled hands began to gently probe the girl's rib cage. She reached up and laid the back of her hand against the girl's forehead. "She might die," she said in a voice that lacked emotion. Her questioning gaze searched Strong Tree's face. "Will her death ease the anger and pain in your heart?"

Strong Tree stared down at the old woman. His mouth opened, but no words escaped. Tangled thoughts spun through his troubled mind. He did not want this girl to die. Her death would serve no useful purpose; it would only make Black Horse's retaliation all the more violent. The Blackfoot warrior hung his head down and stared blankly at the furs that carpeted the floor of the tepee.

His entire tribe would suffer from his foolish actions—and all for nothing, if she died. He turned away from the accusing stare of Bear Woman. "Do what you can for her," he muttered as he bent down and pushed through the flap on the doorway.

The midmorning sun hit him squarely in the eyes. He blinked several times and stepped out into the open. Shy Deer still stood in the same spot. Strong Tree let his gaze meet hers for several silent seconds.

"What's wrong with her?" Shy Deer asked, finally breaking the uneasy silence.

Strong Tree stared at his wife. Her waist-length hair was loose the way he liked it. The dark tresses appeared almost midnight blue in color. Her smooth bronze complexion was flushed, and he noticed her breathing was fast and heavy. The soft doeskin dress she wore rose and fell rapidly over her full breasts with each deep breath she took. He knew every inch of her voluptuous body as well as he knew his own body. But the eyes that watched him now were those of a stranger.

"Bear Woman says she might die," he said. Strong Tree saw the way her mouth was tempted to curve into a smile. "That would be good for you," he added in a snide tone.

"Why do you say that?" Shy Deer asked. She tilted her head to the side and coyly gazed up at her husband.

A crude smile curled Strong Tree's lips. He stepped forward until he was standing directly in front of her. "When Black Horse comes for her, if she is dead, maybe you can take her place." She did not reply, but merely turned and stomped away from him. He shook his head in disgust. That had been a foolish remark, because Strong Tree knew that when Black Horse showed up to reclaim his woman, he would only be intent on one thing, and that would be killing everyone who got in his way.

Chapter Twelve

Back in his tepee, Black Horse still could not shake the strange feeling that something was terribly wrong. He kept reminding himself that White Buffalo was the man who had premonitions and visions. Yet the feeling he had developed down by the river was so strong and frightening that it was impossible for him to ignore.

With a sense of urgency, Black Horse quickly donned his only other ceremonial shirt. This shirt was not as elaborate as the one he had worn for his wedding yesterday. He had left that shirt and the feathered headdress he had worn somewhere down by the river. The memory of his first night with Meadow filled his mind. A contented smile curved his mouth.

Pulling on his extra pair of leggings and a clean breechcloth, Black Horse wondered once again what White Buffalo had wanted to talk to Meadow about. He hoped their discussion would not last long, and most of all, he hoped it would not have an adverse effect on their plans to marry today. As he pondered, he quickly brushed his hair with a stiff grass brush until the raven strands were shiny and smooth. He grabbed a long white cotton headband, which he wrapped around his head and then tied, letting the extra material hang down past his shoulders. Once he had tied his belt around his waist and carefully adjusted his knife sheath at his hip, he was once again ready for his second attempt to become a married man.

With a nervous sigh, he glanced outside. There were no signs of Meadow and White Buffalo. He pushed through the flap and stood out in the warm morning sun. With his arms crossed over his broad chest, he watched the trail coming up from the river until his anxiety threatened to explode inside him.

He stalked to White Buffalo's tepee and peeked inside the empty lodge. Briefly, he recalled the sweet kisses he and Meadow had shared there on that first morning they had awoken together in her father's tepee. Once again he turned in the direction of the trail, but to his dismay, no one emerged from the trees. Perhaps White Buffalo had changed his mind about letting them marry today. Why else would they be gone so long?

When his patience expired, he stalked back into the forest. If there was not going to be a wedding today, he had to know why!

Black Horse's steps lengthened as his heartbeat pounded uncontrollably in his chest. He followed the same path he had followed last night, but when he reached the river he turned and headed up to where they had found White Buffalo earlier this morning. The rock where the medicine man had been sitting was empty.

A loud stomping sound caught his attention, and he instinctively grabbed for his knife. He turned slowly and stared at the bushes where he had heard the noise. The pounding of his heart almost seemed to cease as he waited for the approaching intruder.

A relieved chortle escaped him when a bull moose emerged from the bushes and started walking along the riverbank with a leisurely gait. Black Horse's gaze followed the large, clumsy animal as he moved upriver. As impressive as the big animals were, it had not taken the warriors long to learn that not only were the Canadian moose mean and temperamental, but their meat was not nearly as tasty as the American buffalo that the Sioux so dearly cherished.

Black Horse saw the moose stop abruptly as if something had startled him; then he turned away from the river and moved toward the forest at a faster pace. Black Horse's attention was directed away from the moose as he looked toward the area where the moose had stopped before he had been frightened. Something lying on the ground a short distance away caught his eye.

He stared at the unmoving heap for a moment before his puzzled mind realized that it was White Buffalo. His feet were frozen to the spot where he stood; then he began to run toward the fallen man. He slid to a stop beside him just as he saw the broken arrow protruding from White Buffalo's chest. The painted markings told Black Horse that the arrow belonged to a Blackfoot. His body grew cold. A strangling knot formed in his throat.

Black Horse tore his attention away from the medicine man, and, although he did not expect to see her, his frantic gaze scanned the area in search of Meadow. He was sure he would not find her body crumpled on the ground like White Buffalo's, because he had no doubt what had happened to her. The thought of her being the captive of a Blackfoot was almost more than he could bear.

Black Horse dropped to his knees beside White Buffalo. He laid one hand against the injured medicine man's chest and the other hand above his mouth. His breath was faint, and the beating of his heart was weak in his chest. The Blackfoot who had done this to White Buffalo, and especially the one who had taken his woman captive, would not live to see another day once he caught up to them!

The sound of his tormented cry echoed through the trees as Black Horse approached the village with White Buffalo in his arms. Those who heard the sound rushed out to meet him.

"What happened?" Walks Tall called out as he ran to the edge of the village.

"Blackfoot." Black Horse gratefully accepted Walks Tall's help when the other man easily hoisted the limp form of White Buffalo into his own arms. Walks Tall had earned his name. Not only was he taller than any of the other men in the tribe, but he was as strong as a grizzly.

"How did this happen?"

"Meadow has been taken captive," Black Horse said in a breathless tone. "I'm going after her." He did not waste time talking. The Blackfoot could not be more than a mile or two away, and so he would not need anything more than his weapons and his horse. He should be able to catch up with them before the morning had faded into afternoon.

The villagers besieged Black Horse with more questions as he passed. He did not take time to answer them. From his tepee, he grabbed his rifle, his bow and the quiver that held his arrows, a halter and a blanket for his horse. He glanced briefly at the white marriage blanket that was lying on the furs of his bed. It could not end this way. . . . He would not allow it!

When he stepped back outside, he glanced down and noticed that his shirt was soaked with White Buffalo's blood. He felt the stickiness against his skin, and a feeling as cold as the northern wind blew through him. It did not look good for the old man. He clenched his teeth together so tightly that they hurt as he thought about Meadow's fate. She would suffer the same treatment at her captor's hands that his Blackfoot captive, Shy Deer, had endured when he had kidnapped her. But that had been different. Shy Deer had been willing—even the first time—and he knew that Meadow would rather die than let a Blackfoot have his way with her. He could not let this happen.

As he had been taught throughout his strict training as a Sioux warrior, he cleared his head of all thoughts that could distract him from his goal. He would not think about where the blood on his shirt had come from, or what could be happening to his woman at this very moment. His sole thought would be to recapture her, and once he knew that she was safe, he would see to it that the men who had taken her would never take another breath.

As he headed toward the area where the Sioux ponies were corralled, Black Horse saw White Buffalo being carried into his own tepee. Several of the older women were following him inside so that they could care for the injured shaman with his own mixtures of herbs and powders.

Black Horse bent down and ducked under the crude corral that was constructed of lodgepole pines. His horse—a large black and white paint—could easily be spotted among the other horses. The ponies whinnied and began to move around the enclosure restlessly. Black Horse's stallion, Dusya, pranced back and forth at the far end of the corral. He watched his master approach from the side of his eye as he tossed his head in a defiant manner.

Shaking his head with impatience, Black Horse cursed under his breath. He had not had this horse long, and he still had much to teach the animal about obedience and discipline. Black Horse knew that eventually his strict training would pay off and he would have a horse that could not be equaled. *Dusya* meant *fast*, and this young stallion deserved the name.

"Dusya, come here!" Black Horse called out in a firm voice. The horse responded by running farther away. Black Horse resisted the urge to yell at the stubborn animal, because he didn't want to spook the entire herd. Inwardly, though, he was seething. He frantically twirled around and searched for another horse. But there was not another in this corral that could run as swiftly as Dusya. He faced his own stallion once again.

"Maybe you have finally met a horse that is wilder than you," Walks Tall said as he walked up to his friend. He had grabbed his weapons from his tepee, and now he was ready to join his friend to hunt down the Blackfoot who had stolen his woman and shot the most honored medicine man of their tribe.

"I would like to roast that animal on a spit over the fire," Black Horse spat. He took a step toward the horse. The stallion snorted and pawed at the ground. He continued to back away from his owner until the corral poles stopped his escape. Black Horse took advantage of the horse's moment of hesitation to close the distance between them. He tossed the halter over Dusya's head and prepared himself for the battle he knew would come.

Dusya reared up on his hind legs as Black Horse held tight to the reins. The horse's hooves came crashing down to the ground, barely missing Black Horse's head. Still, he did not release his tight hold on the reins. Dusya tossed his head from side to side several more times before he finally realized that he had been caught once again.

"You would make a better meal for the dogs than you do a warrior's horse," Black Horse spat. He hung on to the halter with all his strength until the last of the horse's energy was spent. Then, without wasting more valuable time, Black Horse quickly threw the blanket over Dusya's back and swung himself up. True to form, Dusya immediately lunged upward and then came crashing back down. He bucked up and down one more time, then, defeated, stopped abruptly and gave several quick snorts. Black Horse held the reins tightly in his hands, kept his legs clamped against the horse's sides and gained control of the animal at last.

Walks Tall held the gate open as Black Horse rode through. He resisted making his usual snide comments about the wild stallion. Pulling the gate closed behind them, Walks Tall jumped onto the back of his own horse. He knew Black Horse would be long gone once he had Dusya out of the forest, and although his horse would not be able to keep up, Walks Tall did not want to fall too far behind.

As they emerged from the thick forest, Walks Tall stopped his horse beside Dusya as Black Horse knelt on the ground and studied the area where he had found White Buffalo lying in a pool of his own blood. The gory sight of the medicine man's blood was now a dark brown stain on the hard ground. Black Horse's gaze focused on the trail of tracks that had been left by the Blackfoot's horse. He glanced up and looked at Walks Tall. Their eyes met; words were not necessary. Walks Tall nodded in agreement when Black Horse motioned with his head westward.

Black Horse swung back up on his horse, and Dusya lunged forward. The power in the animal's legs was evident as his speed began to increase. In a matter of seconds he was keeping pace with the wind. His rider moved with him as if they were one, and for a time it seemed as if they flew over the land without touching the ground. Only moments later, Black Horse and Dusya were no more than a dark speck in the distance.

Though Walks Tall's horse, Hawk, was a strong runner, catching up with the younger horse was an impossible feat. Since this was not the first time Hawk had attempted to keep up with Dusya, Walks Tall knew that if he let Hawk have his own rein, the horse would soon pace himself at a speed that would be comfortable over a long distance. He saw Dusya disappear over the top of a hill, but he was not worried about losing sight of him. Hawk would follow Dusya's trail, just as Walks Tall would always follow Black Horse . . . no matter where the trail led them.

Chapter Thirteen

As Walks Tall rode after his friend, he thought about the events of the past few weeks. Before leaving Montana, Black Horse had led his small band of renegade warriors on a daring raid against the U.S. Cavalry. Supply wagons headed for Fort Keogh had been too tempting for the war party to resist. Not only were the wagons loaded with whiskey and food, but they were also carrying several boxes of rifles and ammunition—all desperately needed by the Sioux on the other side of the Canadian border.

Regardless of the danger involved, Black Horse had planned an attack. At first, it had seemed like a suicide mission, ten warriors against two dozen or more soldiers. But the cavalry unit was careless—and lazy. Black Horse had not made any raids in this part of Montana for a long time, and reports said that he was somewhere in the Dakota Territory. This misleading information made the attack almost easy.

With the cover of darkness as their greatest asset, the warriors had crept into the soldiers' camp. The guards had been easily disposed of, so the Indians quickly loaded all of the supplies and weapons into one wagon. They hitched up a team of the soldiers' own horses. The rest of the soldiers in the camp weren't even aware of the intrusion until the warriors knocked down the makeshift corral and started running off the horses. By the time the sleepy soldiers had their pants on and their weapons in their hands, Black Horse and his warriors were long gone.

The food and the whiskey the wagons were carrying to Fort Keogh were for a large celebration that was planned at the fort. This, combined with the embarrassment over the ease with which the soldiers had been overtaken by the Indians, made the U.S. Cavalry furious. Black Horse's notoriety had quickly grown, and to wipe out him and his followers became the cavalry's top priority.

Walks Tall had been more than a little relieved when his good friend became enchanted with White Buffalo's adopted daughter and decided to stay in Canada for a spell. Black Horse deciding to marry the girl was more than Walks Tall had expected, however. He knew his friend must truly love her to take such a big step, and he hoped this meant that they would stay in Canada for an even longer time—maybe long enough so that the soldiers across the border would get tired of looking for them.

But, should Black Horse lose Meadow now . . . A chill ran through Walks Tall's body. He knew the chief would be so filled with rage that his quest for revenge and destruction would never end until the last spark of life was gone from his body.

At the top of the ridge, Walks Tall surveyed the countryside down below him. The land looked vaguely familiar. He wondered if they had come this way when they had come up from Montana. To his surprise, Walks Tall noticed that Black Horse was waiting at the bottom of the slope. Kicking his horse in the sides, he hurried down the incline. As Walks Tall approached, he could see that the chief's face was flushed, and even though he was sure he knew the other man as well as he knew the back of his hand, there was a strange look in Black Horse's eyes that Walks Tall did not recognize.

"The Blackfoot are moving fast. The cowards know what I will do to them when I catch up to them." Black Horse pointed down toward the hoofprints in the dirt. "See, one horse carries two riders. The man who rides this horse will die soon."

Walks Tall swallowed hard. He barely glanced down at the tracks on the ground. Black Horse's words spoke of death, yet his eyes seemed to hold so much pain. Walks Tall hoped the combination of these powerful emotions would not interfere with Black Horse's judgment.

"We can cut them off in no time. I know of a shorter way, but it will mean crossing over the border to the American side."

"This is not wise, my brother."

"It would only be for a short distance," Black Horse retorted.

"There will be American soldiers patrolling the border."

"When have I ever been frightened by any soldier?"

Walks Tall shrugged his shoulders in defeat. He knew that there was nothing he could say anyway. Black Horse's love for the girl ruled his actions now.

Without further discussion, Black Horse nudged Dusya in the sides. The horse tossed his head back and fought against his master's command. Black Horse yanked on the reins and pressed his knees into the horse's sides as hard as he could until the horse yielded. He kicked him roughly in the sides again. This time, Dusya obeyed without hesitation.

Shaking his head at the insanity of what they were about to do, Walks Tall gave Hawk the signal to follow. Black Horse was no longer pushing Dusya at such a fast pace, and so Hawk was able to stay at the other horse's heels. Walks Tall was not sure when they crossed over into Montana, but he did notice that Black Horse was headed for a stretch of wide-open prairie where only stirrup-high grass grew. A queasy sensation washed over Walks Tall. They would be out in plain sight, defenseless, without one tree or rock to take cover behind if they were spotted.

Oblivious to the danger of exposing himself and Walks Tall to an attack, Black Horse ached with guilt over not being with Meadow when she had been taken captive. If he hadn't waited so long to go back to the river, maybe he could have prevented the attack on White Buffalo and protected Meadow from the Blackfoot. Every second that passed allowed them more time to abuse his beloved Meadow.

He kept being reminded of Shy Deer, his Blackfoot captive. It seemed too ironic that he had stolen a Blackfoot woman, and now his woman had been taken by a Blackfoot. Was it possible that Meadow had been targeted just because she was his woman? He closed his eyes for a minute and swallowed hard. This staggering thought made his stomach hurt and heaviness settle in his chest. If this was all in retaliation for his past actions, how would he ever be able to live with himself? He opened his eyes and looked up at the sky.

"Please don't make Meadow pay for my past evils," he begged of *Wakan Tanka*.

A feeling of helplessness claimed Walks Tall as he watched the chief move ahead. He did not push Hawk to go faster. Instead, he held the horse back for a reason he could not explain. At a slow gait he led Hawk out into the open prairie. With a nervous glance around the countryside, Walks Tall tried to push the rising sense of panic to the back of his mind. Unconsciously, he pulled on Hawk's reins, bringing the horse to a complete stop. His heart pounded like thunder in his chest as he watched Black Horse ride farther away. The chief and his powerful stallion were growing smaller, the black and white color of the horse and the tan shades of Black Horse's buckskin suit all blending together. Something did not seem right.

Walks Tall kicked Hawk in the sides. The horse bounded forward just as a loud sound echoed across the valley. The explosion sent Walks Tall's mind into confusion. His instincts caused him to yank on his horse's reins, but his loyalty to his comrade made him kick the horse in the sides an instant later. In spite of his rider's mixed signals, Hawk charged forward.

Another loud gunshot rang out.

Off in the distance, Walks Tall could see Dusya bucking and twirling around as more shots were fired. Then, although he had not seen Black Horse fall, he realized that the chief was no longer on the horse. Now absent his rider, Dusya was galloping toward him at a dead run.

The events were happening at such a rapid pace that Walks Tall did not have time to think through his own actions. He kept riding toward the fallen chief, but as he drew nearer, he realized his efforts were in vain. He could see the soldiers who had surrounded Black Horse like circling vultures. Because they blocked his view, Walks Tall could not see whether or not the chief was alive or dead. When he was only several hundred yards away from the cavalry troop, one of the soldiers spotted him. Walks Tall heard the soldier shout out to his companions. When they all turned around to look at him, he caught a fleeting glimpse of Black Horse's unmoving body lying in the deep grass.

Walks Tall's first reaction was to try to reach his fallen friend, but in the final seconds before it was too late for him to turn his horse around, his thoughts were jolted back to the many conversations he and Black Horse had had during their long friendship. On several occasions they had talked about what they would do if ever they were in a life and death situation such as they were now. As blood brothers, each had initially said he would never desert the other, but as Sioux warriors they had vowed to do whatever was necessary to benefit their people.

Walks Tall knew what he had to do. He yanked on the reins and leaned to one side, then clamped his legs against Hawk's sides to keep from being tossed off the horse's back when the animal swung around in a swirl of dust and flying grass.

Hawk's hooves pounded down on the hard ground, and beads of sweat flew off his mane as he galloped back in the direction of the forest. Dusya had already disappeared into the thick maze of pines. All coherent thoughts had now fled from Walks Tall's mind. His only goal now had to be to outrun the soldiers quickly closing in behind him. Once he reached the shelter of the trees he knew he would be able to lose his pursuers. Then, he would allow himself to think about Black Horse's fate.

Even though Hawk was not as swift as Dusya, the older stallion ran now as if he understood his master's desperate plight. The trees drew nearer at a rapid pace, and not once did the horse's hooves falter. When they crossed the last of the open field and moved into the trees, Walks Tall did not even have to urge Hawk to keep running. The horse dodged the trunks of the trees with ease.

Bullets ricocheted off the trees as the soldiers attempted to halt the warrior's progress, but Hawk was not startled or distracted by the gunshots. Walks Tall thought briefly of Dusya. Had the paint been as well trained as Hawk, perhaps Black Horse would have had a chance to escape from the soldiers. Silently, Walks Tall cursed the young stallion, even though he knew the horse was not at fault.

Finally, Walks Tall became aware of the silence behind him. Hawk began to slow down; the fast chase had left him winded. He snorted and coughed as his breaths came in labored gasps. Sweat rolled down his neck and over his heaving sides like rain in a cloudburst. Still, Walks Tall could not let the horse rest. He could not chance having another encounter with the soldiers, and until he was certain that he was back on Canadian soil, he would not stop.

His next mission was too important for carelessness. He had to escape so that he could find out whether Black Horse was dead or alive. If the chief still lived, Walks Tall knew he would have to figure out a way to help him escape from the soldiers. Until then, Walks Tall had no doubts about the kind of tortures Black Horse would be subjected to at the hands of the American soldiers. Coldness whipped through him in spite of the sweat that ran down his face and body.

When it seemed that a long time had passed since the sounds of the soldiers' pursuit had disappeared into the distance, Walks Tall felt safe enough to take the time to rest his horse. He turned Hawk in the direction he knew would lead them back to the river, and then he let the horse walk at his own pace until they reached the water. Sliding down to the ground, Walks Tall dropped the reins and let Hawk walk out into the cool water. The horse didn't stop until the water was halfway up his long legs. He bent his head down and began to take loud slurping gulps.

Feeling too weak and sick to drink, Walks Tall fell down on his knees and let his head drop down on his chest. Images of Black Horse's still form lying in the deep grass kept flashing through his mind. Why had such a senseless thing happened? In spite of his sometimes-quick temper, Black Horse was usually a rational man, which was one of the many reasons he had obtained such an honored title at his young age.

Walks Tall knew Black Horse was aware of the danger in crossing over the Canadian border. Yet, because he was so ravaged by the pain of losing Meadow to the Blackfoot, he had sacrificed his own safety. He understood that Black Horse's careless actions were ruled by his love of the woman, and an unexplainable feeling of protectiveness washed over Walks Tall as he recalled the girl who had stolen his friend's heart. That she was a white woman did not enter his thoughts. It had become obvious that regardless of her white bloodline, she was devoted to the Sioux. But none of that mattered now that they had been torn apart by the terrible actions of the Blackfoot.

Walks Tall clenched his hands into tight fists. He would avenge his brother even if it meant his own death.

A splashing noise caught Walks Tall's attention. He jumped to his feet. His rifle was clutched tightly in his hand when he turned around to face the source of the noise.

"Devil horse," Walks Tall hissed when he spotted Dusya standing a couple hundred yards upstream. For a few minutes Walks Tall did not move. The horse watched him with a wide-eyed stare, almost as if he were waiting for the man to forgive him. Compassion for the rebellious horse did not enter into the feelings Walks Tall had toward the stallion, nor did he feel any obligation to care for the horse that might have contributed to Black Horse's capture or possible death.

Raising the rifle up slowly, Walks Tall began to take aim. When the horse was in direct line with the barrel of the rifle, Walks Tall let his forefinger wrap around the trigger. A moment of hesitation claimed Walks Tall's conscience, and a tremor traipsed down his spine. He should just shoot the worthless beast. Yet he continued to stare intently down the barrel until his finger began to uncurl from the trigger. His thoughts were filled with memories of how determined Black Horse had been to train this stupid horse, and of how confident he had been that someday this animal would be worth all the aggravation and work. With a heavy sigh, Walks Tall lowered the rifle. He stared at the stallion as he continued to think of Black Horse.

Walks Tall turned away from the beautiful black and white paint. He looked back at his own horse. Hawk had finished drinking his fill of water and was now staring at the other horse with a curious tilt to his head. He bent down and grabbed Hawk's reins. Without looking back at Dusya, he mounted Hawk and began to lead him away from the river. His thoughts were occupied with the more important tasks he must do as soon as possible. First, he would ride back to the village and gather up the other warriors who rode with him and Black Horse.

Together they would head to Fort Keogh on the American side of the border. It was the largest fort in the area. If Black Horse was still alive, Walks Tall was sure he would be held prisoner there. The constant thoughts of his friend being tortured and humiliated by the *wasichu* made his insides twist like knots. He knew how much Black Horse hated the soldiers, and he believed the chief would rather die than be at their mercy.

Another devastating thought passed through Walks Tall's mind, and a numbing sensation whipped through his body. If Black Horse was dead, Walks Tall knew what he must do next. He would have to fulfill his friend's last wish. It would be up to him to go after Meadow and save her from the Blackfoot, and seek revenge against the men who took her. It would also be his responsibility to Black Horse as his blood brother to look after her and see to it that she would not have to spend the rest of her life alone.

Chapter Fourteen

Meadow lay as quiet as possible while she waited for the right moment to make her escape. For the past couple of days, she had been playing a dangerous charade. The first day they had arrived in the Blackfoot village, she had been incredibly ill. She remembered nothing more than being in terrible pain, and running a fever that kept her drifting in and out of consciousness for most of the day and into the night. As she had slowly regained consciousness, she had been careful not to let anyone else know that she was aware of her surroundings.

An older Blackfoot woman called Bear Woman had been tending to her injuries, and the knowledgeable manner in which she had banded Meadow's broken ribs kept the pain to a minimum. Since the Blackfoot language was similar to Sioux, Meadow had understood enough of what the woman said to know that her fever was probably the result of one of her broken ribs poking something inside of her.

She had heard the old woman telling the warrior who had kidnapped her that she might not survive if she didn't regain consciousness soon. Even in her groggy state, Meadow realized that as long as her captor believed her to be near death, she was safe from him. Pretending to be unconscious had not only allowed her more time to heal inside, it had also given her time to form a plan.

She knew her chances of escape were slim, especially since she would have to be extremely careful not to cause more harm to herself. Because of the extent of her injuries, she knew there would be no room for error in her plan to get away from here. She also knew that she would have to make her escape soon. She could not pretend to be unconscious too much longer. The old woman was wise, and this morning she had leaned over Meadow and mumbled, "Your fever is gone, white eyes. What makes you sleep so long? Are you trying to trick me?"

There were a few times when Bear Woman left her alone, and when she did leave the tepee, the warrior who had done this to her usually came and sat by her side. Sometimes he seemed truly sorry for injuring her, yet at other times he seemed to be filled with so much anger and pain. Even though he believed her to be unconscious, he came and sat beside her and spoke to her as if they were old friends.

But his words made no sense. He talked of how he had to have revenge for the terrible things that were done to someone called Shy Deer. It was the only way he could save face among his people. He told Meadow that she could not die, because then his revenge would never be complete. His anguish was evident in his voice when he talked about Shy Deer. Meadow guessed that she was his wife, but she was puzzled as to why she felt she no longer loved him.

Then, once, his tone had changed drastically as he spat, "But now Black Horse will suffer, just as he made me suffer."

The venom in his voice—and the mention of Black Horse—had startled Meadow so much that she had almost forgotten that she was supposed to be unconscious. She wanted to demand that he tell her what he was talking about, but she forced herself to remain silent and unmoving.

Strong Tree jumped to his feet when the flap of the tepee was pushed aside and Bear Woman said something to him about Mounties being in the village.

Meadow held her breath as she listened to the commotion she could hear outside of the tepee—and, mostly, as she waited to see what Bear Woman was going to do. If she left with Strong Tree, Meadow knew this was the moment she had been waiting for. As much as she hated the Mounties for what had happened at her wedding, she was more than a little grateful for their presence now.

When the flap of the tepee dropped down again, Meadow took a deep breath. Bear Woman did not come back inside. Slowly, she opened her eyes and glanced at the doorway. For several more minutes, she did nothing but stare at the flap. When no one entered, Meadow knew she must make her move before any more time passed. She clutched one arm around her ribs, and with her other arm she gently pushed herself up to a sitting position. Her head spun, and for a moment she felt as if she was going to be sick. She swallowed hard and refused to give into the urge to lie back down.

When her head finally stopped spinning, the nausea also passed. Her ribs throbbed, but the pain was bearable. She gritted her teeth and began to push herself up to a standing position. Her legs were as weak as those of a baby who was just learning to walk, and her knees felt as if they were going to buckle under with any weight. She wove back and forth several times until a bit of her strength began to seep back into her limbs.

The old woman had not undressed her, and her moccasins were standing next to the furs that had served as her bed for the past few days. Lifting her legs up one at a time was pure torture as she slipped her feet into her moccasins. By the time she had accomplished this small task, her face was beaded with sweat.

Outside, the village had grown unnaturally quiet. Meadow took her first agonizing step toward the doorway. Her ribs, though tightly bound, almost seemed to jiggle like mush inside of her with each of her slow movements. A painful moan escaped from her when she bent down to peer through the flap of the door. The area seemed almost deserted; the Mounties' arrival was obviously drawing everyone to the center of the village. She wondered if they had come here to issue the same warning to the Blackfoot about keeping peace in Canada that they had given to the Sioux a few days ago. That day—the day that she should have become Black Horse's wife—seemed as if it had been years ago.

How peculiar, she thought, that she should be in both villages during the Mounties' visits.

The sound of voices made panic wash through Meadow's pain-racked body. She dropped the flap shut again and waited until the pounding in her breast calmed enough for her to take another deep breath. She listened to the distant voices but could not make out what they were saying. All that mattered was that she had only a few minutes to escape, and her fear was causing her to waste them.

Trying to control the panic that threatened to over-power her, Meadow gritted her teeth against the pain and stepped out into the open. She shivered as a feel-ing of complete defenselessness claimed her. If anyone walked out from any of the tepees right now, she would be caught. This thought snapped her out of her frozen state of panic.

Each step she took was filled with agony, but her strength increased with the hope that she was actually escaping. Guessing that the Blackfoot village was laid out in a similar manner to those of the Sioux, Meadow moved in the direction that she believed would take her to where the horses were corralled. She did not look back as she reached the edge of the encampment. A building excitement made her pain dull when she saw a group of horses tied to the trees. In her rush, she did not realize that they were not Indian ponies, nor did she see the man who was standing guard over the horses until she was standing only a few feet away from him.

Meadow's startled gasp was almost simultaneous with the man's surprised grunt. For a moment Meadow considered trying to run into the forest, but she knew that would be foolish. She was in too much pain to run anywhere, and without a horse she would never be able to make it back to the Sioux village.

The Mountie stared at her in confusion, until he finally spoke. "My Lord! You— You're— You—" Brandon's shock caused him to stutter as he attempted to speak. "You're th-the girl from the Sioux village!" He dropped his rifle on the ground and rushed to her side. A million thoughts spun through his head, but his shock over seeing the same girl he'd seen just a few days ago at Sitting Bull's village left him even more confused.

"What in the Lord's name has happened to you?" Brandon asked as he reached out toward her. When he noticed that she flinched and looked terrified, he immediately pulled his hand back. Her appearance was drastically different today than it had been the first time he had seen her. Then, dressed in her wedding finery, she had looked beautiful and healthy. Now, with her hair so dirty and tangled and her dress even more filthy, it was apparent that she had been through hell since he had last seen her.

Brandon's gaze lowered to where she was clutching her ribs. "You're hurt," he said as he glanced in the direction of the village. He thought about going to find Superintendent Walsh, but then remembered that he had been ordered to stay with the horses today because of his outburst at the Sioux village the other day.

Glancing back at the pitiful-looking girl, Brandon decided that his first concern should be caring for her. Slowly, he extended his hand again. "Please let me help you," he asked. To his relief, she did not back away from him again.

"Can you ride?" he asked. His concern was evident as he leaned down to peer into her face. Her green gaze met with his briefly, then she glanced away. He noticed how pale she looked, and the way her blonde hair was matted against her head. She had obviously been badly mistreated in the past few days, but how did she end up here? A sense of rage erupted in Brandon, along with the overpowering urge to protect this girl from all harm, as he realized that the Blackfoot must have kidnapped her from the Sioux village.

As much as she hated to take their help, Meadow knew that these Mounties were her only chance to escape from the Blackfoot—and even then, it was a slim chance. She reluctantly accepted the soldier's assistance when he put his arm around her waist for support. She leaned against him and drew in a relieved but painful breath.

Desperately, she tried to recall the words she vaguely remembered from the white man's language, so she could tell him what had happened to her and how important it was for him to take her back to her own village. But it had been so long since she had spoken in her native tongue that she could not make her mouth form the words. She could, however, still understand most of the white man's tongue. Many of the Sioux had learned to speak and understand the white man's language so that they were not left entirely in the dark when they dealt with their enemies. White Buffalo could speak fluent English, and he had not attempted to force Meadow to forget her own language. However, it was a rare occasion when they would converse in the white man's words.

When Meadow made no further attempt to answer the Mountie, she noticed him glancing toward the camp again. She began to shake her head vehemently. Her frantic mind fought to remember the words she wanted to say. She shook her head again and pointed toward the village. *"Wo winihan"*—I'm afraid—she said in the Indian language.

A confused expression claimed the lieutenant's face.

He tilted his head to the side as he looked down at the girl. "Can't you speak English?"

She shook her head again, then pointed toward the horses. After she pointed toward the horses again, she patted herself on the chest.

The Mountie's gaze followed her gestures as he glanced at the horses, then back to Meadow. "First, tell me how you ended up here," he said. "You were about to marry that Sioux war chief when I interrupted the ceremony."

His words cut Meadow to her core. She stared at the man, remembering now that she had seen this same man just as she was being led away from the fire after her wedding had been interrupted. Her entire body felt as if she had just turned to stone. How could she ask this man for help now?

"Can you understand me at all?" Brandon asked again.

He tried to look into her eyes as he spoke to her, but Meadow would not meet his gaze again. She felt as if she had just gotten caught in a bear trap, and she would have preferred cutting off a foot to being here with this man now.

Finally, Meadow swallowed the heavy lump of fear and anger that had risen up in her throat. In spite of herself, she glanced up at the Mountie and studied his face. He seemed deeply concerned about her, and she knew that she had no other choice but to put her trust in this man—even if he did seem like her worst enemy at this moment.

"Are you being held prisoner here?" Brandon asked. She looked away from him. Defeated, he sighed and looked toward the village again. He had no idea what he should do. He did know what he wanted to do. He wanted to scoop this fragile beauty up in his arms and take her far away from this savage place. Instead, he tried once more to communicate with her, when she pointed at the horses again.

"I can't just give you a horse and allow you to take off on your own," he said apologetically. He motioned to where she clasped her ribs. "Besides, you don't seem to be in any shape to be going anywhere." The panic he saw rise up in her green eyes when she looked up at him made him wonder if she did know what he was saying. He drew in a heavy sigh as he contemplated this dangerous situation. He could not go into the village and interrupt Walsh's meeting with the Blackfoot chiefs, nor could he let this girl have her way. If he gave her one of their horses and let her ride off without an escort, he would never be able to live with himself if something worse happened to her.

He stepped in front of the girl so that he could see her face clearly as he spoke to her, even though she still would not look directly at him again. "It's vitally importantly for me to know what's happened to you. If you can understand me, please, please let me know." Her expression revealed nothing to him, and her silence told him that she was either too scared to reply or truly unable to understand him. Maybe if she had been with the Indians her whole life, she really did not understand anything he was saying to her.

The frightened expression that continued to claim her dirt-streaked face made Brandon feel a growing sense of panic, too. He thought once again about going for his superintendent, but then pushed the thought out of his mind once and for all. Though he didn't know how she had gotten here, it was more than obvious that she was desperate to get away. He recalled all the talk he had heard about the ageless war between the Blackfoot and the Sioux. Had the Blackfoot abused this girl because of her relationship with the Sioux war chief, Black Horse? he wondered. This thought caused nausea to flood through him, and the memory of her standing beside the virile chief only increased this sick feeling. He closed his eyes tightly for a moment in an effort to clear both of the images from his mind. None of that matters right now, he told himself. All that mattered at this time was keeping this girl safe.

"We've got to get you away from here, don't we?" Brandon asked as he considered her precarious situation. He tightened his hold on the girl and glanced over at the horses as he tried to formulate a plan.

Meadow continued to avoid his intense stare as she tried to form a plan of her own, but panic continued to rule her thoughts. The more time that passed, the slimmer her chances became to escape from here, and this would undoubtedly be her only chance to get away.

Meadow's gaze reluctantly moved up to his face. It seemed that he was honestly concerned for her safety. Hope soared through her when she realized that he might be thinking about giving into her request for a horse. Disappointment mingled with her growing terror when he began to speak again.

"I'll have to ride with you, since I'm sure you're not able to ride by yourself in your condition." He turned toward the village again. "Maybe I should hide you somewhere until the rest of the troop returns. It will be much safer if we all ride out together."

Meadow's lashes narrowed slightly as she watched his frantic motions. She just wanted a horse so that she could get out of here—alone—but how was she going to convince this man to give into her wishes without letting him know that she could understand everything that he was saying to her?

Once again, Meadow motioned toward the horses, this time as forcefully as she could manage. The effort caused the pain in her ribs to flare through her entire body. She bit her bottom lip in an effort to hide her pain from the Mountie, but she could tell that he had noticed how much discomfort she was in. That might work to her advantage, she thought.

"I'll get you out of here," Brandon said as he reached for her. "I will not leave you here like this."

Meadow noticed that his worried gaze scanned the area again as he waited for her to take his hand. The woods surrounding the Blackfoot village were not as dense or secluded as those at the Sioux encampment, but there was a scattering of bushes and a forest of scraggily pines surrounding the area. Motioning toward the thickest clump of brush, Brandon tried to convey his wishes with gestures and the simplest of words. "Hide . . . in bushes."

Meadow stared at his outstretched hand as indecision ruled her thoughts. He had said he'd get her out of here, and she had no other choice but to believe him. Her hand shook as she reached out toward him. The idea that she would actually be holding the hand of the man who had ruined her wedding seemed inconceivable to her. She had no other choice, so she let him lead her to one of the nearby horses and allowed him to place his hands around her waist and lift her up into the saddle. The pain this movement caused Meadow almost made her cry out, but once again she clamped her mouth tightly shut and fought back the urge to give in to her agony. When the Mountie swung up behind her, however, she wanted more than ever to scream at him to let her leave here alone. It had been difficult enough to accept his help up to now. If she had any hope of getting away, however, she had to agree to his terms.

They rode a short distance down the narrow trail, and then the Mountie guided the horse into a thicker grove of trees. The horse and riders waited for what seemed to Meadow to be an eternity. She knew now that she would not be returning to her beloved Black Horse or to her father in the near future, and this realization made tears sting the corners of her eyes and a sharp spear of desperation rip through her heart.

Brandon Cornett was a bundle of nerves as they waited down the trail for the rest of the troop to catch up to them. He wondered how Superintendent Walsh was going to react when he saw this girl again. The superintendent's main goal at this time was to try to keep peace among all the tribes that had recently settled here in Canada, and if this girl was the source of any trouble, Brandon feared he might refuse to take her back to the fort with them.

He had not made another attempt to talk to her, since conversation seemed impossible. But he would not rest until he knew how she had gotten here and what unspeakable abuses she had obviously endured at the hands of these Blackfoot savages, and previously, when she had been with those murderous Sioux.

The sound of approaching horses snapped Brandon's thoughts back to his immediate problems. He slid down from the horse, keeping the reins gripped tightly in his hands so that the girl could not try to take off with his horse. Then he pushed the branches apart slightly and peeked out to see who was riding down the trail. He exhaled the breath he had been holding when he saw his troop heading in his direction. Even more to his relief was the fact that there was no Blackfoot escorting them from the area. Now, he just had to face his superintendent's wrath.

When the riders were almost to them, Brandon drew in a deep breath, squared his shoulders and stepped out into the open.

Walsh raised his arm in the air and brought the troop to an abrupt halt. "What is the meaning of this?" he demanded. "I thought you'd deserted when we returned to the horses and you were gone—" He stopped speaking when Brandon led his horse the rest of the way out of the bushes and he saw the girl sitting on the animal's back. The superintendent stared at her without saying a word.

"I know you're wondering where she came from, but trust me, I'm just as confused as you are," Brandon began. "I was doing my duty as you ordered when she staggered up to me in this awful state. How she got here from the Sioux village is a complete mystery. But she needs our help."

Walsh continued to gawk at the girl with a shocked look on his face. Brandon was certain that his commander recognized her as the same white girl who had been about to marry the Sioux war chief. But finding her here now—and in this traumatized condition— left the superintendent speechless for a moment.

When Walsh finally spoke, he used the Sioux language. "How is it that you are here with the Blackfoot? Were you taken captive, or did you run away from the Sioux village?"

"C-captive," Meadow stammered. She would have to be careful around this man, since he spoke the Sioux tongue so well.

"Captive?" Walsh repeated and sighed heavily when the girl nodded her head in agreement.

"That's probably why she is so afraid," Brandon added. "She seems desperate to get away from here, and she has obviously been mistreated." He glanced up at her pale face and noticed that she still looked as if she was about to jump out of her own skin.

"And we should get away from here, too, because once her captors discover that she is gone, they're going to be headed right down this trail to look for her," said Walsh. "They won't be too happy to find her with us, because they weren't real pleased with our visit here today, either." He looked down at Brandon with a narrow-eyed stare. "I will deal with you when we get back to the fort."

Brandon swallowed the heavy lump in his throat and wasted no time climbing back up into the saddle behind the girl. He had no doubt that he would feel even more of Walsh's fury when they returned to the fort this time, but right now he was more concerned with the possibility of the Blackfoot catching up to them.

Chapter Fifteen

Fort Walsh consisted of a scattering of tents, and several long buildings that served as barracks and a stockade. Superintendent Walsh was the first commander of this post, so he had the honor of having the fort named after him. Located on a flat, open tract of land at the base of the Cypress Hills, only a tall wooden fence surrounded the complex. The infirmary consisted of two rooms: one large room that housed the fort's doctor and a smaller room at the back where two beds and necessary medical supplies were stored. Meadow had been brought to this back room a week ago.

The post doctor, Sergeant Roberts, had usually had no more than an occasional cough to treat or a cut to disinfect since he had been stationed at Fort Walsh. The young white girl that had been found at the Blackfoot camp was Roberts's first real patient in months. But since her most serious injuries had already been tended to at the Blackfoot village, there was little else for the doctor to do. Her broken ribs had been bound in such an expert manner that Roberts decided not to remove the bandages until it was necessary to change them. But he busied himself with seeing to it that she was as comfortable as possible.

"How's our patient today?" Brandon asked Sergeant Roberts cheerfully as he entered the back room.

Meadow glanced at the doorway, then quickly looked toward the window again. With her head tilted up in a stubborn manner, she pretended to ignore the lieutenant.

"She's better—I guess," the sergeant said. A deep sigh hinted at his concern for his patient.

"Is there something else wrong with her?" Brandon asked in an alarmed tone of voice.

The doctor shrugged. "Well, look at her. She just seems so . . . depressed."

"I would imagine all the horror she's seen while she was an Indian captive at the Blackfoot camp, and before that with the Sioux, has left her scarred for life."

Meadow continued to stare out the window.

"Have you been able to find out anything about her?" Roberts asked.

"We've wired Fort Keogh, but there's not been a reply as of yet. It's doubtful that we will ever find out who she is, so I guess we'll just have to help her start a new life, now that she's back where she belongs," Brandon answered.

It took all of Meadow's composure to keep from turning away from the window and telling the soldier what he could do with his misguided opinions regarding where she belonged. But she had more important things to concentrate on right now. She knew her ribs were healing nicely; there was barely any pain when she moved now. All she needed was a horse to ride. Her father—although he was stingy about teaching her his medicinal secrets—had taught her a few things about tracking, in case she should ever get lost.

The thought of home also brought about the relentless longing to be reunited with Black Horse. Was he frantically looking for her? He would have no idea that she was here at the fort, and she feared for his life if he should try to go to the Blackfoot village to look for her. A choking sense of panic rose up inside her. She knew she had to escape from here as soon as possible. She had to get to Black Horse to let him know that she was all right, and warn him about Strong Tree.

"It's such a beautiful fall day," Brandon said as he walked up beside her. "I wish you'd let me take you outside for a breath of fresh air."

Meadow looked up at him and shrugged. Then she looked up at him again and wrinkled her brow as if she were confused by what he was asking her.

He pointed out the window and then motioned toward her, adding, "Outside. Would you like to go outside?" He used embellished hand movements to explain his intent as he pointed toward the open doorway.

Meadow was tempted to laugh out loud at the soldier's ridiculous charades. She pointed feebly at the outdoors and gave her head a slight nod. As she rose up to her feet, she pretended to be in a great deal of pain. The lieutenant immediately slipped his arm around her shoulders for support, and although she preferred that he did not touch her, Meadow decided it would be to her benefit not to protest.

The gently blowing autumn breeze brushed against Meadow's skin. She drew in a deep breath and savored the feel of the fresh air on her face. For as long as she could remember, she had never been confined in a white man's cabin until now, and she felt as if she were caged in a wooden box. The outdoors invigorated her and made her feel almost as good as new.

The vibrant hues of gold and orange on the hillsides reminded Meadow that it would not be long before the harsh winds of winter would whip across the Canadian countryside. She had to make her escape before it began to snow. The land would look entirely different then, and she would have a much harder time locating the Sioux village.

Although she wished she could just take off running through the first open gate she saw and not stop until she reached her village, Meadow waited patiently for the soldier to take the lead. She did not want to do anything that would prevent her from ascertaining the location of the horses and the easiest exit from the fort. The lieutenant took the liberty of draping his arm over her shoulders once again as he began to lead her down the stairs and out into the open courtyard.

His presumption that they were on friendly enough terms for him to be so forward irked Meadow. But it was probably another white-man custom that she did not understand. She had not found anything she liked about the white culture. The cot she had been sleeping on was so uncomfortable, compared to her soft, furry bed in the tepee, and the food they had been feeding her the last few days was much too rich for her tastes. But worst of all was the confining outfit they had given her to wear. The dress was made of coarse muslin and had a fitted bodice and waistband, and even though it was a bit large for her body, Meadow still felt as though she were suffocating in the garment. At first, she had refused to wear all the undergarments they had given her, but the coarseness of the dress material had rubbed her skin raw, so she finally gave in and put the white cotton petticoat and bloomers on under the dress.

Regardless of the way the restricting garments hindered her legs as she walked across the courtyard, Meadow felt a renewal of her strength and spirit as the warm rays of the sun continued to touch her face. She drew in a deep breath of the clean autumn air as she vowed to herself that this would be the last day she would spend in the white man's world.

"I wish you could talk to me, at least just to tell me what your name is," Brandon said with a heavy sigh. "But I'm sure it won't be long before you learn your native tongue again. I'll teach you." For a moment he stopped walking and turned to face Meadow. In a serious tone of voice, he said, "And I will do everything in my power to wipe away all the sorrow and horrors you must have witnessed while you were with those horrible savages."

To remain silent and not respond to his degrading comments was one of the most difficult tasks Meadow had ever performed. But, she reminded herself, after tonight it would not matter what he thought, because she would never have to see him again.

She pointed toward the infirmary, indicating that she was ready to go back. He wrapped his arm over her shoulder once again and began to lead her back.

During their brief excursion through the fort, Meadow had learned everything she needed to know.

She had seen where the horses were kept, and had noticed that the gate leading out of the fort was left wide open during the day for people to travel in and out. She guessed it was closed at night for security reasons, so that meant that she would have to get away while it was still daylight. The sun overhead suggested that it was midafternoon.

As they approached the infirmary, Meadow saw two white women walking directly toward them. She hadn't realized that there were any women here. She drew in a trembling breath. She had not seen a white woman for as long as she could remember. One of the women was older, and the other one looked about the same age as Meadow. Were they mother and daughter?

The older woman grabbed the younger girl by the hand before they got any closer, and ducked into the nearest building as if she was afraid to get too close to Meadow. But before they disappeared from sight, the younger girl glanced back over her shoulder. Her gaze locked with Meadow's for an instant, and a slight smile curved her lips.

Meadow's steps faltered as she stared back at the girl. She felt the sting of a tear in the corner of her eye. If the Sioux attack on her family had never happened, she might be walking down the street with her own mother right now.

"Are you all right?" Brandon asked when he felt her stumble.

She choked down the lump in her throat and blinked back the tear. Why would something so devastating come to her mind now?

Brandon glanced at the building where the two

women had just entered. "They are the wife and daughter of one of the officers. There's a boy, too. They arrived just this morning for a visit." He chuckled. "I doubt they will stay long. I don't think there are any women who would actually want to live in a remote place like Fort Walsh. I will arrange a meeting for you. I'm sure they would want to meet you while they are here."

Meadow had to clamp her mouth shout to keep from saying something. The girl's mother certainly had not looked anxious to meet her.

With a sigh, Brandon opened the door to the infirmary and stood back so that she could enter. "When you're feeling a bit stronger, I'll start our speech lessons," he stated.

No need to bother, Meadow thought as she moved away from him. By tomorrow night I'll be back with my man and my Sioux family. She put her hand over her mouth and pretended to yawn, and then she cast a longing glance at the back room.

"I'm going to let you get some rest," Brandon said with an obvious tone of disappointment in his voice. His tone brightened as he added, "But perhaps we could have dinner together later? That is, if I can get out of working tonight."

He shrugged his shoulders and continued to speak as if she was interested in everything he said. "Superintendent Walsh ordered me to do kitchen patrol for the next month. But I'd peel potatoes for the rest of my life if it meant saving you."

Meadow's hands curled into clenched fists at her sides. She almost had to bite her tongue to keep from saying something to him this time. Single-handedly, this one man had destroyed her wedding, which had inadvertently caused her to be taken captive by the Blackfoot, and worst of all, had caused White Buffalo to be injured or even killed. If he hadn't left when he did, she wasn't sure she would be able to remain silent any longer.

She had no way of knowing when the doctor would be back, so with her heart frantically pounding in her breast, she began to search through every drawer in his office and the sleeping quarters until she had found everything that she figured she would need for her escape today. She raced to the back room with her loot and stuffed the bundle under her cot until she was ready to put her plan into action.

The sound of the front door opening nearly sent Meadow jumping through the roof. She tried to calm her rapid breathing as she quickly crawled onto her cot and scooted under the bed coverings. When she heard the sound of footsteps approaching the back room, she closed her eyes and attempted to take deep, even breaths as if she were sleeping. The footsteps stopped at the entrance to her room and did not move for a moment. Meadow did not dare open her eyes again until she was certain the man had walked away from her doorway.

She opened her eyes slowly. Sergeant Roberts was standing by his desk in the center of the next room. His head was bent down, and he was reading a paper that he held in his hand. At last, he put the paper down on his desk and glanced at the pocket watch that hung from a fob in his jacket pocket. He shoved his watch back into his pocket, then headed back out the door.

The instant she heard the front door close, Meadow

was out of the bed. She grabbed the clothes she had stashed under her bed and wasted no time in discarding the dress and undergarments that she despised so much. Since she had no idea where her doeskin dress and knee-high moccasins had been taken, she had no choice but to leave them behind. It broke her heart, though, to abandon the beautiful dress she had worn on the day that she was supposed to be wed to Black Horse.

The pants and shirt she donned now were basic Mountie-issued wool pants with a stripe down the side and a black cotton shirt. She slipped her feet into a pair of black lace-up boots that were several sizes too big, but tightened the laces enough so that the boots would not fall off of her feet. A long red blazer with gold trim topped her outfit and reached down to her knees. It was too heavy for this time of day, but it was an essential part of her disguise now, and Meadow knew she would need it once darkness fell and the night grew cold. With the coat buttoned all the way to her chin, she stuffed her long hair underneath the collar before she placed the large tan Mountie hat on her head. She glanced at herself in the reflection of the window and almost laughed at the ridiculous sight that stared back at her.

The next part of her plan would not be so easy. She had to get to the corral to steal a horse without arousing suspicion. Then, she needed to get through the front gates without being stopped. The plan, she reminded herself, was far from perfect, and the chances of her actually succeeding were slim.

Taking a deep, trembling breath, Meadow stepped down from the front stoop and out into the open courtyard. She glanced toward the area where she had encountered the two white women earlier. They were nowhere to be seen now, but she recalled the way the girl had smiled at her. If she had stayed at Fort Walsh, would she have been able to befriend the girl? Probably not, if the girl's mother had anything to say about it. She reminded herself that there was no time to waste thinking about things that could never happen.

There was hardly any activity in this part of the fort, since nearly everyone was doing drills or finishing chores before the daylight faded. A young boy of about nine or ten years, obviously the visiting son of the officer Brandon had told her about, was playing with a small puppy on the other side of the courtyard. He was not paying any attention to anything other than his pet. Meadow glanced toward the gate—it was still wide open, and only one guard was stationed in the lookout tower. She pulled the wide brim of the hat down lower and began walking toward the corral where the horses were kept.

The distance Meadow walked to the corral was only several hundred yards, but it seemed like a mile. She held her breath most of the way and did not look anywhere other than straight at the corral. When she had reached the corral gate, she finally allowed herself to exhale heavily as she glanced around. She was surprised—and relieved—that no one was guarding the horses. As she entered through the gate, she grabbed one of the halters that was hanging over the top rail. There were saddles lined up along one wall, but Meadow had never ridden a horse with a saddle, and so she didn't give them a second glance.

She wasted no time in picking out the horse she

would use to make her getaway. The stallion was a large dark brown chestnut that in some ways reminded her of Dusya. Black Horse had introduced her to the spirited horse during their courtship. She just hoped this stallion did not have the same bad temperament as Black Horse's prized mount. The moment she walked up to the big horse, it was evident that he was much more mild mannered.

"Whoa, boy," Meadow whispered in Sioux as she held out her hand and gently touched the horse's neck. He whinnied softly, but did not back away. Encouraged by his meek demeanor, Meadow immediately draped the halter over his head and secured the buckle. She led him out of the corral and shut the gate behind her. The horse did not flinch, even when she pulled herself up onto his bare back.

Once they were away from the corral, Meadow pressed her knees into the horse's sides to increase his stride. She did not want him to break into a run yet, but she didn't want to waste time with a leisurely gait, either. The little boy glanced up curiously at her as she rode past him, but his puppy diverted his attention away from her almost immediately.

As she reached the exit, Meadow glanced up at the guard. He was either asleep or in such deep concentration that he was oblivious to everything around him. His back was to the gate, and his head was tilted down with his chin resting on his chest. When he never even turned around as she rode the horse through the gate, her first instinct was to kick the horse in the sides and gallop off in a cloud of dust. But, since she had not drawn the guard's attention yet, there was no need to tempt her luck. In the clothes she was wearing, she knew she would look like any other soldier once she was far enough away. She loosed the reins slightly and let the horse pick up his step until he was moving at an easy trot. She wished she could take off the wide-brimmed hat and let the wind blow through her hair, but mostly she wished that she could give an Indian war whoop in celebration of her freedom that would be heard across the land. For now, she was just content to see the cover of the forest growing closer with every frantic beat of her heart.

Chapter Sixteen

Meadow did not stop riding until the last of the daylight was completely gone and her horse was beginning to stumble over fallen branches and rocks. Even with her fear of the dark forest, she was filled with a sense of freedom and excitement. She could not wait to see her father and Black Horse, and Gentle Water and her grandmother, and everyone else in the Sioux village that she had known for her entire life. Surely, Meadow told herself, they will all know now—after all that she had gone through in the past couple of weeks—that she was completely devoted to the Sioux.

As the long night progressed, the temperature continued to drop until Meadow was sure she was going to freeze to death. She was grateful now for the heavy coat, but it did not even begin to ward off the bone-chilling cold. With the horse tied securely to a clump of branches, Meadow huddled against the rough base of a large pine tree. In an effort to keep warm, she drew her legs up against her body and buried her face into the collar of the coat. Meadow remained in this position for most of the night and only dozed off for a few minutes at a time.

She was worried that the horse would break free, that wild animals would attack them—or worse, that she would encounter the Blackfoot again. A couple of times she heard wolves howling in the distance. The horse would whinny and fidget at the end of his rope every time there was any sort of noise, which only served to increase Meadow's fear and uneasiness.

When there were enough stars overhead, Meadow stepped out from under the tree and looked for the star that her father had taught her to follow if she was ever lost. An endless array of sparkles dotted the nighttime sky, but one glittering orb outshone the others and almost seemed to grow brighter as she gazed up at it. Meadow closed her eyes in relief for a moment. She was sure that she was headed in the direction that would take her back home.

Before it was even light enough for her to ride the horse, Meadow began leading him on foot over the forest debris. She had no doubt that Lieutenant Cornett would be hot on her trail, if he was permitted to come after her. She was not going to give him the chance to catch up with her.

When Meadow came upon the river, she knew that it was proof that she was headed home. She followed the river north. It was midday, and she was finally beginning to relax a bit and was not looking back over her shoulder as often. She tried to stay alert to every noise and movement around her, stopping only when necessary to let her horse drink from the river and to quench her own thirst. In the areas that were too rugged for her to ride close to the river, she was careful not to get any farther away from the water than absolutely necessary. She sighed with relief every time the river came back into view.

At one point, Meadow realized that she was fulfilling one of her lifelong dreams—to ride across the countryside like a free spirit. She even allowed her long hair to blow loose in the breeze and imagined that she was on a vision quest, and that all of the bad things that had happened in the past few weeks were nothing more than a bad dream. But then reality returned.

As the sunlight began to fade behind the distant horizon to the west, Meadow's optimism began to fade, too. She had hoped to be back home before darkness fell a second time, but it was growing dark earlier as the winter months approached, and she wondered how much farther she should travel before stopping for another night. The idea of spending the night alone in the freezing forest again filled Meadow with a feeling of despair. She had wanted so much just to hug her father, and then to fall asleep in Black Horse's arms tonight.

When her horse began to stumble over the fallen logs and low brush, Meadow realized that she would have to stop. She decided to find a tree close to the riverbank to tie up the horse. Then she could sit by the river for a spell and let the gentle flowing sounds soothe her frazzled nerves. Although she was exhausted, she was not ready to attempt sleeping yet. The horse seemed restless, too, not a bit pleased to be tied up again. As Meadow settled herself on a rock at the riverbank, she could hear the horse stomping around and snorting behind her. She wondered if his reluctance to calm down for the night was something that she should worry about. Perhaps he could sense something that she was not aware of. . . .

Finally, the horse quieted, and Meadow's feeling of doom began to ease. She glanced up at the sky, where dark clouds had begun to gather before the sunlight had faded completely away. Now, in the black sky overhead, the clouds looked even more ominous, and the moon was almost completely hidden from view. There would be no starlight tonight. Meadow wrapped her arms around herself in a tight embrace.

When the sound of the river no longer offered Meadow any comfort, and the rock she was sitting on made her backside start to ache, she decided she'd better find a place to settle in for the night. The clump of trees she had tied the horse to would provide her with a bit of shelter, but if the clouds overhead brought rain, she would be drenched in no time. The nighttime temperature was already frigid.

Carefully, Meadow began making her way back up the riverbank. At the top of the slope, something in the air caught her attention. The smell of smoke—of campfire smoke—penetrated her nostrils and brought back a multitude of memories. She drew in a deep whiff of the air again and had no doubt that the odor was coming from a campfire. It smelled as if something was being cooked over the fire. Her stomach twisted with hunger; the last time she had eaten anything was the midday meal at the fort yesterday.

Meadow's heart began to pound rapidly. The smoke had to be coming from the Sioux village, because she was certain she had to be close. If darkness had not fallen, she would be there by now, but there was no way she could stay out here another night if there was any chance that she could make it to the village. Meadow glanced in the direction where the horse was tied. Riding would make her journey harder than if she went on foot the rest of the way.

She quickly untied the animal and took the halter from around his head. If he didn't follow her or find his way to the village right away, she did not want him to get the halter snagged on the branches of a tree. Though he was free, the horse remained rooted to the spot, even after Meadow tried to coax him to tag along behind her.

Since clouds now covered the last of the moonlight, Meadow was forced to feel her way along the edge of the brush that lined the riverbank. With every couple of steps that she took, she stopped to sniff the air to make sure the smell of the smoke was growing stronger, rather than fainter. Her excitement continued to expand as the odor became more noticeable. She was certain that even in the darkness, the area was beginning to seem familiar. Soon she was sure she would be at the same spot on the river where she had first seen Black Horse taking a bath. Then she would also be close to where they had spent their first night together. A shiver of excitement rushed through Meadow as she took another step.

A thunderous roar suddenly cut through clouds in the sky overhead, and an instant later the clouds released a downpour of rain. The thunder frightened Meadow so badly that she cried out in alarm, and before she had even realized the source of the tremendous noise, large raindrops began to pelt against her face without mercy. A few raindrops would not keep her from getting home tonight, she told herself as she struggled to feel her way along the brush and trees.

With every step she took, she would try to inch one foot forward first to check for fallen logs and rocks. Just one careless step and she could be flung down the embankment and into the river. It was raining so hard now that it was difficult for Meadow to keep her eyes open, but the engulfing darkness made it impossible to see anyway. She pulled the big-brimmed hat down over her eyes and moved forward.

The heavy oversize boots she was wearing were becoming caked with mud from the wet, slick ground. She could barely lift her feet. Just as Meadow was about to admit defeat and try to find shelter from the storm, the toe of her boot caught under a large fallen tree trunk.

She felt herself stumble over the log and then attempted to break her fall before she hit the ground. She reached out in the darkness, but her hands scraped against the slick log, and she did not have time to grab on to it before her entire body came crashing down. When her head smacked against the log, she was not even aware of what was happening, because the instant her head hit the fallen tree trunk, all consciousness was stolen from her.

Walks Tall rode Hawk along the muddy riverbank. The sun had just risen, and it was still foggy from the downpour of rain last night. The towering mountain peaks in the distance were topped with snowy white. The snow would soon find its way to the lower ground, and Walks Tall was not looking forward to the cold months ahead. But he was glad that he would be spending the winter here with his sister and her family, instead of running from soldiers and white settlers on the other side of the border, as he and Black Horse had done during the previous winter months.

He sighed heavily and urged Hawk up to the top of

the muddy riverbank. The horse's hooves sank down several inches into the muck, making it hard for him to lift his legs. When they were finally on flat ground again, Walks Tall pulled on his reins and started to turn him around so that they could head back to the village. He had thought he would go hunting this morning, but thinking about Black Horse made him sad, and now the only thing he wanted to do was go back to his lodge and drown his sorrows in the whiskey he had gotten from a couple of French traders yesterday. The bottle had cost him one of his old bone-handled hunting knives, but to forget about his sorrow for a night or two was worth much more.

Just as Hawk started to turn back toward the village, something red lying in the mud caught Walks Tall's eye. He pulled hard on the reins and leaned over to the side to get a closer look at whatever it was that was lying beside a large fallen tree. At first, Walks Tall thought that he was looking at nothing more than a discarded piece of red material, but since it was the same color red as the coats the Mounties wore, he decided to investigate further. He urged Hawk to wade through the mud until they were several feet away from the log. Only then did Walks Tall realize that he was looking at a person lying facedown in the mud.

Jumping from his horse's back, Walks Tall took a couple of careful steps, and then fell down on his knees beside the figure. A sense of dread raced through him when he saw long strands of dirty blonde hair sticking out from beneath the tan hat. He reached out tentatively and rolled the small figure over. Her pale face was nearly obscured by the thick mud, but as Walks Tall stared at her all rational thoughts left his mind. Finally, he thought to check if she was breathing. He reached out a trembling hand and placed it over her nose and mouth, then exhaled a relieved sigh when he felt the faint feeling of warmth coming from her parted lips.

As his startled gaze traveled down Meadow's limp form, he noticed that she was wearing a complete Mountie's uniform. His mind could not even begin to comprehend how she had ended up here, wearing this outfit—especially since they had believed her to be with the Blackfoot all this time. He could not allow himself the time right now, however, to ponder over this strange turn of events. She was hurt, and not knowing the extent of her injuries, Walks Tall knew he had to get her back to the village, if there was any hope of saving her.

As he carefully slid his arm under her neck to raise her up from the wet ground, her hat tumbled from her head, revealing a deep, bloody gash across her forehead. A matted tangle of her hair was clumped against the wound and a fresh trickle of red oozed among the mud-caked strands of hair. A sense of panic tightened the muscles in Walks Tall's chest. He slid his other arm under Meadow's knees and pulled her up with him as he rose to his feet. The cold, frozen mud held her in a deadly grip and made an odd sucking sound as it released its hold on her body.

Very few tribe members were wandering around outside of their tepees on this cold damp morning, but Walks Tall immediately attracted the attention of everyone who was outside when he entered the village. When he spotted Sings Like Sparrow coming out of her tepee, he hollered, "Help me! I've got Meadow, and she's hurt!"

His loud announcement brought Gentle Water rushing from the tepee on her grandmother's heels. "Can she be taken into your tepee?" he asked of Sings Like Sparrow.

The old woman nodded her head and held the door flap open so that he could enter with the injured girl. She followed him in and motioned for the warrior to lay the girl on the closest fur-covered mat.

"It looked like she fell and hit her head on a log," Walks Tall said. "She was down by the river not far from the village, but that's all I know."

Meadow struggled to open her eyes and keep them open. For a moment, the three faces above her were no more than a hazy blur. But, as her vision began to clear, she instinctively whispered, "Father . . . Black Horse."

"Your father is not here, and neither is Black Horse," Sings Like Sparrow said softly. She held out a gourd filled with fresh water. "Drink this, and when you are stronger, we can talk."

Meadow looked at the trio of people hovering over her. Their faces carried strange expressions she could not decipher, and her mind was still too foggy to make sense of anything that was happening around her. She allowed Sings Like Sparrow to hold the water gourd to her parched lips as she took a sip of the cool water. Even the small movement, however, caused her head to throb unmercifully. She started to reach up to her forehead to touch the spot where the pain originated from, but Gentle Water grabbed her hand.

"You've got an ugly cut, but Grandmother will have it fixed up in no time."

"Wh-what happened?" Meadow questioned.

"I found you down by the river this morning," Walks Tall said in response to her question. "When you're up to talking, maybe you can tell us what happened."

"I can talk now," Meadow retorted. "Where are my father and Black Horse?"

The permeating silence that filled the interior of the tepee made Meadow's heartbeat falter in her breast. Her gaze moved to Gentle Water's face. Their eyes met, and Meadow saw the tears that were about to overflow from her lifelong friend's dark eyes. She closed her own eyes in an effort to block out the look of sorrow she had just witnessed. A deep ache inched through her body. . . . She sensed that she did not want them to respond to her question, because she was certain that she would not be able to bear hearing the answer.

Chapter Seventeen

It rained sporadically for another week as the temperature continued to plunge, and then the first snowfall of the season blanketed the low-lying Canadian countryside in pristine white. The days after that just seemed to blend into one another with the daily struggles of surviving in this harsh wilderness as the snow continued to pile up. Food was scarce and some days almost nonexistent. Occasionally, the warriors would come across a deer or elk, but moose was usually the only meat available. The moose's meat was stringy and tough, but it was better than no meat at all. With so many mouths to feed in this large encampment, however, even the biggest piece of venison did not go far.

The winter had been made even more difficult because of the illnesses that had invaded the village. Many died as they succumbed to fevers, coughs and stomach ailments that drained every bit of life from those too weak to fight them off.

Meadow walked beside Gentle Water through the snow-laden forest. They each carried a full urn of snow in their arms. They would dump the snow in a pot over the fire to melt so that they would have water for drinking, washing and cooking. Walking the trails that ran through the dense forest was more treacherous, now that the ground was slick with ice and snow, but the snow surrounding the village was so stomped down now that they had to search through the forest for deeper patches among the trees to retrieve for melting. The only thing that kept the bedraggled tribe going was that spring was getting closer with each passing day, and the renewal of the earth, they hoped, would also renew their spirits and determination to survive.

Meadow stared down at the ground as they lumbered along. When they walked through the area where White Buffalo and Black Horse's tepees had stood last fall, she tried to avoid looking at either location. The bare, empty spaces only served as a reminder that in one horrible day she had lost the two men she loved more than life itself.

When they passed by Walks Tall's tepee, Meadow also avoided looking in that direction. He had been so good to her since her return, but she felt the need to keep her distance from him. Walks Tall had made it clear that he was prepared to serve as Black Horse's replacement, but Meadow was not even remotely ready to think about sharing her life—or her bed—with anyone other than Black Horse. She was still unable to accept the fact that he was presumed dead, but Walks Tall was convinced that even if he did survive the initial attack from the soldiers, he would have been killed once they reached Fort Keogh.

Walks Tall had told her that he had traveled to the fort shortly after Black Horse had been attacked in the meadow, but he had not been able to get in to find out if his friend was being held prisoner there. He was going to return with more warriors and a plan to sneak into the fort to look for the war chief, however, several days later traders passing through the village had relayed the

news that four Indian prisoners being held at Fort Keogh had been hanged recently. Walks Tall knew that
endangering more Sioux lives would be foolish. Black
Horse was surely dead.

But Meadow was not so easily convinced. She prayed
daily that Walks Tall was wrong and that someday her
powerful war chief would ride back into her life. Yet,
as the freezing cold of winter had overtaken the land,
Meadow's hope began to fade. She believed that if
Black Horse still lived, he would have found a way to
come home. As she reluctantly began to accept the
idea that he might actually be dead, she began to die a
little bit inside every day, too.

Once they reached the tepee that Meadow had been
sharing with Gentle Water and Sings Like Sparrow
since her return to the tribe, a loud shout echoed
through the village. Meadow's footsteps froze when
she heard the word *soldiers*. Her mind raced with memories of ambushes and attacks from their days in the
Dakota Territory. As in those past ambushes, Meadow
and Gentle Water ran to their tepee for protection.
Meadow sighed with relief to see that Sings Like Sparrow was already inside the dwelling. At least they would
not have to run through the village looking for the old
woman.

"What is happening?" Sings Like Sparrow asked in
an alarmed voice.

"Soldiers!" Gentle Water gasped. "I thought we were
safe here in Canada!"

If the soldiers were here to attack them, Meadow
hoped that she would be killed right away so that she
could join her beloved father and Black Horse in the
spirit world. She did not hear the voices calling out

from the outside until she realized that Gentle Water was squeezing her hand tightly.

"Meadow," she repeated. "Did you hear? The soldiers are Mounties, and they have brought supplies for our people."

"Mounties?" Meadow asked. "From Fort Walsh?" Would that awful Lieutenant Cornett be one of them? He was the last person on earth that she ever wanted to see again.

Gentle Water chuckled, "Since Fort Walsh is the only fort in these parts, I would imagine they are from there. Let's go see what they've brought for us."

"No!" Meadow said with a strong negative shake of her head. "Remember, I told you how they tried to keep me at the fort."

"Yes, I'm sorry. Do you mind if I go with Grandmother, then?" Gentle Water asked. Sings Like Sparrow was already headed out the door to investigate the goods the Mounties had brought to them.

Meadow shook her head again and pulled the heavy scarf from her head. Her cropped hair fell to her shoulders in unruly tangles. Although she had not been here when the Keeping of the Soul had been performed for White Buffalo—the Sioux ceremony where the unfinished deeds of the deceased are resolved so that they can make the journey into the spirit world—she had still cut her waist-length locks above her shoulders as a form of mourning for her father when she found out that he was dead. "You go. I'll stay here and keep the fire going."

"I won't be long," Gentle Water said softly as she gave Meadow's hand another affectionate squeeze.

Gentle Water saw the now-familiar look of emptiness

on the other girl's pale face as she left her standing
alone in the tepee. It occurred to her once again how
displaced Meadow must feel, now that White Buffalo
was gone. If Black Horse were still here and they had
been married as planned, her place in the tribe would
still be secure. But now Gentle Water worried about
what would happen to Meadow if she continued to
refuse to become Walks Tall's woman. She could only
hope that soon Meadow would realize that she had
very few choices left, and Walks Tall's offer was generous, and definitely not all unappealing.

Thinking of Walks Tall caused a shiver to race
through Gentle Water. He could have his choice of
any of the single girls that were of marrying age, but
he was dedicated to the needs of Meadow because she
had been his best friend's woman.

Gentle Water sighed. She hoped that someday she
would be married and have a family of her own. Her
grandmother was very old, and Gentle Water feared
that the elder woman would not live much longer.
Then, both she and Meadow would be on their own. A
woman alone in the Sioux village lived a difficult life.

Meadow stared blankly into the flames as she stirred
the fire in the pit. She rarely thought about the future; her thoughts tended to dwell on the happier days
of her past. Every day each chore seemed more difficult to do than the day before, and some days she
wished she did not even have to get out of bed. Her bed
offered the only meager comfort in her life—it was
fashioned from the same furs she had slept on when
she had still been living in White Buffalo's tepee.

After his death, all of his belongings had been taken

to Sitting Bull's tepee, and to Meadow's gratification, she had been allowed to take any of her father's possessions that she wanted when she returned. She had taken his cherished medicine pouches, his headdress, and the fur blankets that had made up her bed—the same blankets that Black Horse had also lain on the night he had stumbled into her bed in a drunken stupor. This memory made these furs even more precious to Meadow, and she hoped she could sleep in them for the rest of her life. More important even than the furs was the cherished white blanket that was to have sealed her marriage to Black Horse. Walks Tall had saved it when he had taken down his friend's tepee, and he had given it to Meadow when she returned to the village. She could not fall asleep at night unless she was wrapped in its warmth.

The sound of footsteps approaching the tepee made Meadow's thoughts snap back to the present. A man's voice calling out to her made her jump, and when she recognized the voice as that of Sitting Bull, a sense of foreboding paralyzed her for a moment.

Sitting Bull called out to her again, and Meadow swallowed the lump of fear in her throat. She knew she had to answer him, but for the chief to come here, rather than to send someone else to fetch her, could only mean bad news. After taking a deep breath and trying to brace herself for whatever Sitting Bull was here to tell her, Meadow forced herself to exit the tepee. She was surprised to see Walks Tall standing next to the Sioux leader, but his presence only served to increase her uneasiness.

"There is someone who has traveled here to talk to you," Sitting Bull said.

Meadow stared at the chief, waiting for him to say something more, but he was a man of few words, so he did not offer any further explanation. She looked toward Walks Tall for assurance, but she found none in his blank expression, either.

"They are waiting in my tepee, so we must go there now," Sitting Bull added. He did not wait for Meadow to respond as he turned and started walking away.

Meadow's worried gaze settled on Walks Tall again as she asked, "Who is it?"

When Walks Tall shrugged his shoulders and shook his head, Meadow knew she had no other choice but to follow the chief and face this new intrusion in her life. As she walked past Walks Tall, he reached out and grabbed hold of her hand.

Meadow did not pull her hand away from his embrace. A comforting feeling washed through her. She found that she desperately needed his strength and support right now. Knowing that he had been Black Horse's blood brother made her feel closer to him than she felt to any other person at this time, even Gentle Water.

Sitting Bull had entered his lodge ahead of them, and by the time Meadow and Walks Tall pushed open the flap and walked in, he was already seated among the others. Meadow's gaze went from face to face as her confusion grew. Seated beside Sitting Bull was the leader of the Mounties troop, Superintendent Walsh, and next to him was Lieutenant Cornett. Their presence was not any more surprising to Meadow than that of Gentle Water and Sings Like Sparrow, who also sat around the fire pit in the center of the large tepee.

Meadow looked back up at Walks Tall, but he was

staring at the lieutenant with an expression of disdain on his face. A sinking feeling settled in the pit of her stomach when she realized that this elite group had obviously gathered here because of her.

"Sit there," Sitting Bull ordered as he motioned to Walks Tall and Meadow to join them on the robes surrounding the fire pit. As always, his lined face conveyed an intense expression, and it was impossible to determine how serious this situation was.

Walks Tall led Meadow to the spot the chief had motioned to and sat down beside her. A strange tension hung in the air. Not being able to contend with another second of feeling that an anvil was about to come down upon her, Meadow finally asked, "Why have I been asked to come here?" She looked directly at Sitting Bull, since he was the leader of the tribe and the person she felt she could trust the most at this moment.

"These Mounties have brought us much-needed food and white-man medicine," Sitting Bull replied. He crossed his arms over his chest and glanced at the two white men, then returned his gaze to Meadow.

"We are grateful," Meadow said to Superintendent Walsh. She did not look in the lieutenant's direction, even when Walsh turned to him to repeat in English what she had just said in the Sioux language. Returning her attention to Sitting Bull, she waited for him to speak again.

"They have told us about your time with them after they took you from the Blackfoot village." Sitting Bull's stern expression did not change as he added, "We are grateful to them for helping you and caring for you when you were injured."

Meadow swallowed hard. She was sure she knew why she was here now: she had stolen a horse and clothes from the fort, and the Mounties must be here to see to it that she was punished for her crimes. "Please tell them that I'm sorry I stole from them, but I was desperate to return to my own village, and they can have the horse back," she said in a raspy voice. The horse had eventually made his way to the village and was among the other Sioux ponies in the corral.

Sitting Bull shook his head "They have said nothing of this. But they were worried that you had not made it back to us safely."

Meadow drew in a deep sigh and glanced at Walsh again. "Thank you for your concern. But, as you can see, I am home." He nodded his head and then turned to repeat her words to the lieutenant.

"The Mounties have asked for permission to take you back to the fort with them again," the chief blurted out. "I have asked Walks Tall, Gentle Water and Sings Like Sparrow to join us as we discuss this, because they are like your family now."

"No!" Meadow gasped as her mind frantically searched for the right reply. "Why do you think I ran away from the fort and returned here? This is where I want to be." She looked to Gentle Water. Their eyes met and locked as Meadow silently pleaded with her friend to tell her this was not true.

Gentle Water wiped away tears as she began to speak. "I do not want for you to leave. You are my oldest and dearest friend—more like my sister than a mere friend. But you are filled with such emptiness since the deaths of White Buffalo and Black Horse. I have not seen the sparkle in your grass-colored eyes or a smile on your lips since your return. Sometimes I am afraid that your sorrow will steal the life away from you. I will cry many tears if you must go, but I will cry many, many more tears if you stay the way you are now."

By the time Gentle Water had finished speaking, tears were flowing down Meadow's cheeks, too. "I—I don't want to leave here again," she whispered as she glanced from Gentle Water to the chief.

"We are not going to force you to leave here," Sitting Bull said. "But it is an option you have, and maybe if you are away from the daily reminders of those you have recently lost, it will be easier for you to cope with the loss."

"And we could help you look for your real family," Superintendent Walsh added. "This is the main reason we are offering to take you back to the fort. If any of your real family is still living nearby, they do deserve to know that you are alive and well."

Meadow stared at the Mountie as his words settled in her tormented mind. She wiped at the tears that continued to flood down her cheeks with the back of her hand. Her real family? The idea that she might have living relatives somewhere had never even occurred to her.

"If you still have family . . . Maybe there was a sibling who survived the attack on the wagon train. Or perhaps if you still have a parent or grandparents that have been looking for you all these years, then I truly believe that they should know where you are," Walsh added.

"You would always be welcome to return to our people any time you wish," Sitting Bull added.

Meadow nodded weakly toward the Sioux chief, then looked at Gentle Water again. "I realize that my position in the tribe has changed now, and that I am nothing more than a burden to everyone, but I do love my adoptive people, and I will always be completely devoted to the Sioux." She lowered her voice to a whisper. "And I hate the ways of the whites almost as much as they hate us."

"We will never try to turn you against the Sioux," Walsh said. "If you do not want to go with us freely, we will never bother you again."

Walks Tall had remained quiet since they had begun speaking. Now he felt that it was his turn. "Meadow," he began as he picked up her hand again. "You do have another choice if you want it. My offer to take care of you—to make you my woman—is still a choice you can make. I know that you will never love me as you loved Black Horse, and that is as it should be, but I will do everything in my power to give you a good life."

Except for the superintendent's whispered translations to Cornett, everyone else was silent as they waited to hear Meadow's response to the warrior's heartfelt proposal.

Walks Tall's words spun through Meadow's mind like a tornado. She did not want to go with the Mounties, nor did she want to live with Gentle Water and her grandmother any longer than necessary. But to become the woman of Walks Tall—the dearest friend of Black Horse—was not an option that she could give in to so easily. After knowing one indescribable night of love and passion with Black Horse, she still could not imagine lying in any other man's arms.

His dark eyes met her gaze as he waited for her answer. On his face, she could see an expression of tenderness and hope. "Your kind offer touches my heart more deeply than I can ever tell you, and I wish so very much that I could say yes to you. But—" She saw the disappointment wash through his face the instant she said that word, and she felt a sharp pain shoot through her breast as she continued. "Although Black Horse is supposedly dead, my love for him has not died. It would not be fair to you to be with a woman who still mourns—and loves—another man."

"But in time . . ." Walks Tall began with a pleading tone in his voice.

"Time is not something any of us have," Meadow said, recalling the talks she had had with her father and with Black Horse. She reached up and gently touched his cheek. "If I could love that way again, I would be so very proud to be your woman."

A tear rolled down Meadow's cheek as she looked into Walks Tall's sorrowful ebony gaze. His head nodded slowly, and he looked down at the ground as he pulled his hand away from hers. In many ways he was so like her beloved Black Horse, but still she could only love him as a friend.

As she drew in a deep, trembling breath, Meadow made the most difficult decision of her life.

Chapter Eighteen

"Shall we have another English lesson?" Brandon asked as he placed a steaming cup of tea on the table in front of Meadow.

"Not now. We practice more later," she replied impatiently in her much-improved English dialect. She had her mind on much more important matters right now. A regiment of soldiers from Fort Keogh was planning to pass through Fort Walsh today, and Meadow was determined to talk to them when they got here.

Not to be deterred, Brandon sat down in a chair beside her. He would not give up on her, no matter how long it took or how much she resisted. It had taken him too long and had nearly cost him his career in the North-West Mounted Police to convince his superintendent that they should rescue this girl from the Indians. Only once did he wonder if they were doing the right thing, and that was when she had confessed how much she had truly loved the war chief, Black Horse, when they had been in Sitting Bull's tepee, and Superintendent Walsh had graciously repeated this revelation to him.

"All right then," Brandon said as he settled back in the chair. "We'll just enjoy our tea." He noticed how beautiful she looked today. Obviously, she was making an effort to fit in with her own people. Her golden, shoulder-length hair was brushed neatly behind her ears and held back with two pearl combs. They had bought her some clothes from a trader that had been at the fort, and today she was wearing a black skirt and a white ruffled blouse that buttoned high up to her chin. Her prim and proper look made Brandon wish he weren't such a gentleman. If only he could just convince her to use a white name instead of *Meadow*, the English translation of her Indian name.

"When American soldiers arrive?" Meadow pushed the teacup away and leaned forward to look out the window again.

Her request took Brandon by surprise, and he didn't even bother to correct her language as he usually did. "Midday, I would imagine, but why do you want to know?"

"Just w-wondering." She shrugged her shoulders in a nonchalant manner and pulled the teacup back toward her again. As Brandon had taught her, she picked up the teacup by the handle and daintily stuck her pinky finger up in the air as she sipped the hot brew.

"Well, if you like, I could take you out to meet them when they arrive." Brandon nodded and smiled with approval at the proper way she was holding her cup.

Meadow shrugged again as if she had lost interest in the visitors. "No, I see enough American soldiers to last me a long time," she said.

Brandon nodded his head in a sympathetic gesture. When she turned to look at him again, Brandon felt his chest grow tight. Her beautiful jade eyes seemed to penetrate into his soul, and her full lips were parted slightly as if they were waiting to be kissed. With no thought to the consequences, Brandon leaned forward to fulfill one of many of his dreams about this lovely young woman.

His impulsive action caused Meadow to gasp loudly and push back her chair in a desperate move to get away. She jumped to her feet and stepped behind her chair in a defensive stance. "What you doing?" she demanded.

Brandon also sprang to his feet. He could feel the heat in his face, and he could see the horrified expression on Meadow's face. He inwardly berated himself for being so impatient.

"I'm so sorry, Meadow. I just don't know what came over me. Please . . ." He reached out toward her, but she flinched and backed farther away from him. "It won't happen again, I promise."

"Please leave," she said in a low voice as she turned her back to him.

Meadow waited until she heard the door close and knew that the lieutenant was gone before she turned back around. Now more than ever she had to find out what she needed to know as soon as possible so that she could go home—to the Sioux—where she would stay forever, this time.

By the time the troop arrived at Fort Walsh shortly after noontime, Meadow had rehearsed her speech a hundred times. Even though Brandon's constant efforts to teach her English were annoying, she had made every effort to learn all that she could from him. Since she knew some of the language already, she had been a quick study. It had only been a little over a week since she had returned to the fort and started speaking the white man's language, and she could already carry on a conversation. Brandon was convinced that she was learning so quickly because subconsciously she already knew the English language. Meadow thought it was just because she was smart.

With her heart pounding rapidly in her breast, Meadow grabbed the small satchel that contained her few earthly possessions and hurried out of the cabin. The American soldiers had been in meetings with Canadian leaders to discuss a plan to coax the thousands of Indians who had crossed into Canada in the past couple of years back to the American side. Meadow had heard that they were promising the Indians land of their own if they returned, but this was ironic, because the land already belonged to the Indians. It was the white men who had stolen it from them. And, even worse, the land would be deemed reservation land, which meant the white men would be in charge of everything that the Indians did. They would be like prisoners on their own land. Meadow could not imagine Sitting Bull agreeing to this arrangement for his people. But would he be given any choice?

The American soldiers were stopping only long enough to take a quick lunch break at Fort Walsh and then heading out again, so they were all in the mess hall when Meadow put her plan into action. As she entered the building, she immediately caught the attention of all the men who saw her come through the door. There were still no women at this isolated fort, and the mother and daughter she had seen the last time she was here were long gone.

Meadow focused on finding the man in charge of the American troop. As she passed by the rows of tables, every man jumped up and nodded at her. Meadow thought this white man's habit was foolish, but she nodded back politely and motioned for them to sit down again. As she approached a table in the center of the room, she spotted Superintendent Walsh. Beside him sat a soldier wearing a dark blue coat with yellow shoulder boards. The four bars that adorned each of the boards were the designation for an officer in the U.S Calvary. Meadow knew that she had found the man she was looking for.

Both men stood as Meadow walked up to their table, and she could tell by the perplexed expression on the superintendent's face that he was more than a little surprised to see her there. Since she wanted to waste no more time than necessary, she broke into her speech instantly. "I am Meadow. I lived with Hunkpapa Sioux tribe since I was b-baby." Her uncertainty about how to pronounce some words still frustrated her, so she did not object when superintendent took over and explained her situation to the captain of the American cavalry.

"You must be so relieved to finally be away from those terrible savages," Captain Smith said as he let his gaze rake down over Meadow's body.

The uneasiness Meadow felt under the captain's lustful gaze almost made her forget her plan. Yet her desperation to find out the truth about Black Horse gave her the courage to proceed. "Yes, and eager to find real f-family. I would ask please take me to Fort Keogh with you. I feel I would have better ch-chance to find them if back in my own country."

The captain looked at Walsh and shrugged. "I see no reason why she could not return to Fort Keogh with us." He glanced back at Meadow. "We'll do everything we can to help you find your family. Until then, you would be more than welcome to stay at the fort. We have several families living there, and I would suppose the presence of other white women would be a great comfort to you after your terrible ordeal."

She gave a feeble nod. Out of the corner of her eye, Meadow noticed a man jump up from his seat. She knew who he was even before she turned to look at him. Brandon Cornett's mouth was open as if he was ready to voice his opinion, but to Meadow's relief, Superintendent Walsh did not give him a chance.

"Our only desire for this poor girl has been to help her reunite with any family that she might have." Walsh cast a threatening look in the lieutenant's direction. "And being in the presence of other white women would be absolutely wonderful for her introduction back into civilization." He narrowed his eyes and gave his head a negative shake when Cornett tried to speak again.

"Well, then, Miss—eh—Meadow," Captain Smith said as he motioned toward her and smiled. "We'll be leaving within the hour."

"I'm ready," she answered. She looked back toward Brandon and then at the superintendent as she added, "I thank you much for what you have—" She paused, trying to think of the words she wanted to say.

"It was the least we could do," Walsh said as he continued to cast warning glances at Lieutenant Cornett. "Good luck finding your family."

Meadow nodded and smiled at the superintendent, then let her gaze settle on the lieutenant's disappointed face. Since she hoped never to see him again after today, she decided to cut all ties with him right now. She motioned for him to follow her out of the mess hall, but when they reached the front stoop, he did not give her a chance to speak.

"Why would you want to leave here?" he demanded. "I am going to help you find your family when the time is right and you are ready." He reached out and grabbed her by the shoulders. "Can't you see how hard I have worked to get you back here to your own people where you belong? And I had dared to hope that someday we would have a future together."

His words left Meadow's body numb as a sick feeling began to twist her stomach into knots. This man had ruined her future with Black Horse, yet presumed that they would have a future! She dug her fingernails into the palms of her hands and tried to focus on what she had to do.

"I—I really f-feel I have better chance of finding my family if I go to Fort Keogh," Meadow finally managed to say.

"But that is not a part of my plan for us," Brandon said in determined tone of voice.

"Being here was not my plan," Meadow retorted. No longer able to hide her true feelings, she added, "I was to be wife to proud Sioux war chief, Black Horse, and live among my adoptive people." Tossing her head back, Meadow glared up at the Mountie's face.

Although she was prepared to engage in an angry confrontation, when his tortured gaze lowered to meet hers, she realized that he really did not understand just how deeply his actions had hurt her. Meadow was reminded of another man who had looked at her in the same way not too long ago. The memory of Walks Tall's poignant proposal still haunted her thoughts constantly. But there was absolutely nothing else about Brandon Cornett that could even begin to compare with the Sioux warrior.

"Ever since that first day when I saw you at the Sioux village, I only wanted what was best for you. You must understand that. Will you—? Do you think . . . that you might want to come back here someday?" Brandon asked quietly.

Meadow looked down at the ground and took a deep breath. There was always the possibility that their paths would cross again someday, but she really hoped that they wouldn't. Right now, the only thing she wanted was to learn the truth about what happened to her beloved Black Horse. "Good-bye, Lieutenant Cornett," she said as she turned to leave.

Chapter Nineteen

Fort Keogh had been built even more recently than the Canadian fort in the Cypress Hills that Meadow had just left. After the Battle of the Little Bighorn, the military post was constructed in the hope of being able to control the Indians who were threatening further retaliation against the white men. This fort, however, was already much larger than Fort Walsh, and buildings were still being erected on both sides of the courtyard that stood in the center of the large post.

Even if it was still hundreds of miles away from the wide-open plains of the Dakota Territory that she loved so dearly, Meadow was happy to be on the other side of the Canadian border.

"Miss?"

Meadow jumped at the sound of the voice and turned to look at the man who had suddenly appeared at her side. He was a young, redheaded man, probably not much older than she was, but he was wearing the dark blue uniform of the U.S. Cavalry.

"Hello," Meadow said clearly. Her English was improving daily.

"Hi. Hello. I'm sorry, I don't know your name. Miss . . . ?" He smiled at her as he fidgeted nervously with the hat he held in his hand.

Without hesitation, Meadow returned his smile.

"Meadow—just Meadow. That's my name," she answered.

The young soldier shrugged his shoulders. "Well, I am Private Jensen, and I am here to see to it that you have everything you need."

"My quarters are quite comfortable. I don't think there is anything I need at this time. But I am looking forward to exploring the fort," Meadow answered. This young soldier had no idea just how anxious she really was to learn all about Fort Keogh—especially regarding the Sioux prisoners who had been incarcerated or executed here in the past few months.

The prospect of escorting such a lovely girl around the fort brought an immediate smile to Private Jensen's mouth. In a gentlemanly fashion, he crooked his arm and held it out toward Meadow. She hesitated, but remembered that she was supposed to be acting like a white woman now. She slipped her arm through his as he guided her down the front steps that led from the small private room she had been given at the end of a long row of barracks.

"Many wives and children have already relocated to Fort Keogh, so you will have lots of women to keep you company," the private said as they walked along the dusty street. "We have dances on most Saturday nights, and Sundays are always a very pleasant social event. Everyone attends services at the chapel, and then there is a great meal prepared by all the women. You'll enjoy those gatherings, I'm sure."

Meadow managed a weak nod of her head and a faked smile. She could only hope the white women at Fort Keogh would be happy to meet her, but the activities the young soldier had just described did not sound like anything she would enjoy doing. It made her even more anxious to get the information she sought so that she could return to the Sioux village.

"And this is the mess hall, and also where we have our Saturday-night socials," Private Jensen added as they walked past a large, newly built structure. "Well, that is just about all that there is to see, except for the prison. But I'm sure you want to stay as far away from that place as possible, especially since we have some of the country's most dangerous Sioux warriors imprisoned there."

The soldier's unexpected words took a minute to penetrate into Meadow's thoughts. But, when she was able to grasp the full meaning of what he had just said, it took all her willpower to keep from grabbing the private and demanding to know just whom it was that he was talking about. A rush of blood to her head made Meadow feel as if she was about to pass out, and the pounding in her chest made her entire body shake.

"Oh, I am so sorry," gasped Private Jensen. "I can tell by the look on your face that the idea of having any of those animals from the tribe who kidnapped you so close by is terrifying for you."

He took the liberty of wrapping his arm around her shoulders because she was shaking visibly, and even though the young man's attempt to comfort her was misguided, Meadow knew she must continue to play along with whatever it was that he believed. "Th-There are Sioux h-here at th-this fort?" she managed to ask with the little amount of voice she could muster.

"They can't hurt you," the private said in a compassionate tone. "There are only a few of the younger warriors and several old men, but they are all kept in heavy chains and haven't even seen the light of day for months. If they were considered dangerous at one time, I can assure you that they are as meek as kittens now. There is absolutely nothing for you to be afraid of." His hold around her shoulders tightened when a heavy shudder bolted through her body again. "You poor little thing. You must have suffered terribly at the hands of those savages."

Meadow desperately tried to corral her wild thoughts and emotions until she could get away from the soldier. Until then, she knew that she had to find a way to convince him that his instincts were correct. "I—I am fine. Thank you for your concern. It will take some time, I'm sure, before I will feel safe again." Meadow glanced around the fort. "Just so I know what area to avoid . . . where are the Sioux prisoners kept?"

The young soldier hesitated before answering, "Are you sure you want to know?"

"Yes," Meadow demanded. "Yes, it is important for me to know . . . j-just s-so I can stay as far away from there as possible."

"Well then, you're in luck, because the stockade is all the way across the courtyard, behind the general's quarters. There is no way any of those heathens will ever be able to harm anyone again."

Meadow swallowed hard and fought back the tears that threatened to fall from her eyes. The tone of the young soldier's voice left her with little doubt as to how much he hated all Indians. She took a deep breath and hoped that she could continue with the act that she knew was crucial at this time.

"Th-thank you f-for everything. I would like to rest up for a bit before dinner."

Normally, only the enlisted men without families would eat in the mess hall. Families usually dined in their own living quarters, unless it was a special occasion. Tonight was considered a special occasion, since it was Meadow's first night at Fort Keogh, and it was everyone's opinion that she needed to befriend as many of the women as possible to help her get past the horrible ordeal she had been through with the Sioux. She was dreading the evening.

"I will call for you shortly before six P.M.," Private Jensen replied in a less serious tone. "And tomorrow we can start searching for your family. We have been granted full access to all of General Wray's records regarding any little skirmishes we have had with savages in these parts, so at the very least, we should be able to find a starting date for our search."

Meadow turned away from the private before he could see how much his words had pained her. Little skirmishes? Is that what soldiers called it when entire villages of Indians—or wagon trains of whites—with women, children and elderly were slaughtered and mutilated as if they were nothing more than a pack of dogs? She swallowed the bitter taste in her mouth.

"I'll be ready for dinner when you call for me," Meadow said hoarsely as she hurried into her room. She closed the door behind her and leaned back against it in an attempt to breathe normally again. Was there a white man alive that had any empathy for the plight of the Indians? White Buffalo had told her so many times that all men—red, white or brown—had red blood and hearts that beat the same. She had yet to meet another man who was as insightful as her cherished *ate ate*.

The thought of White Buffalo returned Meadow's thoughts to the important task she had to complete here at Fort Keogh. Somehow, she had to get into the stockade where the Sioux prisoners were being held, for two reasons: to find out if they knew anything about Black Horse and to find a way to get them all out of this hellhole!

The evening was a blur as Meadow nodded automatically to the sea of faces belonging to the officers' wives and daughters she was introduced to at dinner. Although most of the women made an honest attempt to be friendly to Meadow, she sensed that some of them were keeping their distance from her as if they worried that her life with the Sioux had somehow contaminated her. A couple of the women insinuated that decent people would have a difficult time being in her presence, and told her how lucky she was to be at a military base where the residents were more tolerant of women who had been "ruined" by Indian men. Even the girls who looked to be around the same age as she was acted as if they were afraid to sit too close to her. She did not feel a connection with any of them, as she had with the girl she had glimpsed walking down the street with her mother at Fort Walsh the first time she had been there.

Meadow knew she would not be here long enough to care one way or the other how the "decent" women of the fort felt toward her, so instead she concentrated on listening to conversations among the officers and enlisted men in the hopes that she would hear something about the Sioux captives held at the fort. Unfortunately, she did not learn anything useful.

By the end of the long evening, when Private Jensen

walked Meadow back to her own quarters, she was more determined than ever to finish her mission here as quickly as possible, so that she could return to the Sioux village.

As tired as she was, Meadow could not fall asleep. She was sure she would never sleep again until she saw who was being held in that prison and found out whether or not they knew anything about the alleged death of Black Horse.

Holding the door to her quarters wide open, Meadow stared out at the dark buildings and courtyard. The nights were growing warmer, now that summer was rapidly approaching. All that remained of the past winter's snowfall was high on the mountaintops, but on some of the tallest peaks the snow did not entirely melt away all year long.

The first hazy rays of the morning sunlight found Meadow anxiously waiting in her open doorway for her carefully planned day. When she saw Private Jensen headed toward her quarters to escort her to breakfast, she eagerly rushed out to meet him. A fluttering in the pit of her stomach told her that today would prove to be very productive, and she couldn't wait to get things started.

"Well, you're bursting with energy this morning," the private said as she stopped before him. "I take it you slept well?"

"Yes, very well, thank you," Meadow lied. If today turned out as fruitful as she hoped, she would sleep well tonight because she would be one day closer to going home. "Are we still going to research the Indian battles in this area today?"

"We'll start immediately after breakfast," the private

said as he took Meadow's arm and led her down the boardwalk.

Feeling ravenous for the first time since she had left the Sioux village, Meadow devoured two flapjacks, scrambled eggs and some elk sausage as Private Jensen watched in amazement. Although she still preferred the blander Indian food, she was growing accustomed to the more seasoned food eaten by whites.

"I'm ready to get started," Meadow announced as she bounded up from the hard wooden bench that lined one of the long tables in the mess hall.

"I can see that," Private Jensen said with a wide smile. He swung his leg over the bench and stood up beside her. "Well, what are we waiting for?"

As they walked toward the far end of the fort, Meadow felt as though her heart was about to burst out of her chest. Every step toward the general's quarters took her one step closer to the prisoner barricade. Someone there had to know something about Black Horse's presumed execution. As they approached the general's office, Meadow quickly scanned the area surrounding the officers' quarters. The sight of an armed guard standing in front of a square building with window bars caused Meadow's footsteps to falter.

"Are you all right?" Private Jensen asked with concern. When he saw the direction she was staring in, he sighed. "Oh, don't worry. That's not where the savages are kept. That's where we keep enlisted men who have gotten themselves in fights or deserted or something like that." He tossed his head back. "The heathens are locked up in an underground cell behind the prison. There's no chance that they'll ever get out of there!"

A chill ran down the length of Meadow's spine as

she tried to envision the horrible condition of the Indians who were locked in that hellish hole. She drew in a heavy breath, but made no attempt to speak—the choking lump in her throat would not allow her voice to escape anyway.

"Come on, now," the soldier prodded as he forced Meadow to turn away from the direction of the prison. "We've got much better things to think about today— like finding your family."

His words had little meaning to Meadow, since the only thing she could concentrate on was finding a way to get in to those prisoners. She stumbled into the general's office and glanced around absently. With a feeling of relief, she noticed that the general was not there. It was obvious that an important man occupied this office because of the massive desk that sat in the middle of the room and the impressive looking awards and pictures that decorated the walls. Along one entire wall was a row of tall cabinets filled with papers and books.

"I took the liberty of coming over here last night to do some research after I escorted you back to your room." Private Jensen smiled proudly as he strutted over to one of the cabinets along the back wall and pulled open the top drawer. "I think the information we are looking for is in these files, so it shouldn't take too long to discover what happened to your family."

Meadow leveled her flashing emerald gaze on the soldier. "I don't think there has ever been any question as to what happened to them. They were killed fifteen years ago in a battle with the Sioux, and that's why I was taken to live with the Hunkpapa tribe." Her hands clamped down on the curves of her hips. "And the reason our wagon train was attacked was because just days earlier, a village of women, children and old men had been slaughtered by white soldiers!"

Meadow's unexpected outburst left Private Jensen speechless. As he stared at her, she noticed a red blush work its way up from the collar of his navy-blue jacket, not stopping until it reached the brim of his hat. She drew in a deep sigh and inwardly berated herself for letting her emotions get the best of her. "I'm sorry for my rash words. Sometimes, it's hard for me to remember who I am or where I am supposed to be." She was relieved to see the soldier's expression soften and a slight smile curve his thin lips.

"I guess that's understandable. But now that you're back where you should be, you'll see those animals for what they really are."

"Yes . . . yes, I'm sure you're right," Meadow said as she turned away from the soldier and stared out one of the windows toward the distant horizon. She was constantly feeling as though she were being punched in the stomach.

"Now, let's start with these files," Private Jensen said in a tone that suggested he had already forgotten about their previous discussion. "According to everyone's assumptions, it was approximately 1862 or '63 when you were taken captive, so I thought we'd start with the battles that occurred in '62 and work our way up."

A strange feeling passed through Meadow. She clasped her arms around herself and drew in another deep breath. The stack of files the private had just placed before her looked ominous and foreign. Was it possible that the entire first two years of her life was hidden somewhere in that pile of papers?

Private Jensen looked up from the stack of papers he had been diligently reading though all day when he heard Meadow yawn again. The chore of reading through the files was his sole responsibility, since Meadow had never learned to read. "I suppose it is rather boring for you to watch me reading all day. How about if I finish this file, and then we'll go for a walk before it's time to get ready for dinner?"

Meadow eagerly nodded her head in agreement. Maybe they could walk down by the prison area again, and she could get a better look at the layout of the building.

"Oh, I don't believe it!" The private held one of the papers up in the air. "It's all here—all of it." He jumped up from his chair and hurried to Meadow's side with the paper clutched tightly in his hand.

Since the scribbles on the paper meant nothing to her, Meadow gazed at the paper for only an instant, and then looked up at the soldier for an explanation. "What, what is all there?" she asked. A tight sensation was beginning to form in her breast.

"Here." The Private pointed enthusiastically at the paper he held in front of her face. "It's the records from the attack on your family's wagon train. It occurred in October of 1863 and thirty-six people were killed, seven were taken captive and eleven escaped."

A strange sensation crept through Meadow's body as she stared at the document in the private's hand. How could one piece of yellowed paper hold so much information? "D-does it s-say who d-died and who escaped?" Meadow asked in a quivering voice.

"It has a complete list on the back," Private Jensen

announced as he turned the paper over and began to read names out loud. "Simon Phillips—dead; Gene Let—"

"Wait!" Meadow called out. This was happening so fast; in less than a day they had already found the proof that Meadow could not even begin to fathom. Now she had to face the reality that there had been a time when she had been part of another family, her real family—her white family. She drew in a trembling breath and gazed into the puzzled face of the soldier and asked in a weak voice, "The ones who were taken by the Sioux . . . Does it give their ages as well as their names?"

The private's attention returned to the paper as he carefully read down the lists of names of those who were taken captive on that long-ago day. Beside each name was written the gender, and next to that was the supposed age at the time of the incident. "Yes, although there are a lot of question marks beside the ages, so I suppose they are mostly guesses."

Unconsciously, Meadow drew the crocheted shawl she had draped around her shoulders tightly around herself. A small scattering of perspiration beads had just broken out on her forehead. "Th-the ones who were captured . . . Was there a t-two-year-old f-female?" she stammered.

"Mary McBain," Private Jensen announced without hesitation. Then, more excitedly, he looked up at Meadow. "You are Mary McBain!" He held the paper up for her to see; then, remembering that she couldn't read, he turned it over so that he could read it again.

Meadow opened her mouth to speak, but no words

escaped as she continued to stare at the single piece of paper that had just changed her entire life. Mary . . . Her white name was Mary? How strange that name sounded as it echoed through her mind.

"And you are not going to believe this!" Jensen shouted. He did not give Meadow a chance to respond. "You have a brother who escaped, and, oh . . ." His voice trailed off as he closely studied the paper again.

"What? What were you going to say?" Meadow demanded. Her head felt as if it were spinning off of her body. She had a brother? What else was she about to learn about her past life—a life that she had completely ignored until this moment?

He glanced up at her and shook his head as though he still couldn't believe what he was reading. "Well, there have been several notations added to the part about you and your brother. It says here that numerous attempts were made to locate you and the others after your capture. And . . ." He drew in a deep sigh as he paused to glance down at the document once more.

"And what?" Meadow asked in a quiet tone. "What else does it say?" The feeling that her heart was about to pound out of her chest made her words almost a whisper.

"Your brother—your older brother—was raised by a family right here in Montana. After he grew up, he made several more attempts to find you"—the private smiled widely—"before he joined the army. He's stationed at Fort Custer, less than a hundred miles from here."

Meadow felt as if a large band had just tightened around her chest, making it nearly impossible for her to breathe. For an instant the private's face grew blurry before her eyes, and she felt as though her legs were about to give out from under her. Words were lost to the ocean of emotions she was experiencing.

A brother? Who had obviously loved her and missed her and tried in desperation to find her for all these years.

"You'd better take a deep breath before you pass out," Private Jensen ordered. He wrapped his arm around her waist and escorted her to the large leather chair at the general's desk.

"I know what a shock all of this must be to you. To think of the misery and horror you've endured all this time at the hands of those savages, when you could have been living a decent life here with your own kin."

The soldier's words jumbled together with Meadow's own tormented thoughts of the news he had just given her about her past. It was all more than she could bear. Unfortunately, the young soldier was victim to the rage she could no longer control. "Losing my real family at such a young age was tragic, and yes, it would have been wonderful to know my brother," she began in a barely controlled voice, with gritted teeth. Her anger began to show itself as she continued. "But those savages that you speak of took me in and loved me as if I was their own flesh and blood. They raised me and nurtured me and kept me safe when enemies—whites and Indians alike—tried to harm me. And I loved them like my own family, too."

Her fists clenched tightly in her lap as she went on without thinking first about the words that she was about to say. "I also loved a Sioux war chief—I loved him more than life itself, and if he hadn't been killed by murderous soldiers, I would have been at his side for the rest of my life. You talk about savages, Private Jensen. I have known many savages in my life, but they weren't all Indians!"

The private slowly backed away from her as if he could not stand to be close to her. "I see where your sympathy lies, and it is a shame it is not with your parents and your baby sister and other two brothers who were slaughtered during that attack." The soldier twirled on his heels and walked out of the general's office without another word or a glance backward.

Meadow remained motionless at she watched the man's retreat. His parting words left her feeling as though she had just been kicked in the chest. There had been five children in her family, and only two had survived? The realization of how little she knew about her life with her real family overwhelmed her, and for the first time in her life, Meadow cried for the mother, father and siblings that she had never known.

It seemed as though she had been sitting there in the same spot—in the general's big leather chair—and crying for hours as fuzzy, faceless images of laughing children and loving parents crowded into her shocked mind.

Then, the happy images turned to horror as she kept picturing the unimaginable—the murder of her innocent brothers, a baby sister and her poor parents. Although she would never know exactly what had happened on that October day long ago, Meadow knew that from this day forward she could never allow herself to forget that in another lifetime she had once been Mary McBain.

Chapter Twenty

Meadow had not left her quarters for three days, other than to make necessary trips to the outhouse. Soldiers silently brought her meals and collected the trays afterward. With the exception of a visit from the general two days earlier, she was being shunned by the entire population here at the fort. The general had only come long enough to tell her that arrangements were being made to send her back to Canada now that they had helped her find out about her family.

She cringed every time she thought about the way she had reacted when the private had told her what had happened to her real family. She couldn't blame the people here at the fort for thinking that she was heartless and crazy.

But leaving before she had learned anything about Black Horse and the other Sioux prisoners made her feel as if she should beg everyone for forgiveness so that she could stay long enough to get the information she needed.

A loud banging on her door interrupted Meadow's tortured thoughts. She wiped at the tears welling in the corners of her eyes and glanced in the mirror. Her eyes were puffy and red, and her hair hung in long tangled tendrils over her shoulders. She was wearing her wrinkled sleeping gown.

"Who's there?" she called out as she attempted to smooth her hair back from her forehead.

"Open the door," came a stern male reply.

The pit of Meadow's stomach felt like a lead ball. She did not recognize the voice, and the man on the other side of the door did not sound friendly at all. As she slowly took a step forward, another thundering knock echoed from the door.

"Mary McBain?" the man inquired in a loud voice.

Meadow had just reached for the door handle, but when the man asked for her by her white name, her entire body froze. The sound of the man calling her by her white name seemed to strip her of all her identity. She couldn't breathe for a moment. Finally, she forced her hand to clasp the handle as her other shaking hand undid the latch. With a deep breath, she pulled the door open and looked up at a golden-haired man with green eyes the exact same color as her own.

"Good Lord," the man gasped as he stared. "You are the spitting image of our mother."

There was no doubt who this man was, yet Meadow found it inconceivable that she was actually staring into the face of her own brother. Not one coherent thought entered her mind, and her knees began to feel as if they could no longer support the weight of her body. She felt herself sway forward in the doorway, and in the next instant, her brother was scooping her into his arms.

"I'm f-fine," she stammered as he sat her in the nearby chair. "You're just— It's just—" she mumbled, then fell silent as she continued to stare at the man who knelt in front of her.

"I am your brother, Robert McBain—Lieutenant

Robert McBain," he announced. "Are you sure you're all right?"

The concern in his voice sounded sincere, which surprised Meadow, since he had sounded so angry when he had been pounding on her door a few moments ago. "My brother," she repeated slowly. How strange those words felt to her tongue.

"I realize what a shock this must be," Robert said. "You were so little when you were stolen away that you don't remember any of us." He studied her face again, now that he was so close to her. The color of her hair was almost identical to his own golden blond, and the green of their eyes was a perfect match. But it was her uncanny resemblance to their mother that touched Robert to his very core. He had been fourteen years old when their wagon train had been attacked—the oldest of the McBain children. His memory of both of his parents had never dimmed, nor had his memories of his four younger siblings. Now, he found it hard to believe that the chubby, rosy-cheeked toddler that he had toted around on his shoulders was this confused and haggard young woman he saw before him.

"We have a lot to talk about," Robert said after a long, uncomfortable silence. "I hardly know where we should begin." His anger when he had first arrived at her room had faded slightly now that he had met her. When he had first received the wire that his sister was alive and at Fort Keogh, he had been so overjoyed and anxious to meet her that he had immediately requested a leave so that he could go there to get her and take her back to Fort Custer to live with him. Then, when he had arrived today, he had been taken to the general's office, where he had been informed that his sister was a traitor to her own people and that she was such an Indian sympathizer that no one here at Fort Keogh wanted to be near her.

This information had so enraged him that he planned to come to her and tell her all of the gory details of how their parents and brothers and infant sister had been slaughtered. He wondered how she would feel about her beloved Sioux then. But when she had opened the door and peered up at him from their dead mother's face, nearly all anger had fled from him. She appeared to be so lost and helpless that Robert wondered if she had been so abused by those savages that she had lost her mind.

"I can never even begin to understand what you must have been through, but as your brother, I promise you that I will do everything in my power to help you forget the past fifteen years of your life."

Agreeing with him would have been the easiest thing to do, but Meadow refused to let anyone strip away the good memories—the cherished memories—of her time with the Sioux. "I know what happened to our family was horrible and unforgivable, but please try to understand that the Sioux I was raised among treated me with only kindness and unselfish love. I could never forget—" Her words were cut off sharply when her brother grabbed her roughly and pulled her close to him as he yanked her up to her feet. His hands clasped her arms so tightly that she wanted to cry out in pain, but the shock of his actions rendered her silent.

"I don't ever want to hear that kind of talk coming out of your mouth again. You hear me?"

Meadow stared up at him. She flinched at the way

his mouth was curled into a hateful snarl and his green eyes had drawn into narrow slits. A weak nod of her head was her only response to his demand. The instant he released his tight hold on her arms, she started to back away from him.

Robert shook his head and let his gaze rake over her coolly. "I was told that you seemed to love those dirty redskins more than you did your own kind. I hoped and prayed it wasn't true, but I can see for myself that you've been corrupted by those savages, and now I've got to see to it that every one of those filthy thoughts is wiped out of your head for good!"

Meadow continued to step back until she bumped into the wall and could not retreat any farther. Tightness in her throat and chest made speaking impossible, but remembering how her rash words had caused her to be in this situation in the first place, she realized she would be smart to keep her opinions to herself for a change.

"Now . . . ," Robert began in a controlled tone of voice as he straightened up to his full height and drew back his shoulders as if he were standing at attention. "I think it would probably be best for us to head back to Fort Custer first thing in the morning. You can make a fresh start at Fort Custer, and as long as you keep any love you still harbor toward the Sioux to yourself, there should not be any problems."

He stepped toward the door as he added, "I've spent half of my life trying to fulfill two goals: to find you and then to bring our family's killers to justice. Well, here you are, now. That just leaves wiping out every one of those Sioux bastards so that no other family has to go through the horrors that ours has. You'd do well, little sister, to think long and hard about where your loyalties need be."

Meadow's body grew numb from the cold that raced through her as she watched this stranger walk out of her room. Before he closed the door, he turned to her and said, "Be ready to leave at dawn." The hardness in his voice and the look on his face made it obvious to Meadow that a third goal had just been added to her brother's list: to make sure that she became as much of an Indian hater as he was, or rue the day that she had been reunited with him!

With all the energy drained from her, Meadow fell back onto the bed. How had her life ended up so tragic, when just a short year ago she had been the happiest she had ever been in her entire life? With thoughts of Black Horse in her troubled mind once again, she drifted into a restless slumber. Her dreams were beautiful and vivid, of the brief time they had lived and loved among the towering pines. Was it possible to have loved enough in such a short time to last her an entire lifetime?

When Meadow awoke, the sun had not yet risen. She knew she had no choice but to go to Fort Custer today with her brother, but she silently vowed to somehow return to Fort Keogh and learn more about the Sioux prisoners that were incarcerated here.

With an aching head and a body that felt as if it had been run over by a stampede of buffalo, Meadow slowly readied herself for the journey that lay ahead. She did not feel right taking all of the clothes that the women from this fort had given to her, so she picked out a black riding skirt with a tailored jacket and a simple white shirt. The tall, knee-high boots she had been given for riding were pure torture to her feet. Although she knew she would never be allowed to wear her soft moccasins or loose-fitting buckskin dress at Fort Custer, there was no way she would leave them behind. Carefully, she packed them in the bottom of the small leather bag that Little Squirrel had sewn for her when she was a young girl. The white wedding blanket was also in her bag. She still slept with it every night.

When a loud knock sounded on her door, Meadow was ready but not anxious to begin a life with her newly found brother. She opened the door before he had a chance to pound on it again. He looked surprised to see that she was ready and waiting for him. Meadow noticed that two soldiers sat on horseback beside two other saddled horses, which were apparently for her and Robert.

"These men are under my command at Fort Custer, and they accompanied me here," Robert offered when he noticed her eyeing them suspiciously. "Let's ride," he added. "If time is on our side, we'll be at Fort Custer by tomorrow night."

Meadow nodded in agreement and headed for the smaller of the saddled horses. One of the soldiers jumped down to help her mount up, but Meadow had swung up into the saddle before he was able to reach her. She glanced at Robert. The scowl on his face told her that he did not approve of anything she did, and she was certain that he was wishing now that she, too, had been killed in that attack fifteen years ago.

Without another word, the four riders cantered across the wide expanse of the courtyard. The sun was just peeking above the distant horizon, and there was very little activity anywhere in the fort, which was why Meadow's attention was diverted to the movement at the prison barricade. A small group of soldiers carrying rifles walked on each side of a row of handcuffed and manacled Indians. The Indian men walked with their heads bowed and moved slowly, as if they were in great agony. Meadow's heart began to pound like a drum in her breast. These had to be the Sioux prisoners she had been hoping to see, and they were walking right toward them.

Her instinct was to jump off the back of her horse, run up to the men and hug them all and tell them how sorry she was that they were being held here and treated like dogs, but common sense made her remain in her saddle. Still, she could not leave here until she knew if any of these prisoners were men that she might know from her village.

"Robert," she called out as she pulled on her horse's reins and came to a halt. The look of annoyance on her brother's face when he looked back did not deter her. "Could you please wait here for just a moment? I forgot something back in my room."

The lieutenant gave a curt nod of his head and glanced at his two comrades with a look of aggravation, but Meadow didn't wait around for him to change his mind. She turned her horse around and trotted back toward the barracks she had just left. Her hope was that the prisoners would be walking past the same area by the time she reached the hitching post and she would be able to get a look at their faces while she was tying up her horse. In her haste to get away from her brother, however, Meadow reached the building where she had been staying too soon. The bedraggled prisoners were moving at a pace barely more than a crawl, and they were still too far away for her to see any of their faces.

Meadow glanced back at the trio of men who were waiting for her and noticed that they were all looking in her direction. She finished tying her horse to the hitching post and hurried back into the building. Frantically, she looked around for something to grab so that she could stuff it into her saddlebag when she went back outside, since her brother was undoubtedly watching every move she made. A pink gingham dress hung on the back of the chair, so she snatched up the garment, even though that particular dress had been her least favorite of the clothes she had been given to wear.

Feeling as if she was about to explode inside, Meadow's sweating hand could barely turn the knob to let her exit from the room again. As panic flooded through her, she grasped the knob with both hands and yanked the door open. The soldiers and the prisoners were moving right past her when she stepped out into the open. From a distance it had been obvious that they were a pitiful lot, but up close the sight of them caused Meadow's stomach to twist into a heavy knot. There were about a dozen men. Dirt encrusted their dark skin, and their hair hung in heavy clumps down their backs. They wore filthy leggings, loincloths and nothing else, not even moccasins on their cut and bleeding feet. Meadow fought back the urge to cry at the sight of these once-proud men who were now reduced to nothing more than walking skeletons.

As the men moved past her, none of them looked up, so Meadow stepped forward in an effort to see them more clearly. The dirt on their thin faces and the scraggly strands of hair that hung over their shoulders made it next to impossible to tell who they were, but as the last couple of men stumbled past her, one glanced up. His dark gaze met Meadow's without hesitation, and even with all the grime covering him there was no denying who he was. A weak gasp escaped from Meadow, but the strangling knot in her throat prevented her from saying anything or crying out. She grasped the railing of the hitching post for support, because her legs felt as if the bones had just dissolved, and the thudding of her heart had expanded up into her head and made her feel as if she was going to lose consciousness.

Clinging to the post, Meadow stared at Black Horse as he stumbled past her. Their gazes locked, but she could not decipher the strange look in his raven eyes. His blank stare almost suggested that he didn't recognize her, yet that could not be possible. She leaned forward, yearning to reach out and touch him. He was alive—close enough to touch—and she desperately wanted to wrap her arms around him and never let him go again. Her mouth opened to call out to him, to tell him how much she loved him, but the words did not follow.

His eyes—those beautiful dark ebony eyes that had haunted her day and night for so long—were now the eyes of a stranger. She had seen that look in his raven gaze before, when he had talked about his loathing for the white men. She saw his eyes rake up and down her body, then rise back up to her face, but this time he did not allow his gaze to meet hers. Meadow had no doubt now that he recognized her. But he was not looking at the woman he had once loved so passionately. He saw only a white woman—his most hated enemy.

As the group of soldiers and their prisoners walked around the corner and out of view, Meadow clung to the post. If she allowed herself to move, she knew she would not be able to stop herself from running wildly after Black Horse, throwing herself at his feet and telling him that regardless of how she was dressed or where she was, in her heart she was still a Sioux.

Staying quiet and still was the hardest thing Meadow had ever done. Every inch of her being ached from the effort it took to remain passive while the love of her life disappeared from view. Her heart felt as if it had just been ripped in half, her mouth went dry and it was difficult for her take a breath.

"Mary, my God! You're as white as a ghost," Robert gasped as he grabbed her around the waist to prevent her from falling down. She was holding on to the post so tightly that he could not even squeeze his arm all the way around her. Although he had seen the Indians pass right in front of her, he had no idea how profoundly the sight of them had affected her. He had believed that his sister sympathized with the Indians, but from her strange reaction now, he was questioning that belief. The look of horror on her ashen face made him wonder if she was so scared and confused that she didn't even know what she was talking about when she defended the Sioux.

"Let's get you as far away from here as possible," Robert said in a sympathic voice. "And don't you worry—you'll never have to be around another one of those savages again, because I'm going to protect you now, and if one of those animals ever comes near you, I'll kill him with my bare hands!"

Meadow stared up at her brother, unable to speak or to think beyond the agony that was tearing her into a million little pieces inside. The joy she was feeling from knowing that Black Horse was alive was over-powered by the painful knowledge that he now hated her as much as—or more than—he had once loved her. She dutifully allowed her brother to lead her down the steps and help her mount her horse. The thoughts in her pounding head were jumbled with indecision and confusion. How could she leave Fort Keogh now, knowing that Black Horse was a prisoner here?

Still, she was rational enough to think about how foolish it would be for her to refuse to go with her brother, so Meadow took the reins when Robert handed them to her. She stared in the direction where she had last seen Black Horse. She had to figure out a way to get back here soon, and she had to prove to Black Horse that she had not deserted her adoptive people as he had once predicted. She had to show him how much she still loved him, and then she would spend the rest of her life proving it.

Black Horse had lost track of time. Some days he didn't care whether he lived or died. But now, every-thing mattered again.

For months the idea of seeing his green-eyed woman again was the only thing that had kept him going. Now that he had actually seen her and knew what a liar and a traitor she was, he had a different reason to live—to get out of here and tell Meadow how much he loathed her.

He slid down to the ground, leaned his head back against the dirt walls of his cell and closed his eyes in an effort to wipe away her image, that of a white woman through and through. His hand contracted into a tight fist. If he had the strength he would beat something. He thought about the times she had told him about her never-ending devotion to the Sioux, and he had believed every word of it. His heart felt as though a stone-edged lance had just ripped through it. Her lies hurt worse than any of the pain they had ever inflicted on him in this white man's prison.

Chapter Twenty-one

Meadow had thought that leaving the Sioux village was difficult. But that did not even begin to compare to the agony of leaving Black Horse behind at the fort.

She had no idea how far it was to Fort Custer, but she knew she had to make a plan before they had gone too far. Forcing herself out of the shocked trance she had been in since seeing Black Horse, Meadow began to focus on her surroundings. There would be no chance for her to sneak away from Robert and the other two men until they camped for the night. She had to be very certain that she would be heading back in the right direction.

But then what? She could hardly ride right back into Fort Keogh and break Black Horse out of the stronghold without help. For now, she just had to focus on the countryside and the tracking tricks she had learned from White Buffalo.

This part of northern Montana was mostly rolling hills and wide-open prairie. Meadow hoped that making her way through the dark would not be too difficult. Traveling alone was becoming all too familiar, and she had learned that it was far more dangerous than it was exciting. Soon she hoped that she would be riding at Black Horse's side, and then she would never ride alone again.

Spring was rapidly turning into summer, and the air grew hot by midday. Meadow was miserable in the heavy riding skirt and long-sleeved blouse she was wearing. Thank goodness for the black flat-brimmed hat that she had brought with her to shield the sun from her eyes and skin. After spending so much time indoors, she had noticed that her pale skin burned more easily when she was out in the sun.

Robert seemed obsessed with getting back to Fort Custer as soon as possible and pressed the horses and the riders to their limits. They stopped to water the horses several times during the day and only once to eat a quick meal of canned beans and corn bread. The great distance they had covered in just one day was disheartening to Meadow; she would have to ride all night without stopping to get back to Fort Keogh. She just hoped that both she and her horse were able to make the journey.

To her relief, Robert decided to call it a day just as the sun was beginning to set in the western sky. As she helped the men heat up a simple dinner of biscuits and stew that they had brought from last night's dinner at Fort Keogh, Meadow meticulously planned her escape. For the first time since they had met, Robert's mood seemed to mellow, and as they sat around the campfire sipping coffee after dinner, Meadow caught him watching her intently.

When he noticed she was staring back at him, Robert shook his head and smiled. "I just can't get over how much you look like Mother," he said, still shaking his head.

"Tell me something about her—and Father and all the others, too," Meadow asked in a soft voice, knowing that this would probably be the only chance she would ever have to learn about any of them. She leaned forward so that she could see her brother's face more clearly in the flickering firelight. He had removed his gray army hat, and his blond, wavy hair hung softly over the side of his forehead. His thin face was accented by a straight nose and full mouth. There was a barely noticeable stubble of light-colored growth on his chin and above his upper lip. As she watched him reclining back against his bedroll with his long muscled legs stretched out in front of him, she realized her brother was a very handsome man.

"And how about telling me something about you, too. Is there a wife, children?" she asked.

This brought another smile to Robert's usually stern expression. "Nope, neither. I guess you could say I'm married to my career." Noticing the confused look on his sister's face, Robert quickly added, "I mean that I've just never gotten around to looking for a wife, I guess. How about you—?" He stopped and clenched his jaw.

His abrupt change of attitude reminded Meadow of his intense hatred of the Sioux and that she had to be careful what she said around him. To her relief, Robert changed the subject back to their parents and siblings.

"I really wish you could have known our parents, Mary. They were such good people—proud, too. I don't think Dad ever missed a day of work in his entire life when we were back East. He owned a livery stable outside of Boston, and he worked hard to make ends meet so that none of us would ever want for anything." A faraway expression settled on Robert's face as he continued. "We didn't live high on the hog or anything, but we sure ate good, and we had nice clothes to wear to school. I never once felt deprived."

In her mind, Meadow could see the man her brother spoke of as clearly as if she had always known him: a proud, strong adventurer who had thrown caution to the wind to carve out a new life for his family in the Wild West. How tragic that his dream had ended so horribly. Meadow pushed the thoughts of her family's deaths to the back of her mind. She was not ready to think about any of those things, yet.

"What was our mother like?" Meadow asked as she scooted closer to Robert.

Robert smiled again. "Mother," he said slowly. "Mom was so beautiful—just like you. She was just a tiny thing, too, like you," he added as he pointed his finger teasingly at her. "And she could cook like nobody's business. I remember Sunday dinners after church. . . ." Robert closed his eyes, envisioning those happy family times so long ago.

"There'd be fried chicken, mashed taters, this thick white gravy and the best biscuits you ever ate." He motioned toward the leftover biscuits from dinner. "Those are like eatin' rocks compared to Ma's biscuits. Randy, one of our brothers, could pack away a dozen or more at one sitting. And then she would bring out the most perfect apple pie or this dark chocolate cake with sweet brown frosting." Robert paused as his face took on a look of joy.

Meadow stared at the man before her, amazed at the way he had transformed into a little boy right before her eyes as he talked about his cherished childhood memories—memories that seemed so foreign to her. It was almost inconceivable that she had once been part of the life he spoke of now.

Robert laughed as he recalled one incident from the past. "I remember once when you were just a baby, maybe no more than a year old or so. Ma had set one of those delicious cakes down on the picnic table where you had been tied into this tall chair so that you wouldn't fall out. She didn't realize that she had put that darn cake within your reach, and the next thing we knew, you had both your chubby little paws right in the middle of that cake. Before Ma could move it away, you had chocolate cake and frosting smeared all over your face and in that wild mass of curly blonde hair that you used to have." Robert chuckled with the memory.

Meadow joined in his laughter as she envisioned a little girl covered in chocolate. The image of her as a happy toddler surrounded by her mother, father and siblings was so new to Meadow, yet it was becoming easier for her to picture in her mind. A feeling of sadness suddenly intruded into Meadow's merriment as her laughter began to fade. Thinking about her real family somehow made her feel like a traitor to her adoptive Indian family.

"Mary, is something wrong?" Robert asked as he noticed the change in her attitude. When she shrugged in response to his question and avoided looking directly at him, he continued, "I suppose it is hard to hear about a life and a family that you don't remember, but Mary, that is why it is so important for you to realize just how much was stolen from you because of those savages."

Once again, Meadow heard the hatred in his voice

and saw in his face just how deeply he had been affected by the past. She swallowed hard and tried to imagine just how drastically Robert's life must have changed after the attack on their wagon train. Everything and everyone involved in the life he had led up to that point vanished that one tragic day.

Meadow reached out and tenderly wrapped her hands around one of her brother's clenched fists. His hand instantly began to relax in hers as their gazes met. Meadow saw a smile softly touch the corners of his lips once again, and instinctively she smiled back. Inside, her heart felt as if it were being torn apart. She knew the kinship they had just discovered would be short-lived, because once her brother discovered that she had returned to the Sioux to be with the man she loved with all of her heart, he would hate her as much as he hated all Indians.

"Robert," Meadow said in a gentle voice. "Until a few days ago, I did not know of your existence. And because I was so young when I was taken by the Sioux, I never knew of the life I had lived with my real family. The Sioux couple who took me into their home treated me as if I was their own daughter and raised me with kindness and love." Meadow felt Robert's hand begin to tighten back into a fist and she knew her next words had to be chosen with great care. "Hearing you talk about our parents and siblings adds a whole new perspective to everything I've ever known and makes me feel so sorry that I don't have the sweet memories of those days when we were all together."

Robert exhaled heavily and slowly pulled his hand away from Meadow's grip. "I realize that you had no other choice but to become a part of the tribe that kidnapped you." He leaned forward again, yet refrained from taking her hand again. "But what I don't understand is—now that you know what happened to us—how you can still have any compassion for those heathens."

The tone of his voice held no sympathy, and it caused a sinking feeling to work its way through Meadow's body. She knew she could never hope to make him understand her devotion to her adoptive people or her overpowering love for Black Horse. "I feel torn between two different worlds, and I don't know how I am supposed to feel anymore. In my heart"—she raised her hand to her chest as she talked—"I am so sad for all the memories I do not have of you and the rest of our family, and I know that there is nothing that will ever fill that deep hole of sadness. But the memories I do have are of being loved and protected and—"

"Stop it!" Robert cut in sharply. He threw his hands over his ears in a childish gesture. As he rose up to his feet, he added, "I never want to hear you talk about those animals again. The years you spent with them are in the past, and from now on all that matters is wiping those memories away completely." The anger in his voice faded slightly as he added, "I will help you to forget. Now, let's get some shut-eye so that we can head out at first light."

Meadow attempted to keep the trembling out of her voice as she said, "Good night, Robert, and thank you for never giving up on me."

The sunlight had almost faded completely away, and only the small glow from the campfire lit the area, but Meadow could see the tender expression that touched her brother's face before he turned away. Meadow pulled her legs up against her body and hugged them closely in her arms as she watched the last of the flames sink into the glowing orange embers in the circle of rocks.

Today had been a day of such contrasts, partly filled with overwhelming joy at seeing that Black Horse was still alive, yet also with such deep sorrow because of the way he had looked at her. Then, hearing about events of her distant past had evoked a deep sense of melancholy. In many ways it was easier to not know anything about the life she had once lived among her real family.

The dying embers began to blur before Meadow's eyes, and for a brief instant she allowed her lids to close down over her pupils. As it had been almost every night since last fall, the pictures in her subconscious mind were once again filled with only one face and one memory—Black Horse. Meadow's entire body still yearned for Black Horse's touch, and there was not one minute detail of their one night of lovemaking that she could not recall.

Finally, she was forced to open her eyes and face the fact that she had only been dreaming—again. How could it feel so real? Her skin was still tingling with the imagined feel of Black Horse's embraces, and her lips felt as if they were pulsating from his demanding kisses. The urgency that filled her was mixed with fear and excitement, now that she knew these feelings would be a reality again soon. The cold look on Black Horse's face this morning passed before her eyes, and she blinked rapidly to wipe the image away. She would prove her love to him once she had figured out a way to get him away from Fort Keogh.

The silence surrounding her made Meadow aware that she was the only one still awake. Her brother and the two soldiers accompanying them were all snoring softly in their bedrolls. Meadow made her way to her own bedroll as quietly as possible and then rolled an extra blanket up and stuffed it into the center of the flat bedroll. She attempted to make the blanket look like a body, but it was a hopeless task. The best she could hope for was that none of the men would wake up before morning and discover that she was no longer here. As she rose up to her feet again, Meadow looked longingly at the bedroll with the little lump in the middle of it. How she wished she could take the heavy blanket and the bedroll with her for the nights she would be sleeping on the hard ground until she was back in the soft furs of her and Black Horse's tepee. At least she still had her white blanket to ward off the cold. She grabbed several biscuits that were left over from dinner and remembered the story Robert had told her about their mother's biscuits. She glanced back in his direction one last time and blinked back tears.

The horses had been hobbled a short distance from the campsite, and to Meadow's relief they did not whinny or startle when she approached them. It was easy to lead the palomino she had ridden earlier today away from the others after she had untied him from the stake in the ground.

She led the horse away from the camp and did not attempt to put a halter on him or mount him until she was at least a quarter mile from the camp. Then, she swung up onto his bare back and gently nudged him in the sides with her knees. The horse fell into an easy gait, and before long, Meadow felt confident that she had made a clean getaway. There was only a half-circle moon overhead, but it provided enough light to guide the horse and rider along their way, and they only stopped occasionally in the night to rest or get a drink of water when they encountered a pond or stream.

Meadow's plan was simple. Somehow she would break Black Horse out of Fort Keogh. The details were just not clear to her, yet. But as the first gray haze of dawn broke over the eastern horizon while she paused to allow the horse to drink out of a trickling creek, it came to her. She knew now what she had to do and where she must go.

Chapter Twenty-two

Meadow had lost track of how long she had been traveling as the days and nights faded together. The summer heat consumed what little energy she had left, and the lonely nights had almost drained her of the will to go on. But her dream was strong enough to push her forward.

She had not observed anyone following her. When Robert had discovered that she was gone, Meadow was certain that he had been so filled with disgust that he had probably disowned her on the spot. She was grateful to him for the chance to learn about her real family, but it did not change her destiny. Her future had been determined on that autumn day over fifteen years ago.

Although Meadow was sure she was not lost and was still traveling in the right direction, there were times when she became disoriented. The dense forests would always seem strange to her, but they offered camouflage and shelter, and she remained confident that she could find the Sioux encampment once again.

By the fourth day, Meadow was beginning to think she might starve to death if she didn't reach the village soon. She had eaten nothing more than the few hard biscuits she had taken, and they were already gone.

Her confidence in her fishing skills diminished the moment she attempted to catch a trout out of a creek teeming with fish. After numerous attempts, she never even came close to touching one of the slippery little devils, let alone actually catching one with her bare hands. She had seen many rabbits and a few white-tailed deer, but without any sort of a weapon other than a branch, it was useless to attempt to chase after them. Meadow constantly made mental notes of the necessities she would need to pack on her return trip to Fort Keogh. Of course, it was not her plan to travel alone on her next trip.

Exhausted, starving and feeling as if she would never again see her dearly beloved Sioux village again, Meadow knew that *Wakan Tanka* must be watching over her when she scented campfire smoke. For most of the day, she had thought that this portion of forest seemed familiar, but at other times, all of the country-side looked the same.

The smell of smoke guided Meadow back to her adoptive people by late afternoon. As she dug into a hearty meal of Sings Like Sparrow's pheasant stew, she began to tell them all what she had seen at Fort Keogh.

"Are you certain it was him?" Walks Tall asked in a skeptical tone. "Were you even close enough to see his face?"

She nodded her head vigorously. "I was close enough to reach out and touch him. Without a doubt, it was Black Horse. He looked ill. He needs our help soon, before it's too late." Walks Tall stared at Meadow's face as he contemplated this unexpected news. "I thought it was already too late for my blood brother, but if he is still alive, I will do everything in my power to help him."

Meadow exhaled with relief. "We must have a good plan. The prisoners at Fort Keogh are so well guarded that in the time I had spent there, I never even glimpsed any of them until that last day, as I was leaving. It was just as the sun was rising, so I would guess that they are only allowed out of the barricade briefly when everyone else is still sleeping."

Walks Tall rubbed his chin thoughtfully. "That is when we will plan to break him out. We just have to figure out a way to get into the fort without being noticed." He looked at Meadow. "But you know the layout of the fort. That should be all the information we will need."

His familiar smile warmed Meadow's heart and a wide smile parted her lips as their gazes met. "The entire time I was there, I was trying to figure out a way to get in to see who was in that barricade. I know exactly where it is located." The Sioux words rolled easily from her mouth again.

The soft deer-hide dress she wore had never felt so good against her skin, and her feet were still celebrating their return to the comfortable moccasins. Two short braids hung over her shoulders, tied with long strips of leather. A black headband encircled her head. But of all the things she was grateful for again, the most important was the way she had been accepted back into the tribe. Even Sitting Bull had taken the time to stop by Sings Like Sparrow and Gentle Water's tepee to welcome her back to the village. The great chief had said that her time with the whites had given her a chance to find where her true heart was, and now that she had chosen to return to the tribe, they would never ask her to make that choice again. It was at that moment she knew she had returned for good.

As they sat around the campfire digesting their meal, Meadow and Walks Tall continued to discuss a way to get into Fort Keogh. Gentle Water had taken her grandmother in to get ready for bed, and as she exited the tepee, Meadow noticed that she smiled shyly at Walks Tall and then quickly looked away when he smiled back at her.

Meadow glanced back and forth between her friend and Walks Tall, but they would not look at one another again, and they both avoided looking in her direction, too. After an uneasy silence, Meadow spoke. "When Walks Tall and I return from Fort Keogh with Black Horse, maybe we will finally have that long overdue wedding."

"Maybe two weddings," Walks Tall blurted out. He glanced at Gentle Water's confused expression, sure that she had not caught on to what he had just implied. Meadow, however, was giggling like a little girl as her gaze once again flitted back and forth from the warrior to her friend.

"Yes, two weddings is twice the celebration, and our people need to celebrate as much as possible," Meadow said. She draped her arm around Gentle Water and hugged her, even though it was apparent that the other girl was still trying to decipher Walks Tall's unexpected comment.

"Well, first we need to get Black Horse out of that fort," Walks Tall said, returning to the important task awaiting them. He was almost afraid to believe that his lifelong friend was really still alive. He had no doubt of Meadow's undying love for the chief, and he knew that she would do anything to be with him again, but she was not a crazy woman who would make up visions in her head. No, he had been wrong about Black Horse's death, and he would be eternally grateful that he had been mistaken.

"I want to help," Gentle Water offered. She entwined her arm through Meadow's arm and glanced at Walks Tall out of the side of her eye. "I am going with you when you go to the fort to get Black Horse."

Walks Tall violently shook his head. "No, one woman to take care of is more than enough," he stated.

Meadow tossed her head back indignantly. "I think I have proven that I can take care of myself," she retorted as she cast a narrow-eyed glance at Walks Tall.

He shrugged and nodded his head in agreement. "This is true. You have traveled alone farther than some warriors have, and you have survived much sorrow in your life, yet you do not lose the strength to go on. In some ways you are almost as strong as any man."

"Thank you," she said. She had traveled many, many miles alone, endured the wilderness and all its dangers, as well as taken more chances than most men would dare. But, more importantly, her journeys had made her strong in body and mind. She knew now that she was capable of living and loving life to its full extent, and she hoped that she could use the knowledge she had learned from her experiences to help her adoptive people in some way.

She thought about White Buffalo's medicine pouches that she still possessed. The Blackfoot woman, Bear Woman, had been a medicine *woman*. Meadow wondered if she might be able to train herself to tend to the medicinal needs of her people. In spite of her father's refusal to teach her his healing skills, she had managed to learn a few of his secrets when he mixed his potent medicines. Maybe this was a way that she could show everyone that she was a worthy member of the tribe. She was thinking of discussing this exciting possibility with Black Horse when they were together again, when Walks Tall interrupted her thoughts.

"I was going to the river to fetch water." He smiled at Gentle Water and added, "Would you care to join me?"

Gentle Water giggled and shook her head enthusiastically. "I think my grandmother needs water for the morning, too." She smiled at Meadow as she rushed to join the warrior. "I will talk to you later." She paused and leaned down to kiss Meadow's cheek as she passed by her. "I will thank *Wakan Tanka* every day that you have returned to us," she said softly.

This was as it was meant to be, Meadow decided as she watched Gentle Water and Walks Tall disappear into the darkening forest along the same path that she had followed on more than one occasion to see Black Horse. A poignant smile touched her lips. The river was providing them with many treasured memories.

Meadow took her time before retiring to the tepee she was once again sharing with Gentle Water and Sings Like Sparrow. "Thank you, *Wakan Tanka*," she whispered as she glanced up at the sky.

"*Wakan Tanka* listens," Sings Like Sparrow said as she exited from the tepee. She was carrying an elk hide that she had been working on ever since the past winter. The hide was tanned to a soft golden color and was ready to be cut and sewn into clothing. "I couldn't sleep, so I figured I might as well make use of the time."

"That would make a beautiful wedding dress," Meadow said, clasping her hands behind her back and smiling slyly.

"Do you have anyone's wedding in mind?" Sings Like Sparrow asked with a coy smile on her cracked lips.

"Yes. Gentle Water and Walks Tall."

Sings Like Sparrow stopped abruptly, nearing dropping the hide she carried. "Is this true?"

Meadow nodded her head. "Yes, I think it will happen soon. Even as we speak they are getting acquainted with one another down by the river."

Sings Like Sparrow drew in a deep breath. "They are alone?" She gave her head a casual toss and shrugged her bony shoulders. "Oh, it does not matter. Gentle Water is a good girl, and she deserves a good man like Walks Tall. I had suspected that they were flirting behind my back, but I did not mind. He will be a good provider, and then I will not have to worry about who will take care of my granddaughter when I am gone."

Meadow put her arm around the older woman. "You will be around for a long time." Warmth spread through Meadow when the older woman looked up at her and smiled as she squeezed Meadow's arm with her wrinkled old hand. "Come, help me cut the rough edges from this hide," Sings Like Sparrow ordered, although her voice was slightly shaky with emotion. "Walks Tall is a very good man," she stated once more as she began to spread the hide out on a blanket that she had already laid on the ground.

The two women worked quietly side by side by the firelight until Walks Tall and Gentle Water reappeared some time later. Meadow smiled at her friend as they approached, and immediately noticed that Gentle Water's hair was slightly mussed and several tiny tree twigs clung to her ebony braids. Walks Tall's long hair sported similar adornments. Meadow attempted to motion to her friend so that she could pull the twigs out of her hair before her grandmother noticed, but it was too late.

"A man who takes a woman down into the grass had better make sure he also plans to make that woman his wife, especially if her grandmother has a bigger stick than the ones poking out of your hair."

Meadow stifled a giggle when she noticed the horrified expressions on both Gentle Water's and Walks Tall's faces.

"I—I plan t-to," Walks Tall stammered as his frantic gaze slid back and forth between Gentle Water and her grandmother. "But not until my blood brother, Black Horse, is here, so that we all may celebrate together." He smiled and nodded his head toward Meadow. "We will all begin new lives then."

"That will be a joyous occasion," Sings Like Sparrow agreed. Smiling, she turned her attention back to the hide she was working on. Her gnarled fingers worked with renewed vigor as her knife cut through the heavy skin.

Walks Tall motioned for Meadow to walk with him and Gentle Water, so she quickly excused herself from helping Sings Like Sparrow and joined the two of them.

"We will leave for Fort Keogh tomorrow at first

light," Walks Tall announced as soon as Meadow walked up to them. "Take only what you need. We will travel light and fast."

"I'll be ready," Meadow answered without hesitation. "All I need is Black Horse."

Walks Tall nodded in agreement. "There will be many warriors going with us to fight the soldiers if necessary, but only you and I will go into the fort. If you still have any of the clothes of a white woman, take them with you."

Meadow nodded, but did not ask Walks Tall the details of his plan. They would have plenty of time while they rode to the fort to discuss the way they would break Black Horse out of prison.

Meadow shivered when she recalled the way Black Horse had looked at her the last time she had seen him. Wrapping her arms tightly around herself, she struggled to remember the way he had looked at her on the night that they had made love for the first time. Warmth immediately replaced the cold in her body and gave her the strength that she knew she would need when the sun rose up in the sky tomorrow morning.

Chapter Twenty-three

Fort Keogh looked as forbidding to Meadow today as it had on the first day that she had arrived here from Fort Walsh with the American soldiers. But now, everything was different. The knowledge that Black Horse was alive and present, however, gave her hope.

"Are you ready?" Walks Tall asked. His approving gaze traveled over her strange costume.

Since she considered the clothes that white women wore to be pure torture, the only clothes she had kept from her brief stay at the fort were a pair of men's trousers, an old floppy hat and a baggy coat. Even if she did look quite odd in the oversized getup, it did not disguise her identity completely. Her wavy blonde hair had grown out enough so that it now cascaded over her shoulders, and not even the limp brim of the hat could conceal the delicate features of her face. But they were not worried about hiding her identity anyway.

Finding a costume that concealed Walks Tall's identity, however, had proved to be a real challenge. He had found some old clothes among the numerous souvenirs that the Indians had saved from past battles. But the pants and shirt were far too small for Walks Tall's towering frame. Finally, it had been decided that Walks Tall would be easier to disguise if they forwent the white man's clothes for a Mexican costume. Someone located a battered old sombrero and a white serape, and long-legged pants completed his outfit. Now, they had donned their costumes for the final play.

"Are you sure you can do this?"

"*Sha*, I would do anything for him," Meadow answered as she gazed at the buildings scattered in the distance. The torture that he was suffering behind those dark walls gave her the courage to scale the highest mountain or face the darkest demons. "It's time," she stated calmly.

Walks Tall's long form straightened atop his horse. This tiny woman was as brave as any warrior he had ever known, and her endless love for his friend made him believe that there really could be a happy future for all of them. He nodded his head and waved for her to move ahead of him. They tied the horses in a small grove of cottonwood close by the front gate and walked the rest of the way. They had decided to enter the fort under the cover of darkness rather than waiting until daybreak.

At this late hour, Meadow knew that the only soldiers milling about would be the sentries at the front gate and the guard watching the barricade that housed the prisoners. She hoped she could gain entrance once they recognized who she was from her previous stay here. If this far-fetched plan worked, Meadow would attempt to distract the guards while Walks Tall sneaked into the fort. Then, they had to figure out a way to get into the prison to get to Black Horse. Since they had no other plan in place, Meadow could only hope that they would be able to work out the rest of the details once they were inside.

"Halt, there," called out a voice as Meadow approached the entrance to the fort. "State your name and business."

"It's Mary—M-Mary McBain." Her white name still sounded strange to her ears. She stepped closer. "I was staying here until a short time ago when my brother came to pick me up to take me to Fort Custer."

The guard leaned down from his perch to get a closer look at her. "What are you doing back here?"

Meadow attempted to divert the guard's attention by moving to the opposite side of the entrance so that he was forced to turn around to look at her. "It's a l-long story. My brother and I, we were separated from one another, and I was able to s-somehow find my way back here."

The guard hesitated long enough to make Meadow's knees begin to shake. He didn't believe her!

"You were lucky to get back here all alone—and on foot, too!" the soldier finally answered. He rested his rifle against the rail and climbed down the ladder to where Meadow waited. She held her breath as she tried not to give away Walks Tall's hiding place at the side of the entrance.

"What in the devil happened, and where's your brother?"

Meadow swallowed the heavy lump in her throat. "Oh, it's—it's so hard for me to talk about and I really could use some water. I've been wandering around out there in the wilderness for several days now."

The soldier nodded his head. "Of course. Do you need assistance?" He extended his arm for Meadow to lean against.

"Oh, thank you," Meadow said as she let the soldier

help her. She leaned heavily against him as if she were too frail to stand on her own. "It's a good thing I'm finally here, because I don't think I could have made it much farther." Meadow could see the concern in the soldier's face, and she sighed with relief as he began to lead her through the gate without so much as a glance back over his shoulder at the tall man who sneaked silently into the fort behind them.

Once Meadow felt confident that Walks Tall was out of sight, she straightened up and took in a deep breath. "I'm feeling so much stronger now that I know I'm safe. Please, you go back to your post. I can make it to the captain's quarters on my own. I'll tell him everything that happened to me and my brother."

"Are you certain that you're all right?"

Meadow shrugged off his apparent concern. She had other things on her mind now. "Yes, th-thank you so much for your help, but I don't want to get you in trouble."

The young soldier glanced back over at his post and nodded his head in agreement. "I suppose I shouldn't be gone too long. If anyone tried to sneak in while I was on duty, I'd be doing dishes for the mess hall for the rest of my life."

The soldier chuckled. Meadow fleetingly remembered Brandon Cornett saying almost those exact words to her once. "I'll tell the captain how helpful you were," she said as she quickly turned away and headed in the direction she knew the soldier expected her to go. The instant he was climbing back up to his post, Meadow rushed toward the area where she planned to meet up with Walks Tall.

"I was worried you would not be able to get away from him," Walks Tall whispered as he clasped Meadow's arm. They huddled together as they sneaked behind each building and inched closer to the prisoner's barricade.

"That was the easy part. What do we do now?" Meadow's worried gaze moved toward the dark building where she knew the prisoners were kept. On this quiet night, there was only one guard leaning against the door, and it appeared that he was not paying too much attention.

"Only one guard?" Walks Tall whispered. "That looks too easy." He glanced around nervously. Other than the one lonely soldier, there did not appear to be any one else in the area. "Can you distract him as easily as you did the first one?"

"He is all that stands between me and Black Horse," she sighed. "That soldier doesn't have a chance."

The darkness hid Walks Tall's smile as he nudged Meadow forward. He rarely put himself in a bad situation unless he knew that he had a comrade to cover his back; he was confident that this woman would not disappoint him.

Meadow approached the guardhouse as if she knew exactly what she was doing. But, inwardly, she was trembling like a leaf in a windstorm. Every step that took her closer to her man also brought more danger to all of them. Her legs felt as heavy as lead, and it wasn't until she gasped for air that she realized that she had also been holding her breath. The guard looked up just as she drew near.

"Sorry to startle you," Meadow said without a trace

of the terror she felt inside. "I just needed a breath of fresh air and thought a walk around the fort would help me to sleep better."

The soldier slowly lowered his gun. He squinted as he sought to focus on the woman standing directly in front of him. "Are you staying here at the fort?" he asked as he lifted up the kerosene lantern that was sitting on a chair beside the door.

"I'm Mary McBain," Meadow said as she extended her hand in a friendly gesture and stepped closer to the soldier.

He sat the lantern back down, along with the rifle he had been holding, and took another step toward her. He never got any farther.

Meadow threw her hand across her mouth to keep from crying out when Walks Tall rushed out from the shadows and hit the soldier in the back of his head with the butt of his gun. The sickening thud against the man's skull made Meadow's stomach feel as if it had just twisted inside out, and when he crumpled to the ground, his limp form reminded her of a rag doll that White Buffalo had given to her when she was a child. As Walks Tall dragged the soldier around the corner of the barricade where he would not be seen, Meadow remained unmoving and numb.

"Let's go," Walks Tall commanded as he proudly held up a key he had taken off the unconscious guard, then grabbed Meadow's arm and led her down the narrow stairs that led into the dimly lit barricade.

The smell of feces, urine and spoiled food assaulted Meadow's nostrils, and she had to throw her hand over her nose and mouth again, but this time it was to keep from gagging. Please, please, let Black Horse be all right, she prayed as they made their way down the stairs and to the back of the dirty, foul-smelling basement. The uneven sounds of the prisoners fitfully sleeping could be heard as they reached the cell area. Lanterns hung sparsely along the walls, barely providing enough light for Meadow to make out the forms of the men lying on the floor.

She frantically searched among the dark shapes, looking for anything that would distinguish Black Horse from the other men. Then, even though the light was so poor, her gaze locked with the pair of dark eyes that seemed to be staring straight through her.

Unlike the other men, Black Horse was not sleeping. He was sitting against the back wall with his knees pulled up under his chin and his arms wrapped tightly around his legs. When Meadow realized that he was staring directly at her, it was all she could do not to cry out to him. Instead, she quietly leaned up against the steel bars and held her hand out toward him. For several seconds, he remained unmoving as if he was in a trance and didn't believe what he was actually seeing. When Walks Tall stepped up beside her, however, Meadow could tell that Black Horse finally realized they were more than just a vision in his mind. He slowly rose to his feet and did not speak as he carefully stepped over his two cellmates. Nor did he make a sound when he approached the bars where Meadow's outstretched hand waited for him.

Without acknowledging Meadow's presence or her waiting hand, Black Horse looked at his friend and nodded his head slowly. Meadow observed the silent gesture and gradually pulled her hand back against her breast. She forced herself to turn away before she cried out for Black Horse's forgiveness and got them all killed with her foolishness. No one else in the prison even seemed aware of their daring escapade so far, and Meadow knew that she could not let Black Horse's rejection affect her now. When they were safe again, she would find a way to convince him of her love, and then he would remember his love for her . . . she was *almost* certain.

Walks Tall wasted no time inserting the key into the lock on the cell, but the clanging of the key ring against the metal bars made a loud noise that seemed to echo throughout the building. He grabbed the dangling ring, but the damage had already been done. Men in every one of the cells began to stir and awaken.

The panic that had only been a threat to Meadow's sanity before was now raging out of control. She threw her shaking hand over Walks Tall's hand in an effort to aid him in opening the cell door, but he was already pulling the barrier open. Black Horse was out of the cell, and Walks Tall was pushing Meadow back along the corridor before she even realized what was happening.

"Are we just leaving the others behind?" Meadow whispered as they ran toward the front door.

"I left the keys," Walks Tall answered. "We can't take the time or we will all be dead."

"We need to be out of the fort before the soldiers realize what is happening," Black Horse added.

At the front doorway of the barricade, the trio paused while Walks Tall inched out into the open. When he motioned for the others to follow, Meadow felt Black Horse's hand clasp her upper arm tightly as he led her out of the rank-smelling building. The sounds of the other prisoners breaking out of their cells grew louder with each passing second. As they ran across the dark courtyard, Meadow's fear threatened to consume her. She could not feel her feet touch the ground, nor could she focus on any of her surroundings as they raced toward the front entrance. It was impossible to imagine they would get out of the fort without being shot or captured.

She did not have long to wonder how they would get past the guard at the front gate, because before she realized it, they were being ordered to stop.

"What's going on here?" The guard stepped forward with his rifle pointed directly at Black Horse's chest.

Meadow felt her entire body go numb as she stared at the gun that threatened to end his life. Walks Tall, however, was still standing in the shadows where the guard had not yet seen him. He jumped from the side of the opening and knocked the guard unconscious so quickly that Meadow barely had time to do more than gasp before Walks Tall grabbed her by an arm and dragged her out through the front gate. She glanced over her shoulder and saw Black Horse limping behind them as fast as his weakened legs would carry him.

As they left the fort behind them, Meadow could hear loud noises, but nothing was coherent. She didn't even realize that they had reached the horses until she was being thrown onto the back of the horse that she had been riding earlier and Black Horse climbed up behind her. She felt his arms close around her and his legs grip her hips between them. It didn't matter that the entire fort was probably chasing after them, because for the first time in a very long time, she felt safe.

Once they met up with the rest of the warriors that waited in the trees beyond the fort, Meadow expected Black Horse to get on one of the extra horses they had brought along, but he made no effort to switch mounts. They continued to ride and stopped only to water the horses and themselves, and were always, always looking over their shoulders and listening for the sounds that would signal approaching danger. Although she hadn't realized it at the time, the unexpected chaos that followed the dangerous prison break had aided their escape. She shuddered to think about what had happened to the rest of the prisoners when they ran out into the open and met with the soldiers and their deadly weapons. Meadow had heard many rounds of gunfire before her party had ridden out of earshot, and she was certain that all the rest of the prisoners had met with a tragic end. She tried not to dwell on the men they had left behind. Instead, she concentrated on the fact that Black Horse was alive. He was sitting right behind her, and they were headed home at last.

She desperately waited for him to speak, but he barely even acknowledged her presence, even though they were molded intimately together on the back of the horse as they rode through the darkness. Several times, Meadow had felt his hold on her grow slack, and she had feared that he was going to lose consciousness and fall off the horse. She had asked him repeatedly if he was well, but his only reply had been a quick grunt. She tightened her grasp on his arms where they encircled her waist, and each time, to her relief, she felt him straighten up again. Still, he was growing weaker with every passing mile.

As the first streak of daylight broke through a starless sky, they reached an area where a hillside harbored a small cave. Meadow slid to the ground and grabbed the pack tied to the back of the horse and then reached up to help Black Horse down. He refused her help as he eased down to the ground. She opened her mouth to speak.

"No, not now," Black Horse said in a tired voice.

She nodded her head. The pained expression on his face told her that now was not the time to try to talk to him. In the growing daylight, his poor condition was more evident than ever. The sight of his face—swollen and discolored, it was obvious, by beatings—made her knees weak and her stomach twist. There was hardly an inch of his body that did not appear to be black and blue, but the dirt that covered his skin made it difficult to determine the severity of his injuries. Though he was coated with filth from the white man's prison, Meadow could tell how thin his frame had become. She would nurse him back to health, and as she never planned to leave his side again, he would have no choice but to listen to her reasons for being at Fort Keogh with the white soldiers. She would make him understand—somehow! She only hoped that the wound of the betrayal he believed she had committed would heal faster than his other injuries.

"There are no animals or snakes," Walks Tall announced after he checked the interior of the cave. He reached out to help Black Horse enter the cave, and when he glanced at Meadow, he gave her a reassuring grin.

"The others and I will take care of the horses and find a place to hide them," Walks Tall said.

"I'll try to make him as comfortable as possible," Meadow said as she bent down to enter the small opening at the mouth of the cave behind Black Horse. The inside of the cave was small, only about six feet wide and maybe double that in length, and not high enough for even Meadow to stand up straight. Black Horse hunched down and made his way to the back of the cave. He said nothing as Meadow spread out the fur blanket that she had in her pack. The heavy sigh he gave was the only sound he made as he laid back. There was enough light coming through the cave entry that she could see that his eyes were already closed. She took one of the medicine pouches out of her pack and removed a soft cloth. She dampened it with water from her flask and gently began to wipe the dirt from his upper body. Afterward, she carefully packed the cuts that she could see on his chest and stomach with a mixture of the herbs and powders that were in the bag. She noticed that there was a deep scar on his left shoulder, only inches from his heart, and it did not match the old scars that had been made during the Sun Dance Ceremony when he was inducted into manhood. This scar was from a much more recent wound. Meadow wondered if this was where the soldiers had shot him when he had been captured. She rubbed a tiny bit of bear grease on the scar. He slept through the entire process.

With a weary moan, she leaned against the hard wall of the cave as she listened to him sleep. She had so many things to tell him, but would he even want to hear them?

"You should try to rest, too," Walks Tall said as he ducked into the cave opening. "We have plenty of men to keep watch."

"Do you think they followed us?" Meadow asked.

He shrugged. "Maybe, but they had prisoners going every direction at the fort." He shrugged again. "Even if they did come, they will not catch us before we cross over into Canada. The American soldiers cannot follow us there."

The confidence in his voice gave Meadow a very small amount of hope that there was a chance that they could find some sort of peace, once they returned to their village. Then, Walks Tall spoke again.

"We are not going to travel far into Canada. Only far enough to make sure the American soldiers have given up on catching us."

"Where will we go?" Meadow glanced down at Black Horse. "He needs time to heal."

"He will get it, but not in Canada, and not at the Sioux village. After Black Horse's escape from the prison, the Americans will ask the Canada soldiers to help them bring him back for punishment. We will put the entire village in danger if we are anywhere near there." Walks Tall sat down at the front of the cave opening where he could see the landscape below. "We will be staying here in Montana until he is better. There is a small band of Oglala Sioux in the mountains that we will join for a while, and eventually we will travel back to our homelands in the Dakota Territory," he added.

"We can't," Meadow gasped. "It's too dangerous."

"There is no place that is safe for our people anymore, but at least here we have a chance for survival. In Canada, we do nothing but wait to starve to death or die of disease." He looked at his sleeping friend. "That is not an acceptable death for men like us."

Meadow knew there was no use arguing with him. His mind was made up, and Black Horse would undoubtedly agree with him. So, where did that leave her and Gentle Water? Her dear friend believed that she had a future with Walks Tall, and Meadow wondered what would become of her once Black Horse woke up.

Chapter Twenty-four

"I thought I was dreaming," Black Horse whispered when he opened his eyes. "But then I saw you, my brother, and I knew this was real."

A smile bloomed on Walks Tall's face. "I can tell you are doing better. I wasn't too sure about you when I first saw you in that white man's prison. You are lucky you had a good medicine woman to care for you."

Black Horse ignored the other man's comment. He grimaced as he rose up to a sitting position and let his eyes adjust to the dim light in the cave. He took the water flask Walks Tall held out to him and drank deeply. He could feel Meadow's presence beside him as she stirred slightly. "Why did you allow her to come with us? She does not belong here."

"She saved your life. I foolishly believed you were dead all of this time. If not for Meadow, I never would have known that you did not die that day you were attacked by the soldiers."

"I saw her at the fort, dressed in the clothes of a white woman and surrounded by our enemies," Black Horse said, his voice filled with venom. "She said she would never leave the Sioux, but I saw her with my own two eyes!" His voice grew louder, and he noticed that Meadow began to move slightly as if she was waking up. Black

Horse scooted as far away from her as the cramped area would allow him to move.

"There is much that has happened," Walks Tall retorted. "You must understand that we all thought you had been killed."

"But she said she would never leave the Sioux, no matter what happened. She wasn't as strong as I thought she was."

Walks Tall lowered his eyes to the dark ground. "White Buffalo was gone, and we thought you were, too."

Silence engulfed the dark cave for a moment as Black Horse digested this sad news. "But she ran off to be with her own kind, instead of returning to our village when the Blackfoot released her?" he finally asked in a low voice.

"There is much more, but it is her story to tell. I'll check the horses and give the two of you some time to talk."

Even after Walks Tall exited from the cave, the silence remained. Black Horse knew Meadow was awake, because he had heard her sniff as if she was crying. His pride would not allow him to be the first to speak.

Meadow pushed herself up to a sitting position and wiped away the tears that escaped down her cheeks. She searched for the right words. He would only give her one chance. "I don't even know how to begin to tell you what the past several months have been like—"

"You were there, surrounded by white men," Black Horse interrupted, "dressed as a white woman and acting like one, even after you had told me that you would never return to the whites." His voice trembled as all his hurt and anger came rushing out, "Your promise—and that night we shared together—meant nothing to you."

His callous words caused a deep pain to slice through Meadow's heart. Did he really believe that she would turn her back on her adoptive people?

"I thought you were dead," she cried. "And White Buffalo was gone, too. I was a burden to everyone in the village. Even Sitting Bull thought I should go with the Mounties. I went, but only because I had to know what happened to you. In my heart I couldn't believe that you were dead, and I was right."

"Sioux women do not become traitors when their men are gone—they survive. But you had a choice didn't you? You've always had a choice. Lucky for you that Mountie saved you from becoming my wife. I used to think I would hunt him down someday and kill him for what he had done, but now I think I should just thank him."

The coldness of his voice made Meadow wince. She was glad the dimness in the cave did not allow her to see clearly the hatred she knew must be in his eyes. "My choice was to be with you—ever since the first moment I saw you—and that will never change." Meadow answered in a quivering voice.

The permeating quiet made the atmosphere almost unbearable, and she felt as if she couldn't breathe. She would not beg him to forgive her, because she had not done anything wrong. He had to realize that what she did was because of their love and her devotion to her adoptive people, and until he was ready to accept the truth, there was nothing else to say.

She crawled past Black Horse and out through the

narrow opening of the cave, and he said not a word. By the time she had stood up in the open, the sting of his rejection was ripping a hole in her heart, and she could not stop shivering. She wrapped her arms tightly around herself and glanced out at the broad expanse of prairie that stretched out below the hill where she now stood. The tall grasses were a goldenrod color and blew slightly with the breeze. Almost a whole year had passed since she had first set eyes on her beloved Black Horse, and so much had happened since then, most of it bad. They had had such a brief time of happiness during their courtship, and that one perfect night. Was it enough?

She sighed heavily. For as far as Meadow could see, there did not seem to be anything other than the waving prairie grass and a few distant hills. As badly as she had wanted to return to their homelands here on this side of the border, she almost wished now that she was back in the deep forests of Canada. At least there she could hide behind the tallest tree while her heart shattered into a million tiny pieces.

"We should not spend much more time here," Walks Tall said as he walked up the slope. "The others are getting the horses ready."

Meadow blinked back the tears as she tried not to meet his inquiring gaze. She did not want him to see her cry any more than she wanted Black Horse to.

"He has been through a horrible ordeal, Meadow. Give him time to heal. He will understand."

She shook her head in a defeated gesture. "I'm not sure that he will. He only sees an enemy when he looks at me now."

Walks Tall reached out and rested his hand gently

on her shoulder. "But his love for you will eventually overcome his anger."

"What do I do until then?" She looked directly into Walks Tall's eyes, hoping to see the answer, but he seemed to be nearly as worried as she was. "I knew it might be difficult to make him understand, but he does not even want to hear my explanation."

"I will talk to him," Walks Tall replied.

"There's nothing to talk about," Black Horse said as he climbed out of the cave. "She did not remain true to our people, and for that, I can never forgive her."

As he straightened up to his full height and started walking toward them, the agony he still felt was obvious. He grimaced with each step. His wounds, however, looked much better since Meadow had cared for them. She thought his pain would eventually go away—unlike hers.

"We need to get moving," the war chief stated in a flat tone. He did not look at Meadow again as he limped past her and started down the incline.

With a heavy heart, she began to follow the two men to where the horses were tied. When they reached the horses, Meadow held back, not sure if Black Horse would ride with her again. He walked to one of the spare horses and mounted. A sharp pain tore through her breast as she climbed onto her horse alone. She let her horse fall in behind his when they headed out. He made no effort to speak to her throughout the long day.

They did not stop riding until darkness set in and the horses began to trip over rocks or uneven ground. By the time the sun had disappeared Meadow had convinced herself that no matter what happened between her and Black Horse, she would never regret what she had done to save him from certain death in the white man's prison. She only hoped that someday he would realize the depth of her love.

"We should stop for the night," Walks Tall announced, after his horse stumbled for the third time.

"Yes, I think we are far enough now that the soldiers will not catch up to us," Black Horse answered.

Meadow noticed that he sounded exhausted, and for the past few miles she had seen his body slumping farther and farther down on the back of his horse. A couple times she had thought about suggesting that they stop, but anything she recommended would probably not be welcome. She sighed with relief when Black Horse decided to make camp for the night.

She sipped water from the flask Walks Tall offered, and then handed it to Black Horse, who took it from her without saying a word.

"We should reach the camp at Hidden Springs in two days' ride, but we will have to slow our pace. The ponies are tired," Walks Tall said. He handed each of them a strip of jerky. "We should find food, too."

"Ask a couple of the warriors to go hunting for small game, but tell them to use arrows or knives, not guns. We can't take any chances," Black Horse said as he reached toward the spot on his hip where his knife sheath usually hung. He pulled his hand away slowly and turned back toward his horse.

As if he knew what was going through the war chief's mind, Walks Tall pulled out a brown leather sheath that hung from a worn leather belt from his saddlebag and handed it to the other man. A nod of Black Horse's head was his only reply as he took the gift and wrapped the tattered belt around his waist.

Meadow watched the men's exchange in silence. She would make him a new sheath, and it would be sewn with love.

Black Horse grabbed the pack from the back of her horse and removed a fur blanket and a smaller woven one. He held the fur blanket out to Meadow.

She opened her mouth to argue with him about which of them needed the heavy blanket worse—he was wearing nothing more than a breechcloth and the ragged leggings—but decided it would be useless. She took the fur blanket and retreated to a spot by a nearby clump of sagebrush. The men tied the horses to the sturdiest bushes they could locate in the darkness, and then they all settled down for a restless and uncomfortable night.

Wrapped tightly in the fur, Meadow did not even see where Black Horse had bedded down. A terrible hurt gripped her heart when she thought of him lying alone on the cold, hard ground with nothing more than the flimsy cover, especially after all the torturous months he had spent at that horrible prison. She had heard Walks Tall offer him his fur blanket, too, but he had stubbornly refused.

Meadow could not make her eyes close without seeing Black Horse's eyes filled with hatred every time he looked at her, or hearing the sound of his cold words when he had said she was a traitor to the Sioux. He thought she had chosen the easy path by going to the fort. She knew that life as a white woman was simpler than the hard life of an Indian, but if all she wanted was an easy life, she could have stayed with Brandon Cornett or her brother. They would have taken care of her. But she had chosen to return to the Sioux, and until he realized her loyalty to them there was nothing else she could do.

As tired as she was, sleep would not come on this night, so Meadow rolled onto her back and stared up at the velvet black sky that sparkled with millions of stars. White Buffalo and Little Squirrel were up there with *Wakan Tanka*, and she sensed that they were watching out for her even now. They would always be her guiding lights, and she knew that they would never lead her astray. That was why she was here now.

The night was not totally dark, and by the light of the nearly full moon she could see Walks Tall and the other warriors snuggled up in their blankets. Somewhere close by she knew a couple of the men stood watch over the camp. She closely searched the area until she spotted Black Horse's form curled into a tight ball beneath a shaggy sage bush far away from the other men. She was sure, by the way he was huddled up, that he must be freezing.

Slipping from beneath her cozy fur, Meadow rose up to her feet and gathered up the blanket. As quietly as her clumsy, boot-clad feet could carry her, she crossed over to where Black Horse lay and carefully laid the blanket over him. He did not react to the gesture, but when Meadow started to turn to walk away, she was stopped abruptly when his hand reached out and grabbed her ankle.

She gasped. "I—I was unable to sleep, and I thought you needed the fur more than I did." His tight grasp on her ankle remained for a few more seconds, but then he pulled his hand back as if he had been bitten by a rabid dog.

"Thank you," he muttered. "For the blanket and tending to my wounds. You did well." He rolled over.

Meadow hesitated. She wanted to tell him about her decision to continue with her father's work, but his silence told her that this was not the time. She turned to walk away, holding her breath; she still hoped that he would say something else. But the night engulfed her as she walked away from him. Each step that took her farther from him grew harder, and the pain in her chest threatened to break her heart in two. How could she even continue to breathe if he never wanted to be with her again?

When it seemed she could not make her feet take one more step, Meadow twirled around. She would run back to him, and tell him again why she had been in the fort, and this time she would not stop until he really did understand. But she had barely turned around when she was pulled up hard against his lean body. He had moved so quietly that she had not even heard him come up behind her. She gasped as his warm lips claimed hers.

His kisses were so filled with demand that they were almost painful and rough. Meadow responded urgently. They had been apart far too long to worry about tenderness now. She raked her fingers through the tangled mass of his waist-length hair and drew herself even closer against him. Their lips melded in hungry kisses, and she felt him pull up one of her legs until it was wrapped up around his hip. His manhood pressed rockhard into her abdomen, causing such a fierce ache in her loins that it made her feel faint.

As her body swayed in his arms, Black Horse seemed to sense her weakness and with one swift motion swept her up from the ground and into his arms. Meadow moaned weakly as she let her entire body grow limp within his embrace. His sudden burst of strength surrounded and protected her, and at that moment she realized that every beat of her heart depended on this man's touch.

He carried her to the more secluded spot where he had just been lying. The fur felt cool against her back as Black Horse placed her on top of the thick blanket. As he lowered himself down next to her, he grabbed one end of the fur and rolled it over both of them so that they were huddled together within its warmth and protection.

"I never turned my back on the Sioux or you," Meadow whispered.

Black Horse pressed his finger against her lips to silence her. "I should have believed you—I should have believed in our love."

A small cry escaped from Meadow. *Wakan Tanka* had heard her prayers.

He fiddled with the annoying buckle on the belt Meadow wore to hold up her baggy pants for only a second before she reached down and yanked the clasp apart for him. Meadow kicked the loose boots and pants away from her feet in one quick movement while Black Horse pushed the coat and shirt away from her shoulders. Buttons flew into the darkness as he ripped the last of the shirt away from her and tossed it aside.

Meadow's entire body was exposed to his touch, and she shivered in anticipation. The one night they had spent together had burned like an eternal flame deep inside of her, and the memory ignited such a fire that now she could not control her body's frenzied response to him.

Once the tattered clothing that Black Horse was wearing had been discarded, their bare skin molded intimately together, and she eagerly allowed him access as his hips slid in between her thighs. She fought the urge to cry out loud when she fleetingly recalled that Walks Tall and the others were nearby. She would have to remain quiet on this beautiful, fateful night.

Black Horse's longing seemed equal to her own, and, as he pressed relentlessly inside her, Meadow heard him groan as though he was almost unable to control himself. They moved together in perfection and desperation, clinging to one another as if they would die if they loosened their hold. As Black Horse's hips moved harder and faster, Meadow's hips matched each and every movement. She wasn't aware that her nails dug into his back or that her vow to keep quiet was broken as they reached a climax that left her weak and trembling.

Black Horse lay atop her for a couple of moments as if he was too spent to move. When he did rise up, it was only far enough so that he could bring his lips to her mouth in a hot kiss that devoured her breath with its intensity. Then, keeping her within his possessive hold, Black Horse rolled off of her and cradled her against his side. Meadow curled up as close as she could get to him and laid her head on his chest. Everything in their tumultuous lives was calm when she was in this man's arms.

Chapter Twenty-five

Meadow woke to the chill of the morning. She burrowed underneath the blanket to cover her freezing nose and realized with a start that she was alone. In spite of the cold, she threw the blanket off and sat up. There was no sign of Black Horse or any of the other warriors. Panic began to well up in her chest until she spotted two horses still tied to the bushes not far away—Walks Tall's horse, Hawk, and the horse that Black Horse had ridden yesterday. But where were all the other horses and the men?

Maybe they were hunting for breakfast. The thought of a roasted rabbit or sage hen made her mouth water. She wrapped the fur blanket around herself until she located the shirt and pants she had been wearing last night. The pants where still wearable, but the shirt was now without buttons, and the buttonholes were ripped wide open.

Meadow couldn't help but smile as she donned the shirt and remembered the way he had torn it off her. She clutched the shirt together until she found the bag that held her Indian dress and high moccasins, and also the white wedding blanket that she still carried everywhere she went. Slipping under the cover of the blanket, Meadow quickly discarded the uncomfortable pants and shirt and slipped her soft hide dress over her head and her feet into the comfy knee-high moccasins. As she tightened the laces that ran up the front of her moccasins, she vowed to herself that she would never wear white man's clothes again.

Meadow stood, smoothed her dress down over her hips and ran her fingers through her tousled hair. She would try to braid it later, but first she had to find her man. She knew from past experience not to call out to them. Enemies—or even wild animals—could be close by, and the sound of her voice could alert them to her presence. Meadow wandered cautiously toward the horses and glanced around. Off in the distance she could see a towering cascade of mountains, and she assumed that they would be headed in that direction, since Walks Tall had mentioned that they would be meeting up with other Sioux—renegades, most likely— that lived somewhere in the mountains.

Meadow drew in a deep breath and stared at the distant mountains. Would Black Horse really take her there with him? Even though their actions the previous night had held more raw passion than she had ever known could exist between a man and a woman, she realized now that they had hardly spoken a word to one another during or after their impassioned lovemaking. If he was trying to punish her, she thought, he had definitely picked the wrong method. She had not felt anything but pure pleasure.

As she stared at the two horses, another thought came that made her insides twist with terror. She leaned against a tree for support when she realized that Black Horse might actually be gone. What if he and the other warriors had ridden off in the middle of the night and left Walks Tall here to take her back to the village? Maybe he had decided that last night had been a terrible mistake and that he never wanted to see her again. Her nervous gaze scanned the area again as she started to walk toward the horses.

Being alone with her insecurities and fears was making her frantic. Forgetting the caution she had been taught, Meadow opened her mouth to call out for them. The words stuck in her throat as a hand clamped roughly over her mouth and fingers dug into the side of her face. Meadow reached up, intending to claw the face of her attacker, but he grasped her wrist as if he had known what she was about to do. She struggled helplessly as she was dragged back into a clump of heavy brush and pulled forcibly down to the ground. She felt the prickly branches of the bushes scratching her face and arms as her bottom hit the hard ground, but she was as defenseless against them as she was against her attacker.

In the shelter of the bushes, Meadow's captor forced her to turn around so that she could see his face. As her gaze met his, the shock nearly rendered her incoherent. But she could see the silent warning in Black Horse's ebony eyes and knew that they were both in danger. She tried to swallow the constricting lump in her throat as she also tried to convey to him that she understood that he was trying to protect her from someone or something.

Meadow felt his grip around her mouth and jaw loosen, and she nodded her head as he slowly pulled his hand away from her face and raised his forefinger to his mouth in a gesture for her to remain quiet. He also released his tight hold on her wrist and then motioned for her to remain on the ground. She swallowed hard again, hoping that she could catch the breath she had been holding and not start coughing or gasping. With her own hand clasped over her mouth, Meadow turned to look in the direction that held Black Horse's attention.

The sight that met her eyes made Meadow grateful that she had clamped her hand tightly over her mouth, because it prevented the scream that threatened to escape from her. Riding straight toward them were a half dozen soldiers, and the one in the lead was none other than her own brother, Robert McBain!

Meadow's startled gaze moved back to Black Horse, and she noticed that he held the old bone-handled knife that Walks Tall had given him last night. Walks Tall and the other warriors had rifles, and she could only hope that they were hiding somewhere nearby with guns aimed at the soldiers, because the knife Black Horse clasped would not offer much protection. A rush of strange emotions flooded through Meadow—blinding fear for the man she loved and for their friend, Walks Tall, but also sadness and guilt that she would rather see her own flesh and blood die than lose either one of them.

The image of her brother's hate-filled expression when had he told her that he never wanted her to mention "those animals" again flashed before her eyes. He undoubtedly had heard about her part in Black Horse's escape, so she was certain that he must really despise her now. That he had come all this way to find them was proof that he would never forgive her for wanting to be with the Sioux more than with her own family. A shudder racked Meadow's entire body as she realized that her own brother had probably come here to kill her.

The troop of soldiers was almost to where the two horses were tied, and Meadow knew it would be just seconds before the men knew that they had caught up to their prey. A feeling of helplessness mingled with her terror; they were trapped like animals in a pen. She looked to Black Horse for encouragement. His dark lashes were narrowed into thin slits around his eyes, and his full lips were drawn into a tight line. Even after everything that he had suffered in the past months, the power he still emitted was staggering. But did he have the strength to go into battle so soon?

A fleeting memory of the previous night passed through her mind, and in spite of their precarious situation, Meadow felt a heated blush rush into her cheeks. Last night he had seemed plenty strong enough to fight any war. But last night he had not been fighting for his life.

Lieutenant McBain and his contingent were stopped beside the two Indian ponies now, and they were all looking around cautiously as if they expected to be ambushed at any second. Meadow heard him order his men to spread out and search the area. The pounding of her heart sounded so loud to her own ears that Meadow wondered if the soldiers could hear it. Her frightened gaze moved back to Black Horse. He had scooted away from her and was crouched down on his heels and ready to pounce forward, like a mountain lion stalking his prey. His deadly expression had not changed.

Meadow drew in a trembling breath. She was prepared to fight, too. She was, after all, the main reason these soldiers were here. She could not escape from the image of her brother's ruthless expression when he had talked about the Sioux. There would be no reasoning with him, but she had to do something.

The soldiers were on foot now as they began to search through the sparse cedars that grew in the area. Meadow knew it would only be a matter of seconds before they spotted her and Black Horse. She panicked, jumping up from the protection of the brush and lunging forward before Black Horse had a chance to stop her.

"Robert," she called out. She thought she heard Black Horse say something to her, but she did not acknowledge him as she hurried out into the open to face her brother alone. Her legs felt wobbly beneath her, and she worried that she would fall if she couldn't control her shaking. She spoke English, but it was impossible to talk without her voice quivering. "It—it's m-me that you want, Robert," she cried out. "I know that y-you think I've shamed you a-and the memory of our f-family, but—"

"But what, little sister?" the lieutenant spat, cutting off her words. His gaze raked up and down as if he was assessing her Indian attire. "Do you want me to forget that you are a traitor to our race, and a complete disgrace to our family's memory? Just look at you." He raised his rifle up and aimed it directly at her head. "You are no better than the dirty savages that you are trying to protect," he added. His tone of voice was filled with venom, and the disgusted expression on his face showed the disdain he felt for his flesh and blood.

Meadow's vision focused on the end of the gun barrel pointed straight at her head, and she tried to think. Would her impulsive gesture give Black Horse—and, she hoped, the others—time to make a stand against the soldiers, or had she just sealed their fate? "R-Robert, I can't help the way I feel. I know that you will never understand why, but please—"

"Where are they!" he screamed, cutting her off again. "That buck you broke out of the prison and the other ones that you were riding with. Are you lying with all of those dirty animals?"

As his horrible accusation reached Meadow's stunned ears, she did not have time to react. In the next instant, a barrage of gunfire accompanied a flurry of activity that Meadow did not see, as she was knocked to the ground when Black Horse rushed from his hiding place and pushed her out of the line of fire.

Meadow felt her body hit the hard ground, but she did not have a chance to protect herself as the back of her head thudded against a protruding rock. Darkness stole away the last of the morning sunlight from her eyes.

Chapter Twenty-six

The cool rag against her forehead was soothing, but it did not mask the throbbing pain at the back of her head. "You are a foolish woman," Meadow heard as she forced her eyes slowly open. Her vision blurred for a moment before she was able to focus on the handsome face that loomed above her. She opened her mouth to speak, but only a weak moan escaped.

"You could have been killed," Black Horse continued in an aggravated tone. "That was a crazy thing that you did."

"She saved your life—again," said Walks Tall. "The soldiers would have walked right up on the two of you if she had not distracted them for a few minutes, and your one little knife was a pitiful match for six guns."

"It hit its target," Black Horse retorted.

Meadow gasped as she touched the back of her head, which was throbbing even more violently now. "Wh-what happened?" she asked. Her fingers gingerly felt at the open cut that oozed blood. She quickly pulled her bloodied hand away.

"You will live," Black Horse said. He carefully began to tie a rag around her head to help stop the bleeding as he softly thanked *Wakan Tanka* over and over again that she had not been hurt too badly when he pushed her out of the way.

Meadow's gaze rose up to his face as he spoke the harsh words, but his expression and the tenderness in his actions told her that he was not as angry as he sounded. "What happened?" she repeated. She attempted to sit up, but the back of her head felt as if it was about to explode like a cannon, and Black Horse's hand against her shoulder gently pushed her back to the ground.

"The soldiers are dead."

Black Horse's brief statement did not register for a few seconds. But as his words slowly began to sink into her foggy brain, she whispered, "All of them?"

Black Horse nodded his head. He stared down at Meadow as if he was afraid to speak. She wondered if he had understood any of the exchange between her and Robert. But before she had a chance to ask him, he responded as if he had read her mind.

"I heard the words you and the soldier spoke," Black Horse said in a low tone of voice.

Not only had he understood their words, but Meadow sensed by the way he was looking at her that he was finally beginning to understand just how devoted she was to her adoptive people—and most of all, to him.

"I have killed your brother," Black Horse whispered as he leaned down closer to her. He slid his arm under her neck and carefully raised her up so that their faces were only a couple of inches apart.

"He would have killed me without a second thought," she answered. "He would have killed you, too. You only did what had to be done."

Black Horse did not respond with words, but rather by pulling Meadow up tight against his chest. She could feel the pounding of his heart against her cheek. The throbbing in her head almost seemed to disappear now that Black Horse was holding her as if he was never going to let her go again. But when she heard Walks Tall clearing his throat loudly, she knew that this tender embrace was about to end.

As Black Horse slowly released his tight hold, Meadow tilted her head back and looked into his eyes. There she saw the man that she had missed so desperately, and as the reflection of her own face became evident in his ebony gaze, Meadow felt there was nothing that could ever tear them apart again.

"We should leave here as soon as possible," Walks Tall said.

"*Sha*," Black Horse replied as he pushed himself up from the ground. He extended his hand down to help Meadow to her feet.

Standing up made her head swim, and the fall against the hard ground had also made her entire body feel as if she had just been kicked by a wild stallion. When her legs threatened to give out, she once again felt Black Horse's strong arms encircle her floundering form as he swept her up and carried her to their horse.

With a nervous glance around, a trembling sigh escaped from Meadow. There was no evidence of the deadly battle that had just been fought.

"I have asked my warriors to bury your brother and the others," Black Horse stated as if he could read her mind.

"Thank you," she whispered as a fiery tear escaped from the corner of one of her eyes. An engulfing sadness filled her as she thought about the boy that she did not remember, and the man—the brother—she would never forget. In some ways, she realized now, he really had died with the rest of her family on that October day long ago. Only his hatred for the Indians had kept him going all these years, and it had finally been his demise. Still, a part of her would grieve for him, now that she had learned of his existence, and she would be eternally grateful to him for the brief glimpse he had given to her of her past life.

"I will not be going up into the mountains with you," Walks Tall said as he rode up beside the couple. "Not yet, anyway. I have something I must take care of in Canada."

Meadow glanced over at the warrior and met his gaze. When he winked at her, she knew what he planned. "We will look forward to seeing you and Gentle Water soon. Then, we can have those two weddings we talked about," Meadow answered.

"I see there is much I have missed," Black Horse added. He nestled his face into Meadow's golden locks. "You can tell me all that I need to know when we reach the safety of the mountain camp."

As she reached her hand up to cradle his chin in her embrace, Meadow replied, "All you need to know is that I love you with all my heart and that I will never leave you again—not intentionally, anyway."

"I know," he whispered, and then he kissed the inside of her palm. "I will never doubt that again."

Walks Tall began to turn his horse away from them as he said, "I will bring Dusya when I return. He has missed you, my brother."

Black Horse smiled and nodded. "I will be glad to see that evil horse again, too."

Walks Tall met his friend's gaze as he loosened

Hawk's reins and let the stallion break into a trot. "We will meet again—soon."

As the rider and stallion became a small dot on the distant horizon and then disappeared altogether, Meadow was finally able to swallow the heavy lump that had settled in her throat. "What do you think will become of us?" she asked Black Horse as they continued on their endless journey.

A heavy sigh echoed from the war chief before he finally spoke. "I wish I could tell you that everything would turn out the way *Wakan Tanka* meant for it to be for our people . . . that our bellies would always be full of buffalo and sweet berries and that the white men would go back to their own lands and leave us to live in peace on the lands that have belonged to us since the beginning of time. But that is apparently not what destiny holds for us. We will continue to fight with our enemies, and every single day will continue to be a struggle for our people. Yet, in spite of all of that—and because of all of that—we will always, always find a way to survive. We will have many children so that our people will never fade away completely, and most of all, we will love one another with a passion that cannot be equaled until we take our last dying breath."

Meadow felt Black Horse's hand gently touch her stomach as he spoke of the children they would have. Maybe they had already planted the seed of their first son last night. His brave words filled her with hope and gave her the courage to face whatever the future held for them. She felt the warmth of his strong arms surrounding her, and knew that wherever this trail led them, she was exactly where she belonged.

SHIRL HENKE

The Cheyenne Seer

Since childhood the amber-eyed, red prairie wolf has filled Fawn's dreams. After being educated in the white world, she returns to the Cheyenne to guide them with her medicine dreams.

The Red Wolf

With his cunning and his Colt, Jack Dillon has become a feared lawman. But he faces his toughest job ever when he agrees to protect Fawn and her people from the scum trying to steal their land.

The Grand Design

When Fawn meets the amber-eyed, russet-haired Irishman, she is both infuriated by his cocky self-confidence and irresistibly drawn to his charismatic charm. He is the wolf totem of her dreams who holds the key to unlocking her visionary powers. Together they can save her people, if only he chooses to love the...

CHOSEN WOMAN

ISBN 13: 978-0-8439-6248-2

CONSTANCE O'BANYON

"Constance O'Banyon is dynamic, one of the best writers of romantic adventure." —*Romantic Times BOOKreviews*

The Blue Norther swept across the Texas plains with a fury that would alter lives and change destinies. It killed Shiloh's father, leaving her to run their struggling ranch and raise her little brother alone. It also stranded a feverish young Indian girl in their barn. Shiloh knew the Comanche would come for Moon Song sooner or later, but nothing could have prepared her for the fierce war chief who appeared at her door.

Shadowhawk was full of restless energy, like a wild animal that couldn't be tamed. And now he owed the blue-eyed beauty a debt of honor for saving his sister's life. Shiloh was *his* to protect, his to shield from the dangers of the frontier. He would spirit her away to his village, woo her in the way of his people and make her a woman beneath the magical light of a

Comanche Moon Rising

ISBN 13: 978-0-8439-6265-9

Kate Lyon

"Kate Lyon . . . is worthy of standing up with the greats like
Cassie Edwards and Johanna Lindsey."
—Kristal Gorman, Romance Reader At Heart

Angelina Sanchez didn't hold much stock in men. The ones who
weren't slimy fortune hunters weren't interested in a young lady
who would rather spend time with her horses than flirt. But when
she saw a handsome stranger in town, there was an instant connection, a spark of familiarity like nothing she'd ever felt. And no
matter how fiercely her father warned her away from Jeremiah
Baldwin, nothing could have kept her from his side.

When her father had him beaten and left for dead, Angel's soft
hands and sweet voice coaxed Jeremiah to stay, to fight. In her
arms, it seemed he'd finally found a place to belong. But how
could he protect her when it was her father who'd led the raid
that had slaughtered his family? His spirit guides had told him he
would feel true joy only if he made peace with his greatest sorrow.
But unless he could find a way to win Angelina's heart without
forsaking his family, he would remain . . .

Destiny's Captive

ISBN 13: 978-0-8439-6283-3

INTERACT WITH DORCHESTER ONLINE!

Want to learn more about your favorite books and authors?
Want to talk with other readers that like to read the same books as you?
Want to see up-to-the-minute Dorchester news?

VISIT DORCHESTER AT:
DorchesterPub.com
Twitter.com/DorchesterPub
Facebook.com (Search Pages)

DISCUSS DORCHESTER'S NOVELS AT:
Dorchester Forums at DorchesterPub.com
GoodReads.com
LibraryThing.com
Myspace.com/books
Shelfari.com
WeRead.com

☐ **YES!**

Sign me up for the Historical Romance Book Club and send my FREE BOOKS! If I choose to stay in the club, I will pay only $8.50* each month, a savings of $6.48!

NAME: _____

ADDRESS: _____

TELEPHONE: _____

EMAIL: _____

☐ I want to pay by credit card.

☐ **VISA**　　　☐ **MasterCard**　　　☐ **DISCOVER**

ACCOUNT #: _____

EXPIRATION DATE: _____

SIGNATURE: _____

Mail this page along with $2.00 shipping and handling to:
Historical Romance Book Club
PO Box 6640
Wayne, PA 19087
Or fax (must include credit card information) to:
610-995-9274
You can also sign up online at **www.dorchesterpub.com**.
*Plus $2.00 for shipping. Offer open to residents of the U.S. and Canada only.
Canadian residents please call 1-800-481-9191 for pricing information.
If under 18, a parent or guardian must sign. Terms, prices and conditions subject to change. Subscription subject to acceptance. Dorchester Publishing reserves the right to reject any order or cancel any subscription.